Twelve Essays in Love

Andy Matheson

twelve essays in love

Andy Matheson

Chapter 1: These Four Walls

Ruth sat at her desk and allowed her eyes to glance at the clock on the corner of her laptop screen. 16:47 – nearly time when it was deemed acceptable to head home for the night. The day had been full. Back-to-back meetings, conversations, discussions, but all of them with arms-length relationships on topics that, in the grand scheme of things, mattered little. Ruth defined her job by the number of discussions she had each day. A day was busy when she started at 8:45 and left eight hours later, having managed to have no gaps in her schedule at all. Lunch was 'on the go' and coffee drunk in disposable cups with plastic lids. On an average day, Ruth might interact with ten, twenty or even thirty people. The same cup of coffee might be sipped in multiple rooms.

The trouble was, she reflected, she didn't really know anyone. Oh, sure she talked to them. They exchanged a few pleasantries but only at a superficial level. Ruth worked in the Corporate Communications team of a large financial services firm based in the City. A job that meant she spent most of her days in meetings with a cross section of people from within the business. She could count only a couple of people who had crossed the border between friend and colleague. A few she knew pretty well — enough to send Christmas and birthday cards, at least. But most people remained mere names and desk locations. Incredible to think it was possible to share the same space with so many and yet know so few. She was the mistress of superficial conversation and informal pleasantries, the unwritten code of conduct allowing employees to engage in discussion about the weather, travelling to work, travelling home again and TV programmes, or office gossip about babies, appointments, resignations, illnesses, bonuses and sackings. Beyond that, most subjects were off limits.

Over time, Ruth also began to notice a direct correlation between her phone battery level and her attitude to work. Like most people she would charge it overnight and start her journey to the office in a reasonable level of readiness. A packed Tube train could mean that by the time she got to work, the level was already down to 80%. By mid-afternoon, it was hovering around the 20% mark and she was lucky if there was any life in it at all by the time she got home. Once indoors, she needed to plug the phone into the wall and herself into a comfy chair with some wine and then both she and her phone could recharge. She had also noticed the battery seemed to be holding less charge these days. She was sure when she first bought the phone it would last longer; after all, it was top of the range at the time. Now it was struggling with a single evening out or a day in the office. Life was like that, it seemed.

***

Will, on the other hand, was 'in between jobs', as he liked to call it. His work as an IT contractor recently came to an abrupt end when the project deliverable schedule was revised to 'take account of changing market conditions and the need to rationalise the existing product portfolio'. In other words, he was no longer needed. So, after a leisurely breakfast, Will found himself in a faded T-shirt browsing Facebook and looking for work.

Will was reassured that so many of his friends led such fulfilling lives. Simon, for example, had just eaten the most spectacular of breakfasts and had supplied a nice photograph in case there was any uncertainty about the quality of the bacon. Stella was delighted to announce that it was her mother's birthday and her mother had won the best mother in the world competition. This no doubt depressed Stella's other Facebook friends, who may have been under the impression that they possessed the best mother in the world but were in fact mistaken.

Will was also pleased that Dave had supplied some interesting video links to cute cats in strange locations doing odd things. One cat could open a refrigerator door. Another was seen to strike a well-aimed paw at a large dog and seemingly win the fight. The cat videos were quickly followed by a video of a man making something impressive from a single piece of wood. Using a lathe and some hand tools he took an old log and created a perfect replica of the Hanging Gardens of Babylon. This whole experience apparently only took him eight minutes and forty-three seconds.

Will could carry on like this for hours. Five hundred and forty-three friends on Facebook and a daily competition for who was having the best life. Will used to post things and try to win the competition. But his photos were long out of date, his postings had become weekly, then monthly and now he found himself a mere voyeur. He watched other people's interesting lives by clicking on links.

His own Facebook page offered few clues to the complex being known as Will Graden. Hidden amongst his five hundred and forty-three friends were a few from primary school days who had reconnected over the years. A selection from secondary school and college, many of whom had started as playground mates and ultimately progressed to drinking buddy status. The majority had been added at university when it was a popular pastime to add random people as friends. Flicking through the list now, Will would struggle to recall the connection.

In addition to his friends, you could discover that he had 'liked' a number of bands and bars and listed his favourite movie as *Les Amants Du Pont-Neuf* (which he was accused of adding as it sounded pretentious). He had also clicked 'like' on The 100 Club, Gordon Ramsay, Amazon, David Lloyd, Waitrose, John Lewis, West Ham United, *The Big Lebowski*, *Star Wars* and Big Big Train amongst others.

When he reflected on the five hundred and forty-three people linked to his profile, Will couldn't help but feel something of a fraud. Despite the numbers, Will could only really consider six to be proper friends. The kind of people who would be there when you needed them, could be relied upon to help out in an hour of need or simply be around to share a cool beer on a summer's day. Most were the kind to whom you would send a 'happy birthday' message when prompted by the good people at Facebook. Something that took all of twenty seconds of thought and effort.

To add insult to injury, he would often get reminded of the length of a friendship. *Celebrate!* proclaimed the automated headline. *Nine years ago today, you and Gill Wands became friends on Facebook!* The post then displayed photos interspersed with cartoon fireworks and figures high-fiving, followed by the ultimate in patronising statements: *And while there are billions of friendships … there's only one like yours.* The reality being that Will had never breathed the same air as Gill Wands. At best they had liked or commented on the same post a few times. Once Will contemplated culling the list to make it more realistic. He decided that a true friend would be defined as someone who would come to his funeral or feel sorry to miss it – a macabre test of friendship, perhaps, but strong nonetheless. Unfortunately, that criteria decimated the friends list, so he left it as it was.

***

Ruth picked up her coat, water bottle and bags, and

headed out the door. A few colleagues looked up as she shuffled past and uttered a simple farewell and a hope that she had a good evening. Gerry on the third floor even asked her what she was up to and like many people, she pretended to be pleased to be going home to an evening of her own company.

'I am doing absolutely nothing, thank God,' said Ruth. 'I'll be glad of a sit down, although I have a feeling I will have to get the laptop out and do a few emails.'

Gerry knew exactly what she was talking about. He too was heading home via the supermarket and was looking forward to a takeaway and a nice glass of Chardonnay. Somehow the two of them seemed to connect over this simple ritual. Culturally, this had become an acceptable response. All were agreed that work was busy and that time at home was meant for solitude, reflection, Chardonnay and an hour or two of TV.

Ruth wandered outside into a damp city street where the rain did more than sum up the mood. Her battery was definitely feeling drained.

***

Will was on Series 2, Episode 3 of *24*. He had decided to watch all seven series one after the other and really get under the skin of being a counter-terrorism agent. Sadly, some of the drama was reduced by the fact that Kiefer Sutherland's face appeared prominently on every thumbnail preview of each episode. It was forever apparent that, despite being tied to a chair by a terrorist who was holding him in place with knives, bare electrical wires and guns, Kiefer (or Jack, as Will preferred to call him) would be home in time for dinner.

It seems that the boxed set had become a replacement for real-life action and adventure. For a few hours, Will could become wrapped up in a plot and find himself on the edge of his seat with anticipation. So excited, in fact, that as one finished, he could allow the automatic play of a second episode and then a third. When the series was originally broadcast, people would have to wait for days before they could find out the next plot twist. Will could now press Play and fuel his energy with bags of Doritos and cups of tea. Only when he finally turned off the TV would a sense of disappointment overcome him, with the stark realisation that the boxed set had become an excuse for inactivity and a device for ensuring the rapid passing of time. But with an unpleasant aftertaste that lingered on the tongue long after the dust of the tortilla had been licked from the fingers.

***

Ruth squeezed onto an overcrowded Tube train at Holborn. Here the rushed, overheated and uncomfortable collided in a small space where personal boundaries evaporated with the heat from the train. Ruth found herself wedged between a steel pole, two rucksacks, a man in an ill-fitting suit and a young woman who reminded her of someone she worked with. As the train rattled through the stations, Ruth couldn't help but reflect how physically close she was to people and yet how mentally remote. This was as close as she could imagine being to a stranger and yet all she wanted to happen was for the doors to open and the steaming mass of humanity to exit and disappear into the distance. Ruth figured that, when you are this close to people, all you want to do is escape as fast as possible, never to see them again.

She opened her bag in search of a tissue. You can tell a lot about a person from their bag and the contents. Ruth's was a medium-sized black leather tote made by Radley, the small dog logo indicating a recognisable brand but not one of the super expensive ones. Loose change wrapped up in taxi and restaurant receipts added not inconsiderable weight. A quick analysis would confirm Ruth as someone who'd eat out as much as she ate in and who didn't like wandering streets or pubic transport alone. Hidden in the pockets you would find a low-calorie brunch bar, a replacement for lunch perhaps. A notebook and pen that was rarely used, a Kindle loaded with many books by unknown authors, an iPhone (not the latest one) encased in a leather cover, a large bunch of keys but none that started a car, a curved box that had started the day holding a banana, a makeup bag containing a selection of Mac cosmetics, a small bottle of Pomelo perfume courtesy of Jo Malone with her Jo Loves brand, a new packet of tissues, a second packet of tissues already opened, a third packet of tissues which had been opened but now covered with the black fluff that seems to accumulate at the bottom of every bag, a small mirror and a hairbrush. She was indeed ready for any random eventuality, even though nothing had ever come up.

***

Will went out for some milk. It felt good to be out. A chance to breathe in some fresh air and to witness the wild goings-on between his flat and the newsagent. Will was a regular and now on nodding terms with the shopkeeper. They exchanged pleasantries and Will handed over the cash for the milk, a packet of mint imperials and a lottery scratch card. Deep down, Will knew he had more of a chance of being asked to join a new band with Chris Martin than he had of winning any of the top lottery prizes. Given that Will could neither sing nor play an instrument, the Chris Martin thing was a remote and rather random idea.

Will was now on nodding terms with local people other than the shopkeeper. He had, over time, progressed from the 'staring at the floor and avoiding eye contact' stage to the 'looking up and nodding in the general direction' stage. This took about eighteen months in Will's neighbourhood. At this rate, he would be exchanging Christmas cards in about nineteen years.

***

Ruth reached the front door and fumbled for her keys. She was glad to be home at last. Time to escape the chaos of the commute and to collapse on the sofa. She walked into the house and spotted a rarely used house phone blinking in the corner. An answerphone message, no less. Something of a rarity these days. Quickly she pressed play to find half a message from someone asking whether she had ever paid for PPI insurance. She pressed the delete button just as quickly and went in search of tea.

***

Meanwhile, Will arrived home sucking a well-deserved mint imperial. His step counter had hardly registered his effort but deep inside he felt better for the exercise. Even though it was a mere four minutes each way, he could now say he had been out, and was now going back home.

***

And so it was that Will and Ruth sat down in the lounge. Miles apart and with no knowledge of each other's existence, but bound by a common set of circumstances.

***

Will reached for the remote and began channel hopping. A strange blur of images blended on the screen, forming a surreal animation. He finally settled on *Amateur Celebrity Love Island*, in which people he had never heard of met other people he had never heard of whilst being trapped on a desert island with only a tin of pineapple, two coconuts, a bottle of white rum and a seventeen-strong film crew and an advertising budget to sustain them. The idea of the conquest was apparently to engage in enough flirting and showing of cleavage to secure maximum TV coverage. All being well, this would convert into TV ratings and with any luck the winning participant could be asked to become a contestant on *I'm a Celebrity … Get Me Out Of Here!* In this show, people you had hardly heard of met other people you had never heard of, together with an ageing US TV star you felt sure had died. If said winning participant did enough flirting, showing of cleavage and eating of kangaroo testicles, even higher ratings could be achieved. The pinnacle of this career path being a quarter-page spread in *The Sun* newspaper and a backstage pass at the Brit Awards.

Will reflected that this wasn't a bad career option. In fact, complete unknowns had managed to convert their status from 'never heard of them' to 'the girl from the TV show hosted by Ant and Dec'. Perhaps this was his path. He did worry that he had neither a cleavage nor a six pack (which seemed essential for the ultimate in career trajectory). He was also worried that he might be too clever. Will was aware that his many opinions on topics of national and indeed international importance, might prohibit him from entering. He also felt too well read and perhaps authentically opinionated. Will had some bright friends and he enjoyed the cut and thrust of verbal debate. In 'celebrity land' it seemed these were a positive disadvantage.

After forty-three minutes of *Amateur Celebrity Love Island* where the whole conversation seemed to revolve around how to peel a banana without using your fingers, Will turned off the TV. He looked around his apartment. Tidy? Yes, it was. Homely? Well, not too bad. Stylish? Will was doubtful other people would think so. The black leather armchair didn't match the floral carpet that had been there since he moved in. It was hardly a bachelor pad. Will had often had fantasies about his apartment and bringing back women to wine, dine and seduce (not necessarily in that order). The reality had been somewhat different. Eleven months into his tenancy and his claim to fame was a single night with Claire Hadlow from PC support after the office Christmas party. The spontaneity and surprising nature of her arrival meant he wasn't quite as ready for her as he'd previously imagined. In his head, he would have had sensual music playing. Probably some Ludovicio Einaudi to demonstrate his potential for classical romanticism. He would have had flowers, chocolates, seductive lighting, grapes, clean linen, fresh scents and wine in crystal glasses, all combined with a sense of adventure and mutual abandonment of sexual inhibitions.

This image was a far cry from the reality of the leftover dinner plates containing congealed chicken tikka dhansak and the pile of pants and socks on the bed waiting for a drawer to find them. Oh, and the lighting that should have been discreet was either full-on 60 watts of illumination or complete darkness. Will and Claire engaged in what could only be described as drunken fumbling in the dark whilst their senses were aroused by stale cumin, coriander and garlic. Claire left fairly quickly, claiming the need to get home and be somewhere early the following morning.

Will stared at the blank TV screen, checked his phone and decided to go to bed. He could hear vague sounds coming from the people next door but not enough to disturb him. He was sure they were delighted to have him as a neighbour, as his apartment was always so quiet. Even the Xbox explosions were contained by the volume control. In fact, Will wondered if they could tell whether he was in or whether he was out. The noise level would be pretty much the same.

'Goodnight all,' he sighed to no one in particular.

***

Ruth was halfway through many things. She was halfway through a book by Hilary Mantel, which was halfway through the life story of Oliver Cromwell. She was halfway through a bottle of Pinot Grigio and halfway through a plate of cheese and crackers. She was also halfway through an email she had started writing and halfway through sorting out the pile of magazines in the rack by the armchair. She was halfway through the ironing and halfway through the housework. She was debating going away for a long weekend with some girlfriends and was on the way to saying yes to the Algarve in June. She had also been asked by some work friends if she fancied going to see Justin Bieber at a big show in Hyde Park. She was undecided and would perhaps let them know tomorrow. That was providing they could get the tickets, of course. She was also halfway through deciding what to do with her life.

She found herself in a position where she quite liked her job but also found it boring. She liked where she lived, without being in love with the neighbourhood. She liked the idea of commuting to work, but didn't enjoy the journey. She liked the feel of her house and the comfort she felt when she walked in. But she felt it was time to freshen up the paintwork and change the furniture and the white goods ... oh, and the pictures. She now found herself bored of Monet and feeling more Renoir. She liked going out but part of her longed to say no to people and to stay in. Oh, and one more thing. She was halfway through getting over Dan.

Dan had made her feel like a whole person. What was it Tom Cruise said in *Jerry Maguire*? 'You complete me.' For a while, that was Dan. He was fun, charming and full of compliments. Ruth always felt better in his company. When Ruth debated her own self-esteem and self-image, Dan could raise her all the way up to a six out of ten. He made her smile. He had a way with words and made the company of others easy. He was also a great person to be alone with. It was so easy to be in a room with him and say nothing at all. Right now, it wasn't his company she craved but the bliss of silent companionship. Ruth could look up from her book and know that Dan was there. She didn't need a conversation or words of reassurance. She missed the idea of him.

Since their split, she had carried on as best she could. She consoled herself that she would be going through a period of mourning and then she would give herself a good talking to and be ready to join the human race. Then she discovered match.com and realised that the human race had in fact been infiltrated and all men had been replaced by arrogant, self-opinionated pains in the arse.

She recalled with some affection an evening with Peter Templeton. It seemed that Peter was able to talk about himself all evening without stopping. And such an interesting life he seemed to lead. The stories about the nights out with the lads, excessive drinking and his love of football was just what a girl needed. Ruth did some adding up. Ruth, 3 – Peter, 847. That was a rough estimation of how much information they had shared. From Ruth, she was fine, yes this was only her second date and a white wine would be lovely. From Peter, among many other interesting facts she learnt that the Sale of Goods Act of 1979 part II was relevant to Peter's experience in buying a used car from Kingsland Auto in Bristol when the car did not meet expectations. He could also talk at length about the best places to go out in Ayia Napa without seeming to care whether she ever planned to go there. At the end of the evening he had the audacity to suggest 'it had been great meeting you' when in reality he hadn't met Ruth at all. He had merely shared the same space for a while and looked in the general direction. The only 'great' thing about online dating was the ability to block and delete profiles.

Deep down Ruth knew she had to get out more, to experiment more, to say yes more and to escape more. The house had become her safe place, her fortress, her sanctuary. Perhaps it was time to unlock the door again. But the implication of this was always worrying. She risked lowering her already fragile self-esteem and running back inside to hide.

Ruth put down her book and washed her plate and wine glass. Tidying the kitchen was a painless activity these days. She flicked off the lights in the living room and mumbled, 'Goodnight room,' underneath her breath. If these four walls could talk, she pondered, they would have nothing much to say.

Corporate Invisibility

Excerpt from an essay by Peter Stephens, published in Journal Management & Leadership Today, Feb 2018

I want you to imagine a radar screen, the sort used by air traffic controllers. It is green, glowing and shows a rough map of terrain, using radio waves to determine the position, angle, or velocity of objects such as aircraft, ships, missiles and vehicles, and even the weather. We have all seen movies where a frantic radar operator struggles with the arrival of unexpected blips or perhaps the disappearance of one of the blips on the screen.

I began to play around with the idea of using radar technology on organisational life. I imagined a CEO sitting in the boardroom with a big green radar screen, checking out the progress of the employees and ready to bark orders for those underperforming.

In this scenario, your blip would appear the day you started work. The strength of your glowing icon would depend on your performance. So, for example, if you helped a customer in need, came up with a great idea, supported a colleague who was struggling or saved some money for the company, then your light would glow even brighter. Likewise, the CEO could spot the lights glowing dim and be able to demand more input from you.

I discussed this idea with select colleagues, who agreed this sounded rather stressful. It was suggested the best move would be to start work (thus triggering salary payments) and then to quickly fade away and disappear from view completely. In fact, we were able to pinpoint a couple of colleagues who appeared to have already achieved the enviable feat of corporate invisibility.

Fascinated by the ability of some people to live under the radar, immune from the watchful eye of the CEO, I began to research this phenomenon further. Here are the top ten ways people can disappear at work whilst still getting paid to turn up:

1. Blend: Observe the dress code from those around you. If suits are the norm, then buy the same colour and design as everyone else. Copy the accessories and merge chameleon-like into the background.

2. Eye contact: Avoid this for the most part. Keep your head down and only connect if you have to.

3. Mobile focus: Keep your phone with you at all times and bring it out whenever new people are in the vicinity. Continue this behaviour while walking along or using lifts.

4. Agree: Master the art of agreeing with everything you hear. Be wary of too much enthusiasm. A simple nod of the head and the words 'that might work' are all you need.

5. Meetings: Be on time and don't leave early, no matter how dull they are. You will stand out more by showing contempt for the time-wasting monotony that they are, so develop coping mechanisms to stick them out until the end.

6. Get busy: When anyone asks how you are doing, always respond with a reply that suggests you are busy, on top of things and will be glad of the weekend.

7. Avoid controversy: If asked for feedback, always err on the side of reasoned moderation. Balance is always the diplomatic way.

8. Connect: Find out what other people are listening to, watching or reading and do the same. Nod with appreciation during discussions about the latest

news/developments. This enables you to appear to contribute to conversations when all you are doing is agreeing with general points made by everyone.

9. Report: Make sure the number of management updates you provide exceeds the amount of work you do. People read updates much more than they look at project content so this will give the illusion of progress without the need for controversial work to surface and be discussed.

10. Network: If you go to a networking meeting, only mingle with the people you already know. This avoids having to answer awkward questions.

Does this behaviour pay dividends? We found some worrying data and correlations:

• Those operating below the radar were consistently rated 4/5 on a performance appraisal: statistically the highest average in our sample.

• There were no cases of disciplinary action amongst the target group we surveyed. Those being fired or going through some sort of disciplinary process were either high performers (but often controversial) or truly terrible employees who caused problems.

• There is a direct correlation between length of service and below-the-radar behaviour. It seems the longer you can disappear, the longer you will work for the company.

Chapter 2: Close Encounters

Will's phone buzzed in his pocket.

You free tonight?

It was a text from Steve. *Maybe – what's up?*

Fancy a beer?

Is the Pope Catholic?

I should ducking hope so.

What?

Bloody spellchecker. Take it from me, I will never use the word ducking in a sentence in my whole life – C U l8r.

***

Ruth's phone rang.

'Hi Megan.'

'Hi Ruth. So tonight we are meeting for a quick bite at Intermezzo and Helen wants to call into the Royal to see her boyfriend's band.'

'Yeah okay, so what time shall we meet?'

'I'll pick you up in a cab at 7:30.'

'Do we have to see the band? The last one we saw was a few blokes with acoustic guitars droning on for ages…'

'Apparently we do. And, according to Helen, we will like them. She has insisted that they practice all the songs and promise not to play any Ed Sheeran.'

'Okay, bring it on. But if one of them starts retuning a guitar while telling stories about the potato famine, I am leaving.'

'Don't worry. I'll text Helen to tell the band to ban any mention of the potato famine.'

'And Ed Sheeran.'

'Yes, and Ed Sheeran.'

'Okay, see you later.'

And in that moment some strange atmospheric currents began to stir. Perhaps a butterfly spread its wings and flew through a window in South Korea. Perhaps as a result a flicker of a breeze started, causing a flock of birds destined for the South China Sea to make a slight detour. Perhaps a whisper of the wind blew the clouds over the mainland near the Bay Of Bengal. Small changes of temperature were detected over Pakistan. The reduction in air pressure resulted in a minor change in the jet stream through Turkey, across Europe, and finally blowing a storm cloud over Oaklands Road near Hanwell, where it started to rain, just in time to greet Ruth as she walked home from the shops. This particular rain cloud seemed to know that she was carrying two bags of shopping and was unlikely to raise her hands and bags above her head. Now she would have to wash her hair.

In Ruth's mind, there was a big difference between 'popping out' and 'going out'. Popping out was a quick visit to the shops, running errands, spontaneous actions and necessary diversions. Popping out tended to serve a purpose, albeit an often trivial one. When popping out, it was fine to wear a comfy sweatshirt and flat shoes. Going out meant something different, more meaningful. Going out meant that Ruth needed time to think about the image she wanted to present to the world. She needed time to reflect on shoes, jackets, makeup and hair. Dan used to complain that she was 'only going out with the girls' and 'why are you taking so long?' Ruth would try and explain that going out with the girls was always the most complex of experiences. She had to consider the location, the time of day, the weather, the venue and, perhaps most importantly, what everyone else would be wearing.

So tonight involved: showering – shampoo and double conditioner – rinsing – towel drying – hair drying – teeth cleaning – teeth flossing – hair straightening – foundation – light makeup – most recently purchased underwear – jeans (the posh ones) – cream top – black jacket (goes with everything) – Tiffany necklace with the padlock – cream FM shoes with slight heel (not too agonising) – a generous squirt of perfume – a long look in the mirror and all finished off with killer red lipstick. This process took a mere ninety-seven minutes. At least, it would have done had she not had doubts about the shoes and jacket, which resulted in several more minutes of internal angst and indecision. In truth, Ruth would never describe herself as 'ready'. All that happened was the arrival of other people who demanded to leave, forcing her to stop her eternal preparation. So Megan arrived at 7:40, which coincided with Ruth now being ready to go out. Sort of.

***

Will owned three pairs of shoes. Black ones, a pair of trainers and some brown ones. Black ones for work, trainers for daytime at weekends and brown ones for nights out. When a pair showed signs of wear and tear he would buy a direct replacement. He would then keep the old ones in the bottom of the wardrobe for a couple of years, just in case he needed a slightly scruffy version of the style. He never did, of course. He owned two pairs of jeans; one pair needed a wash so he wore the Levi's. Choice of shirts: a black long sleeve polo would be fine. Squirt of BOSS Orange aftershave – a present from his sister at Christmas which made him smell like a satsuma. Hair seemed fine. Final rub of deodorant under the shirt and he was ready. The whole process of getting ready took Will just under eight minutes.

Will never thought about 'getting ready'. He was more of a 'ready now' kind of bloke. He had learnt (to his cost) that T-shirts and weddings don't mix – especially ones with slogans saying *I Married Her, Because She Looked Like You*, which he thought would amuse the married couple. Apparently not. He also knew that, no matter what he wore, his BOSS leather jacket would go on the top. It always did. He could, of course, dress up if the situation required it. He could be suited and booted for work, interviews or funerals. But going to the pub required minimal thought.

Will stood outside his apartment waiting for an Uber driven by Mohamed Abhan – a Toyota Prius, registration number MX16 LTF. Apparently, the driver had a love of ancient history, was married with three children and liked listening to Capital FM. Okay, Will invented the last bit but he did wonder if Uber would ever supply conversation starters for passengers. Surely cab drivers were bored beyond belief by the 'how long have you been on duty today' question. Maybe they could enrich their few short minutes together and perhaps offer discounts for lively conversation or the discovery of new facts that would enhance the journey of other passengers. Will could, for example, mention that before the war, there was an old church on this site but it was demolished after receiving a direct hit from a doodlebug. And now in its place stood a kebab shop and an estate agents. This gem of information could perhaps be worthy of a 10 per cent discount.

One of Will's favourite movies was a kids' film called *Up*, featuring, among other things, a talking dog. Will loved the way the dog, mid conversation, suddenly said 'squirrel!' and became completely focused on the possibility of a small rodent with a long tail. Will was aware he'd developed a similar trait, but not about rodents. About women. He put it down to being single and aged thirty-five. And so, his thoughts about Uber drivers came to an abrupt halt when a rather stunning girl came into view. She was walking down the other side of the road and looked dressed to go out. Pretty, not too tall, nice hair, good shape, right sort of age. In fact, she had all the qualities Will might look for in a woman. He wondered if she might fancy joining him and Steve at the pub, what she might be doing afterwards (damn, he should have cleared up the lunch things). When faced with such a moment in life, Will did what he always did. He breathed in, stood slightly taller and looked the other way. The girl didn't look up at all, which perhaps was a sign of attraction. She wandered around the corner, never to be seen again.

Will was aware that his approach wasn't exactly working for him. But he had always had a problem with the moments of bravery required to start anything with a stranger. His friends and colleagues often told him to be more up front, to find the courage to walk up to a stranger and offer to buy her a drink. The trouble was, those moments were fraught with potential danger and rejection. How did you know, for example, that a girl who had caught your eye was not already in a long-term relationship? Her boyfriend might arrive and discover you trying to chat up his beloved. Said boyfriend would wave you away with a patronising smile and you would have to beat a hasty retreat to the bar stool from whence you came. This sort of thing had bothered Will ever since he asked Debbie for a slow dance at the school disco and she announced she was too tired. Only for Doug Ealing to ask her three minutes later and for her to have demonstrated a remarkable recovery. Moments of such humiliation run deep.

***

'Hi Megan, you look lovely.'

'Thanks Ruth, so do you.'

'New bag – I bought it in Aspinal and just love it.'

'I noticed. It goes so well with your outfit. So, what's the plan?'

'Well, a quick bite of pasta at Intermezzo. We have a table booked for 8:00, and then off to the Royal. Helen says the band starts at 9:30, so we should be there for the beginning.'

'I had a quick look on TripAdvisor and apparently we should avoid the Caesar salad. Dripping in sauce, making the lettuce soggy and inedible. We should also avoid one of the waitresses, not sure which one, who is extremely rude. Otherwise, the pizzas seem to go down well and the owner is lovely if slightly overfamiliar.'

'Fab. Let's go, then. Shall we grab a cab?'

And so Megan and Ruth headed out for the night. The cab ride became a blur of anticipation and the world disappeared. Conversation sparkled and the cab driver navigated his way around the backstreets of Hanwell and Boston Manor. Hammersmith was, as usual, busy on a Thursday night with far too many buses and cars for the small amounts of tarmac offered by the A4. They stopped outside Intermezzo and hurried in to meet Helen and Abi.

Once inside they were absorbed by the buzz of the restaurant whilst inhaling wafts of garlic, oregano and crushed tomatoes. The pasta was delicious; the wine was cheap, drinkable and inoffensive; and the glasses were enormous. The waiter did not disappoint with his lavish handling of the deluxe-size pepper grinder. What was it with pepper? When Ruth was a kid, pepper came in a silver pot with four holes. You needed to fill this pot up once every two years. She had noticed that the grinding of pepper had since been turned into a whole phallic experience. Men (it was always men) would ask seductively whether you would like black pepper and perhaps some parmesan. This was inevitably before you tried the food to know whether it needed any additional flavour. They would then grind and sprinkle small flecks of pepper and/or cheese all over the food. Some people (mostly women) would leer back and demand lots of pepper and lots of cheese. They spoke as if this ritual had some sort of erotic undertone. One could almost imagine Eric Idle being cast as the waiter. 'Would you like some pepper with that dinner, madam? We can sprinkle it all over, nudge, nudge, wink, wink, say no more. Like a bit of pepper on your pasta, do you? Nudge, nudge, say no more!'

Two bottles of wine, three salads, pasta and a side of asparagus later and the girls were done.

'Okay,' said Helen, 'Let's head over to the Royal. I hope you like the band. They play mostly Motown and soul.' Apparently, Abi had already seen the band (Ruth noted that Abi and Helen had clearly been out a couple of times on their own) and seemed to think they were pretty good.

The four of them wandered into the bar, on the way in paying a scruffy man £5 for the privilege of him smudging a black stamp onto the backs of their hands. Said stamp was impossible to read and easily forgeable with any old scribble, a quick lick and a rub with a finger.

***

There is something about an English pub that no other country can replicate. You can go to a pub in the USA, or Switzerland, or France and even if they pretend it is an English pub, it isn't. There is something about the colour, the feel, the sound of them that is so, well, English. Will and Steve wandered up to the bar and surveyed the range of beers on offer. Will ordered a craft beer – a bottle of

Brewdog – while Steve went for the London Pride. Steve also ordered some pork scratchings, which are pretty disgusting no matter how you think about them. The smell, texture, taste and indeed the idea of eating salted and dried pork skin, seemed repulsive to Will. Steve commented that their one redeeming feature was that no one took any when offered, so you could eat all of the packet.

Steve and Will propped themselves up near the bar and where they could see the band going through the final motions of setting up.

'One two, check, one two,' came the sound of the man at the mic. 'Testing one, two, three…'

'Well, that works,' said Will. 'You'd think they could think of something more creative to say, wouldn't you?'

At that the microphone burst into life again as the man began to chant in a monotone:

> *As mortals we drift into silent slumber*
> *Counting our blessings and falling in number*
> *Doth winter descend on the earth that surrounds me*
> *Do prophets and harlots battle to find me*
> *Do those with the power urge me for more*
> *I respond with a metaphor and show them the door…*

'Blimey,' said Will, 'he must have heard me; that's not what you expect to hear, is it?' Perhaps the sound man was indeed a pseudo intellectual who would take any opportunity to preach his teachings to the assembled masses. Perhaps the sound check represented a perfect opportunity to influence a captive audience. However, he soon resorted to type with a quick 'Check one, two three'. It seems intellect lasted mere seconds and the monosyllabic sound man had reclaimed his place.

'Thank goodness for that,' said Will. 'You know where you are with "Testing one two three."'

Just as Will and Steve were chatting about the merits of the philosophical sound man, four girls walked in. They wandered up to the bar and waited until the barman replete in T-shirt and tattoos offered to serve them. Quickly, they were surrounded by members of the band who were noticeable only by their black ill-fitting shirts and black shoes that seemed out of place in the Royal. The girls found a place to stand and to pile up their assortment of bags.

At 8:45 the band started their set for the evening. They were most enthusiastic and sung songs made famous by dead people who used to be on the Motown record label. Some of the band's eight members had even learnt some rudimentary dance moves in time to the music. They were okay if you like that sort of thing.

At 8:57 two things happened at once. Will asked Steve if he fancied another pint and Ruth, who was now standing in the corner, announced it was her round. And so it was that Ruth walked up to the bar with a £20 note in her hand and another at the ready. At this point, the band were in full swing, playing 'Let's Get It On' by Marvin Gaye with the crowd nodding in appreciation. If ever a song signalled the start of something, it was that one. Conversation was incredibly difficult at that point but, had you been close, able to listen hard and, in part, lip read, you might have been able to make out Steve saying, 'Nah. Let's go somewhere else and get away from this shite.' And so it was that Will left the bar while Ruth ordered a round of gin and tonics.

Moments of Truth: Kismet or Chaos

Excerpt from an essay by Professor L W Jenkins, published May 2017

To what extent is life defined by random moments? How much is the path of our existence pre-determined and to what extent does the course of our lives depend on an arbitrary sequence of events?

In my study I interviewed a selection of people from the London Borough of Islington to explore how random moments had forged their current lifestyle. My sample consisted of working married couples aged between twenty-five and fifty. Following are some of the excerpts from recorded transcripts (the full recordings are available from the University of Sheffield Audio Cognitive Library, Ref: Audio.Kismet.Jenkins 2016):

1) Interviewees Mr & Mrs J Jackman

I was walking down Peckham High Street and the heavens opened. I ducked into a doorway to shelter from the rain and a few people joined me. One of them offered me an umbrella and the other offered to walk me home. We got soaked and got married, and would not have met had it not been for the rain.

2) Interviewees Mr & Mr Delwyn

I had two job offers open to me. One in Brighton, the other in Kensington. Both jobs seemed interesting and I struggled to decide. In the end, I phoned a friend and they convinced me that Brighton was the best bet. So, I took the Kensington job where I met Arun. He was the first person to offer me a coffee, the first person to ask me what I thought and the first person to open up to me. If I had taken the advice I was given, we would never have met.

3) Interviewees Mr & Mrs Lightbody

Do you recall the frost of May 2012? We do. An unseasonal frost played havoc with our bedding plants. We both went to the same garden centre in search of protective covers for our early shoots and we bumped into each other as we both reached for the last garden fabric cover. Had there been no frost or indeed a larger stock of what we were looking for, we would never have met at the centre or argued over who could take home the cover. We settled things over a cup of tea and a scone and now we plant things together, don't we, dear?

4) Interviewees Shaft & Missy

We met at rehab. I was coming down from methadone and she was recovering from an addiction to crack and she stole my fucking watch. Bitch! Anyway, I found it and she confessed. She had a nice smile and now we are cleaned up and happy.

5) Interviewees Mr & Mrs Driver

It's all a bit embarrassing. I was walking the dog on the heath and he disappeared. I ran after him but couldn't find him. After about twenty minutes, I heard some yelling and ran over to see if my dog had anything to do with it. So, there was Spike next to a cute poodle called Pippa. Pippa's owner was shouting and yelling and shoving at Spike. It took me a few moments to realise that Spike and Pippa had somehow become joined at the hip. Well, not quite the hip, if you know what I'm saying. It seems that Spike had been in the mood and Pippa was quite receptive. It was only her owner who was not at all happy. We exchanged phone numbers and I think she threatened to sue me, although I pointed out it wasn't me who was conjoined with her precious. Anyway, one thing led to another and now we walk the puppies together. If it weren't for my damn dog, we would never have met.

Essay note: Everyone I interviewed had a story like this. Lives were populated by 'if only', 'would you believe', 'as luck would have it' and 'if it hadn't been for'. There is no doubt that the randomness of connections and meetings owes a great deal to luck and timing.

The counter argument to randomness is design. The belief and concept that there is someone for everyone. The belief that some higher power or fate determines who we might meet and the circumstances under which the world conspires to place two people in the same space at the same time. For some, it is a religious experience. God is looking after them and has managed to create a moment of interaction that will spark a relationship. Some believe in spirits and the power of psychic energy to bring likeminded souls into the same space.

For me, I believe that love forces a unique perspective on history and creates an aura around the random choices we make. Life is more like a pinball machine. We are catapulted into an unfamiliar territory but the combination of buffers and flippers and tilts all add up to a destination we would struggle to predict, but with hindsight seems to have been a perfect choice.

Chapter 3: This is the Moment

'When you think about it, a kebab shop is a strange thing. They have all the salad stuff in a nicely presented cold cabinet. Nice fresh lettuce and sliced tomato. Cucumber, onions, that strange chilli stuff they have. Then they have a giant rotating slab of God knows what and hidden supplies of random sauces. Seriously, Will, what exactly is this?' Steve eyed the meat inside his kebab.

'I saw a movie recently where a kebab shop owner accidentally kills an abusive customer,' Will replied. 'He doesn't know what to do with the body, so he uses his mincing machine and passes the deceased off as a lamb doner.'

'That is disgusting but if this is that shop, then I have to say the taste is better than expected.'

'Beware of fingernails.'

Steve and Will were near Hammersmith Broadway, soaking up the effects of a couple of pints. A pleasant enough evening. They had put the world to rights. They had agreed the government's economic policy, developed some clear plans for dealing with the European Customs Union, resolved the leadership crisis for the Liberal Democrat party and discussed at length the problems of winning the Championship when your name is Liverpool. Funny how easy it is to resolve world issues when you don't actually need to do anything or make any decisions.

They left the kebab shop feeling satisfied but with fingers in need of a good wipe. Steve said his goodbyes heading towards the Hammersmith & City Line while Will grabbed his phone and opened the Uber app. He could see the image of one cab nearby together with a note that informed him there was peak time excess charging. He looked at his watch and realised that 11:10 near Hammersmith

Broadway was always a popular time. With no black cabs in sight, he ordered the Uber and leaned against some railings, looking out for another Toyota. As soon as he had placed the order, three empty black cabs came into view. Will ignored them but cursed quietly under his breath. He then scrolled through his phone, wondering what world events or key messages he had missed since 9:58, when Steve had gone to the Gents. Funny how any small gap in the day results in phone checking. Nice to see, though, that Adam had enjoyed what looked to be a delicious selection of tapas and that Jenny's uncle was celebrating a birthday.

Gradually Will became aware of the sound of a motorbike approaching. Or was it a scooter? He looked up just in time to see a gloved hand reaching out in his direction. A flash of a helmet, the lunge of some fingers and Will's phone was gone. He spun around, stumbling from the shock of the moment and his reaction to pull away from the attacker, albeit too late. He began to shout, only to find a second rider on top of him. This one drove straight at him, forcing him to fall over into the railings. The sound of the small engines disappeared around the corner and into a labyrinth of back streets. His iPhone had gone as had the cashpoint card that he kept in its case. Will was left with £10 in his pocket, and a lot of anger. He scrambled to his feet.

A couple of people came over to see how he was. A tall guy asked if he was okay and when Will said, 'Yeah, I think so,' he seemed pleased and wandered off, presumably concerned enough to ask but not concerned enough to do anything. Then Will found himself surrounded by four girls. Even in the midst of his distress, Will was alert enough to allow himself a flicker of the thought, *Every cloud*.

The girls fussed around him, asked what he had lost, how he was, did he recognise the attacker, did he know which direction they had driven, had he called the police (obviously not), how many fingers were they holding up, how was he getting home, was he okay, would he fancy coming back to their place for a party later as the night was still young, could they call anyone for him. Will responded with as much information as he could muster. Although perhaps he misheard the question about the party.

It transpired that one of the girls, Megan, had seen what happened. She was the first to shout out to the others that she had seen the bike thieves and the first on the scene to see how she could help.

'You need to go to the police station,' said Megan, assertively. 'This sort of thing needs reporting.'

***

On Sunday morning two things occupied Will's mind. One was the new phone and the need to see that all his data was backed up. The other was the scrap of paper bearing two phone numbers. The girls had been kind in his moment of need. They had offered to help, offered to ring people, offered to buy him cups of tea, but Will refused, saying he was fine. The one called Ruth had written down her name at Will's insistence after she'd ordered an Uber to take him to the police station on the Shepherds Bush Road. The other number was from Megan, who said she could be contacted if he needed a witness.

Will's evening had ended with a ninety-minute experience in the police station. Here he got to witness the late-night chaos of the station and the seemingly excessive bureaucracy of the reporting process. Will couldn't help but reflect that this should have been so simple. What did they need from him, after all? A few personal details and a statement of what happened, which in this case amounted to: 'I was playing on my phone and some opportunistic blokes on motorbikes saw a moment and grabbed it. No idea who they were or where they went.' It seems that this event needed to be spread over several pages of forms with many signatures.

Will found it easy to sort his phone. A few minutes in a store, a new contract. More forms signed and logged in. He sent a text to Steve:

An eventful evening after I left you. Came home with phone numbers from two girls. See what happens when you leave me? I become a magnet.

Steve's reply was laden with sarcasm and a hint of envy.

And so it was that Will found himself staring at the scrap of paper. Ruth seemed a nice girl; so did Megan, come to that. It was pretty rare that he had a phone number and a good reason to call. It was also pretty rare not to have Facebook or LinkedIn to review. You could tell a lot about a person from the pictures they posted. Here he had nothing to go on but a number, a name and a brief experience of a smile and compassion in an hour of need.

As Will stared at the numbers, he began to run through a variety of possible outcomes if he called.

1) She would be pleased to hear from him and would love to meet up

2) The phone would be answered by an angry-sounding bloke who would swear at him, track him down and arrive armed with a hunting knife

3) He would learn that she didn't in fact like men at all. She would be an ardent feminist and a founding member of UK Feminista and choose this opportunity to loudly condemn him for seeing her as a potential date

4) She would be a bit tired right now (the ghost of Deborah at the school disco ever present)

5) She had purposely written down the number of someone else

The thing is, Will was a worrier. Some blokes seem not to care about these things. They figure that asking someone out is a lottery with nothing to lose. 'What's the worst that can happen?' they would preach. But Will's response to his situation was a continuing spiral in the reduction of self-esteem. Loss of job + no girlfriend + rejection = perpetual loser.

Will made a coffee and thought some more. Perhaps he would ring later. He checked Facebook on his new phone and was pleased to see that Simon had chosen a poor place for lunch. Certainly his lamb shank (whatever that was) looked rather bland and the gravy did appear somewhat congealed over what he presumed was crumpled green paper impersonating some cabbage.

And so it was that Will sat in his kitchen and experienced fifty-three minutes of self-doubt and self-loathing. The thought of spending the day checking out Simon's photos of food appalled him. But at least this delayed any potential feeling of rejection. At least by not ringing, he could fantasise about the endless possibilities of a flourishing relationship without the fear of actually being in one. Fortunately for Will, at precisely 13:21 he experienced eleven seconds of courage. Enough courage to pick up the phone. Sufficient courage to keep on the line while the phone connected and rang. Ample courage to stay on the line when a voice said 'hello'.

**

They arranged to meet at The 10 Cases wine bar in Covent

Garden, just around the corner from the Tube. As it turned out, a trip along the Piccadilly Line for both of them. To Will's delight, Ruth had chosen Outcome 1.

Will had made many right moves. A nice central place, wine not beer, a meet at 18:30 which implied informality and the potential to extend the evening or cut it short. A bar near lots of other places to eat, drink and wander. In other words, a perfect zone for a chat, a chance to get to know someone but also quite a respectable answer when in twenty years' time someone asked how they met and where they went for the first date. He also had the perfect chat-up line on the phone. All he had to do was thank Ruth for the kindness showed by her friends, to answer the inevitable questions about the police station and progress since the robbery, and then to offer to buy her a drink to say thanks.

***

Ruth was browsing the shops when her phone rang. It was a number she didn't recognise, so she responded with a quick 'hello'. She then stood and listened to the guy from a couple of nights ago. He seemed grateful, which was nice. He wanted to repay her for the Uber, no need. He wanted to pass on his thanks to her friends, which of course she would. What happened next in the conversation was interesting. Ruth was quizzed about it by her friends afterwards. All Ruth said was, 'Well, I am glad you are okay. Please don't worry about the Uber and get in touch if you need anything.' In her mind, she meant that if he needed any help with the police report, or something like that, meaning she was wholly unprepared for the 'Would you like to meet for a drink?' question.

The problem was, she had already offered to help him in any way. Normally she would have made an excuse but she had already announced her willingness to assist, so the only words she could utter were, 'Oh … that would be great.'

Several hours later she found herself debating what to wear for a drink with a virtual stranger in a bar she didn't know.

Ruth decided to go out in 'advanced casual wear'. Roughly translated, this was relaxed, informal but with a touch of class. So nice jeans and top, finished off with a belt that matched the shoes and a small bag with just enough room for the essentials and not enough room for anything else. A finishing touch of an Alexander McQueen scarf completed a look that would be perfectly acceptable in most bars in London. She'd looked up The 10 Cases bar and it looked like her kind of place.

She did have doubts about going. Of course she did. It had been a few months since her last date (and she wasn't even sure that this was a date she was going on). Will seemed genuinely grateful; she liked the sound of his voice, which seemed calm and sincere. She also didn't like changing her mind. If Ruth said she would do something for someone, she would do it and this would be no exception.

Ruth arrived at the wine bar fashionably late. Will had already sent a text to say that he was sitting a table near the back on the right. She liked his style, as this made everything a bit easier. To be honest, she struggled to remember what he looked like. It was all a bit of blur, not helped by gin and tonic vision. She walked in to see a man in the corner waving a hand and mouthing the word 'Ruth'. It turned out that Will couldn't remember what she looked like either and had been doing this to any single woman who peered through the window for the last ten minutes. He would now be gathering a reputation for slightly strange behaviour and the tendency to call everybody Ruth.

Looking at Will, Ruth saw someone smartly but casually dressed. She started from the bottom up. Nice brown shoes, stylish and polished (a good sign). Blue chinos and a white shirt with a button-down collar. A clean-shaven face, framing a warm smile. Ruth reached for his outstretched hand and for the only time in their relationship, greeted him with a reciprocal shake.

Will stood up and motioned for Ruth to sit down. He did remember her but she seemed prettier today than the other night. Perhaps the lighting was better or perhaps he was more focused on her and less distracted by lost phones and motorbikes. He viewed her from the top down. Will was a bit of a 'long hair man' and was pleased to see a cascade of auburn that just reached the tip of Ruth's shoulders. She had a sunny disposition, and her whole face radiated a welcome. *Good figure*, thought Will, despite the fact that it was hard to tell given what she was wearing. A black top with a high neckline topped with a silver dolphin necklace. Jeans looked cute, fitted well and revealed curves in all the right places. Significantly no ring on the finger. He already liked her.

The first test for them both was the 'what do you want to drink' debate. Everyone knows that you learn an awful lot about people in the first few minutes. Ruth chose a chilled Pinot Grigio, so Will chose the same. What Ruth didn't know was that Will had been doing his research on how to impress on a first date. His choice of meeting place was recommended in the *Location Location* section from the dating blog he had been reading. It had emphasised the need for somewhere slightly classy where you could get a table, and not be drowned out by music or people. Without this bit of research, he might have suggested a beer at the Dog and Duck followed by a Chinese at the Happy Dragon, but he did worry about whom he might bump into there. The blog also made several suggestions on eating and drinking. It suggested taking the lead from your date. So when Ruth ordered the white wine, he followed suit. He would do the same thing over whether to order food, whether to have a starter, how many courses. Will felt this all seemed rather subservient but was assured by the blog that this was most respectful and would be seen as kind and considerate. The blog also mentioned the need to ask lots of questions and do lots of listening. This particular lesson Will forgot at first.

Ruth spotted his new phone on the table. 'You sorted a phone out okay, then?'

'Yeah,' said Will. 'The great thing with cloud computing is that you just need to log in the new phone with an ID, click reload from existing data and the whole lot is streamed to the new phone within minutes. It's brilliant. I noticed that even the song I had been playing was paused at the same point. Mind you, I did need to do some work on the email configuration and the diary access. I think the software engineers need to take a look at that in the next IOS release. I am also having some problems matching the data on my laptop and iPad, but I think I can sort that by resolving duplicate Apple IDs. I'm not sure I like the new AirPods, though. I am sure I will forget to charge them up so they won't Bluetooth to the phone. That means no catching up with podcasts on the Tube –'

At this point Will noticed a slight change in Ruth's disposition. Something about her attention had gone.

Ruth listened to Will expound on the detail of how to synchronise a new phone. *What have I done?* she thought. *I have come out with a prime geek. As if anyone cares. You buy a phone, plug it in and things happen. As if this is remotely interesting.* Ruth had an image of tumbleweed rolling through the abandoned corridors of her mind. She was beginning to lose the will to live. Fortunately, Will seemed to detect this.

Will had been surfing a website called Quora where you can ask questions on anything and people from all sorts of backgrounds and experiences will share thoughts and responses. He was flicking through the answers on what it was like to work with Steve Jobs (evidently an obsession with Quora surfers) when he stumbled on a question about the art of conversation. He read an interesting response and determined to try it out for size. Now seemed a good time. The respondent to the question had suggested the acronym FORD, which stood for Family, Occupation, Recreation and Dreams. Apparently, you could do a lot worse than ask about these things. (He also remembered that when he told Steve about this, Steve had ventured an alternative that was Foreplay, Oral, Rubbing and Dive right in). Fortunately for Ruth, Will went for the Quora version.

'So, tell me about you, Ruth. Brothers, sisters, parents, weird relatives?'

Ruth felt a little broadsided by the sudden change of direction but at least it stopped the boring stuff about Apple IDs and Wi-Fi coverage.

'One sister who lives in Reading, parents in Winchester and one uncle who isn't really that strange, although some of his Christmas presents are definitely interesting. You?'

'A brother who is in the USA doing amazingly well and always impressing my folks back home in Watford. I do have a couple of weird relatives. Aunt Margaret is a determined green campaigner. A child of Greenham Common, dedicated to bringing down fascist dictators everywhere and poisoning her nephews with excessive broccoli and artichokes and no burgers. Uncle Walt is clearly gay and living with someone called Michael but my folks never seem to mention it.'

A waitress arrived with drinks and menus. Will, of course, took the lead from Ruth, who was 'happy for a light bite'. She ordered the haddock fish cakes so Will went for Fish Pie. Fortunately, she avoided the vegetarian menu and Will managed to avoid falling into the trap of pretending to be vegetarian too. He couldn't remember what the blog had said. But he did wonder whether a veggie and a meat eater could be friends. What if they kissed and tongues found bits of chicken between the teeth? Would that be repulsive to a vegetarian? He assumed so.

The conversation meandered roughly around Will's FORD agenda, which he had to admit worked pretty well. Ruth noticed he was leaving his peppers in the side salad and asked if she could eat them. Will couldn't believe they had reached this level of intimacy already. 'Sure,' he said and felt this was a good time to reveal his well-thought-through peppers theory. 'You see, I have this theory that the production of peppers is governed by the European Parliament. I think peppers grow readily across the continent and the EU have provided incentives to farmers with subsidies. As a result, thousands of farmers are growing peppers of all colours in huge quantities. This results in a giant pepper mountain, which they then have to dispose of in an environmentally friendly way. So they offer incentives to chefs and restaurant managers to create recipes that include peppers. Restaurants are given a 10 per cent rebate on the use of peppers in a recipe and a 15 per cent rebate in an inappropriate recipe.' Will was on a roll. 'What happens in places like this is that, regardless of what you order, they throw in some peppers. Salad, throw in some peppers. Fish pie. I bet there are few in here. Order a crème brûlée and I wouldn't be surprised to find a pepper garnish.'

'Wow,' said Ruth. 'That sounds terrible for you. But I love peppers so it suits me. I wonder if it keeps the prices down?'

'Not according to the prices on this menu,' said Will, wondering if this was a mistake to say out loud. Too late.

Call it chemistry, call it lively conversation. Neither would admit to love at first sight but something changed right then in The 10 Cases wine bar. Ruth and Will upgraded from being strangers to being friends over a glass of wine and smoked haddock. People looking at the two of them would have described them as close. While the subject matter spun from one topic to another they both had similar thoughts. Will felt like ringing Steve to let him know he thought he'd found someone. Ruth, perhaps more reserved, felt completely at ease. An emotion that is so hard to find in the company of strangers. She noticed that she quickly stopped trying to impress with her answers and relaxed into authenticity. 'I want to know what it's like on the inside of love' went the song on The 10 Cases wine bar sound system. Neither of them noticed the tune but it seems even the stereo felt the mood change and switched the song choice to something more appropriate. Nada Surf would have been pleased to witness the vibe they had created.

Love at First Sight: Real, Love, or Illusion?

Excerpt from an essay by Dr Frances Wordman, published 2014 Random Press

Many people claim to have found love at first sight. On meeting a new person, they experience a rush of emotions that tie them to the new partner. Our research sets out to explore whether this is real or illusionary. We looked at a number of hypotheses:

1) Love at first sight does exist. People can feel chemistry that triggers an almost involuntary or uncontrollable emotion that this is 'the one'.

2) Two people who are ready and willing to forge a connection meet and describe the realisation that they have found a kindred spirit and claim they have fallen in love. We will argue that they were in love with the idea of love already and just needed someone to be the recipient of fully charged emotions. This 'love at first sight' is better described as relief at finding a target for emotional outpouring.

3) Love at first sight is a myth that human beings exploit. They spend their life in search of a partner and have learnt the tricks of the trade to ensure a mate, for example, 'I loved you from the moment I saw you' being one of many lines used to foster feelings of loyalty.

4) Love at first sight only exists with hindsight. People need to interact many times before they forge a clear view of the person they are with. They then project backwards their current emotions and re-invent their first meeting as love at first sight.

5) Human beings are purely animalistic. Just as birds and animals have colours, routines and rituals of courtship, humans have the same. In finding a mate, people are no different from the dominant lion in the pack or the preening pigeon in Trafalgar Square. Love is a competition with winners and losers. The idea of love at first sight is really nothing more than relief that the chequered flag has been flown in your face or the ticker tape has touched your chest as you cross the finish line.

Chapter 4: Feels So Good

Ruth got home at 10:30. The evening had started with a handshake and ended with clumsy but well-intended kisses on the cheek and the commitment to see each other again. Not two minutes after crossing the threshold, she received a text from Will, whose number was now programmed into her phone, along with his picture.

It was lovely to see you tonight. Am I allowed to say that I can't wait till next time? x

Ruth grinned and typed, *Why, I believe you are. x*

***

Will sank back into his sofa and allowed himself a smile of contentment. He picked up his phone. Funny how he was an avid user of social media. He read all about people's lives, everything from the food they ate to the celebration of marriage or the loss of a loved one. Now, sitting here with his fingers hovering over the screen, he had so many thoughts and yet nothing he wanted to share. He didn't want to tempt fate by announcing anything about how he felt. Usually, whenever anything remotely interesting happened he would be tempted to post something somewhere. Without doubt, Ruth was the most interesting thing to have happened to him for some time, but he felt an overwhelming need to keep her his secret. For now, at least.

His thoughts drifted to their next date and Will decided to make it impressive. He would demonstrate his sophistication and class whilst remaining sensitive and something of a romantic. This, Will determined, was another job for TripAdvisor. He hadn't been on many proper dates lately so he figured he would need all the help he could get.

He had three days to plan and organise a spectacular day out that would present him in the best light possible.

Will consulted the blogs and decided he needed a number of factors for the day to work. He made some notes. First, he wanted a place to meet for mid-afternoon coffee. Somewhere classy that perhaps sold nice cakes. Looking through TripAdvisor, he found a five-star coffee shop in Wardour Street that looked perfect. Everyone was full of praise for the excellent coffee and impressive service. He made a note of the name and location and was pleased to be able to suggest somewhere upmarket to meet. Even better to avoid the Starbucks or Costa chains of this world. He wanted this date to feel special. Then he needed somewhere interesting to go. Something to visit and talk about. Will checked through the list of top attractions and didn't feel that a trip round Buckingham Palace accompanied by ten thousand tourists was the ticket. An art gallery seemed to fit the bill. Sophisticated, potentially intellectual and he could sound impressive. Ruth had mentioned a love of art and this would forge Will as an art gallery kinda guy. The Royal Academy was showing an exhibition of Russian art from 1901-1945. This sounded a bit bleak but the poster on the website looked okay so he added that to his list. Will was then temporarily distracted as he researched Russian art during this period and made lots of notes. Returning to his planning, he decided on an early dinner in nearby Chinatown, followed by some kind of theatre or show. Something that would entertain but also be a conversation piece and part of a whole day of overwhelming excellence. He browsed through a variety of websites and found a great offer on some contemporary dance at the Festival Hall. This sounded great to him as he figured they could do cocktails in the OXO tower afterwards and then have a romantic stroll along the Thames before heading home.

There. It was sorted. A relaxed coffee, a bit of culture, a nice Chinese and a show followed by a glass of wine or two. Will dropped Ruth a text.

I have sorted out a great day on Saturday. Bring comfy shoes! x

The response arrived quickly.

I am a girl. I don't have comfy shoes. In fact, none of my shoes are designed for walking. I will give this some thought. xx

Will was pleased to see two kisses at the end. Always a good sign. He figured that one kiss was affection between friends. Two kisses were a guarantee of intimacy. Three kisses and beyond meant you were heading for a night of wild passion.

Great! he replied. *See you at Bar Bruno, 101 Wardour Street at 13:30 xxx*

***

Saturday couldn't come fast enough and Ruth was genuinely excited. She got up early and spent only a short while getting ready, starting at 10:00 and finishing by 12:00. She worked out that it was about forty-six minutes to the coffee bar Will had chosen so she planned to leave at 12:15 just to be on the safe side. She was pleased the weather looked okay. Nothing worse than worrying about hair being soaked on the way to something important. She dressed casually but with a hint of class: a blue floral jacket with jeans, shoes with a slight heel and a delicate bow that matched the colour of her handbag. She had soaked and polished most parts of her body and had smothered the rest in body cream. She was worried that if Will gave her a hug, she might slip out from his grip and slide down the road.

The Piccadilly line was not too bad but got busier as she neared Knightsbridge and the lure of Harrods and Harvey Nicks. She emerged from the underground at Leicester Square and wandered along Shaftesbury Avenue towards Wardour Street. She never tired of this town. The place was alive with the sight, the sound, and even the smell of the people. Every pedestrian crossing contained a complete cross section of humanity all waiting to traverse the road for different reasons. Some heading into the amusement arcades, some clutching theatre tickets; others heading for street food, bars and restaurants from every walk of life. Tourists mixed with office workers, chefs, dancers and buskers. She loved this town.

She walked up Wardour Street past a variety of conventional coffee shops as well as a few well-placed massage parlours and gay bars. Soho still contained its fair share of sleaze despite the modernisation of much around it. She finally spied Bar Bruno and to be honest, it wasn't what she'd had in mind. Small tables with plastic cloths, a massive cold cabinet containing many varieties of meat and salads. Above the counter was a huge blackboard which contained many dishes, all served with chips. Eggs, sausage, bacon, steak, chicken could all be served with chips. The all-day breakfast was £5.95 or the all-day 'gut buster' breakfast was £8.95. Both options came with tea and a portion of white toast.

Ruth was early, and there was no sign of Will. There was a free table in the corner and she squeezed past two men with yellow safety jackets to sit down. A quick glance around confirmed she was in what she might describe as a 'salt of the earth café'. All the diners were men and all were eating vast quantities of egg, beans and bacon. She looked at the menu, which conveniently included pictures of the food (just in case there was any doubt about what a cooked breakfast looked like). A waiter ambled over, wiped her table with a cloth that looked like it had also been used to check the oil in several cars, and asked what she would like.

'I'm waiting for someone so perhaps just some chamomile tea?'

'Sure,' the waiter said and minutes later a tea arrived. The mug was blue and the sort of thing you might expect to see dished out by a tea lady in the 1950s. In fairness, the tea was fine and Ruth peered over the rim of the teacup and began to hum 'Streets Of London' by Ralph McTell to herself.

Minutes passed and no sign of Will, so she sent a text.

Lovely coffee shop. Wondering where you are xx

Ruth made her tea last as long as possible but soon realised she needed to either order something else or get out of there. This wasn't a place where you could occupy a table for a whole lunchtime. It was a city café where the fast turnaround of customers was the only thing keeping it afloat. She considered ordering a salad but there was a distinct lack of anyone eating anything with greenery. She stole another quick look at the faded yellow menu, which was laminated with peeling corners. Was this Will's idea of a joke? Had he set her up to sit in this place for the afternoon?

She checked her phone: no reply.

I am going for a wander. Text me when you are free, she typed, thinking she would be better off wandering than sitting among the local workmen and their fry-ups. She paid for her tea with a £2 coin and left a £1 tip, and was just getting up when a frantic Will burst in and rushed over.

'God, I am so sorry! Bloody Tubes were stuck. I have been underground for nearly half a bloody hour with no signal.'

Ruth felt fairly unimpressed since she knew Will used the same Tube line as her. She was on time and he was not. In her head she said, *Well, I guess that shows how important I am, doesn't it?* but the words came out as, 'Don't worry, it's fine.'

Will sat down and gushed with more apologies. 'So how long have you been here?'

'I was early, so about forty-five minutes.'

He took in his surroundings. 'What is this place? It's supposed to be a five-star café with exceptional food and cakes. I checked.'

'Well, I guess it is if you happen to be in need of breakfast and some lard.'

'Damn, it looked great on TripAdvisor. Have you eaten? Can I get you anything?'

'How about we get out of here?'

'Are you sure I can't get you some bread and dripping?'

'Tempting but no. Follow me.'

With that they left to the sound of the street and even the noise from the cars and nearby jackhammers was drowned out by the sound of Will's continued apology. Ruth led the way through a labyrinth of narrow roads. They crossed Regent Street and ended up in New Bond Street. Ruth tucked down an alleyway called Lancaster Court and announced, 'Let's have something here.'

Will was immediately humbled. The whole street was cosy, intimate and packed with welcoming restaurants, with outside seating warmed by overhead patio heaters. The glasses on the tables were polished, the cutlery shone under the soft lighting that supplemented the daylight. Couples and professionals chatted and giggled and discussed matters of great importance and matters of trivia under the open skies. A few were smoking or vaping as here they could take advantage of one of the very few places where you could eat, drink and smoke. This was the perfect location for a date.

'How did you find this place?' Will asked.

'The girls and I often come here,' Ruth replied. 'It's a hidden secret that many people walk past without knowing it's here.'

'It's lovely.'

'Yeah, but sadly I don't think they serve egg and chips.'

'Okay, okay. Point taken.' Will took a breath. 'You look great by the way, love the shoes.'

Ruth suspected that Will had learnt this line. But it worked. It was the right thing to say and she hoped he meant it.

***

A glass of wine and some nibbles to keep them going seemed fine. Their second meeting seemed a lot easier than the first. The nervousness of anticipation had gone and was replaced with easy conversation.

They arrived at the Royal Academy through the impressive gate on Piccadilly and made their way across the giant and imposing quad, which surprisingly had nothing on a central plinth but the word, *Empty*. It was at this point that Will noticed the Russian Art Exhibition wasn't starting for a couple more days. Instead they had arrived just in time for *Minimalism & Abstraction: 1942-Modern Day*. Will strode confidently to the ticket office and parted with £26 for two tickets and led Ruth by the hand up the staircase to the main galleries. He was more than a little disappointed that his research into Russian Art under Stalin was to be so worthless today. He had hoped to sound impressive but realised he was now going to have to busk his way through the gallery. Ruth seemed fine to look at anything.

And so it was that Ruth and Will wandered into Gallery 1, which was apparently a metaphor for the standardisation of urban society. In this room, the blurb said, one was confronted with consistency, conformity and the repression of the spirit. The work was titled *Magnolia* and contained an enormous canvas painted in, well, magnolia. In one corner sat a Lego brick-size square of red, which was the only point of note in the entire painting. Will and Ruth stared at the large square and were soon surrounded by other people, many of whom looked like academics or students who nodded quietly and took notes.

Will leaned over to Ruth. 'This reminds me of the hall back home.'

'Oh, well, perhaps that's the intention. To challenge your thinking and to connect you to your own sense of decay and demise into urban monotony.'

Will spotted the wry smile in Ruth's voice and secretly breathed a sigh of relief. She thought this was complete bollocks as well.

'You know,' Ruth continued, 'I often think of becoming an artist, but when you see work of this sophistication and complexity, it puts you off. So humbling, isn't it?'

'Very true.' Will nodded sagely. 'What do you think the red square is all about?'

'Clearly this represents the small fragment of embarrassing non-conformity. The last bastion of hope for your life as a unique human being. In this square we find your last remaining hopes and dreams or even your dirty secrets. And deep down inside, we know that someone is going to come along with a large paintbrush and cover it in a nice shade of magnolia, thus rendering you invisible and your life blending in with everyone else's.'

'I see where you're coming from,' said Will. He was amused to see two students taking notes as Ruth espoused her theory. Who was to say she was wrong?

And so to Gallery 2, where a series of unfinished paintings hung on the wall. At least, they *looked* unfinished.

Each painting showed a vase with some green stems poking out, but no flowers. Not even one. The vases were different and the stems changed from picture to picture. The pictures were called things like, *Still Life without Petunias*. Or *Still Life without Roses*. Or *Still Life without Hydrangeas and Ferns Number 1*. The blurb announced that the painter had taken a radical approach to still-life painting by using clear descriptions of well-known items and then not including them in the picture: *In this way, we allow our own memories and creativity to complete the image. Far from being a uniform experience, everyone sees a unique image.*

'Will, do you think this bloke didn't really know how to paint flowers?' asked Ruth. 'The vases and the stems are not that great, to be honest.'

'Oh no, I think we are dealing with a genius, Ruth. The bloke was clearly a master with the brush but shows great integrity by choosing not to use a brush to create a great work.'

'I wonder how much this would cost you?'

'Probably £20,000 or so, I would imagine.'

By Gallery 3, Will and Ruth were getting the hang of the mindset required to appreciate this exhibition. Healthy cynicism seemed to be the only way to go. *This gallery,* said the blurb, *was all about the potential for creative thought. Each artist attempting to capture the moment between thinking about an image and committing it to paper.* On the left they encountered a frame containing five stapled pages of A4 paper, each featuring a single large question mark. The work was entitled *The Difference Between Thought and Action*. Next to that was a small canvas on which someone had written the word, *Potential*. The title of this work was *Realised Potential*.

'Ah,' said Will. 'I see what they have done there. Note the clever use of the word "potential" to suggest that this canvas could in fact be something great. And then the title suggesting that it already is. Pure genius.'

Gallery 4 was a video room. Art galleries often have these. The work was entitled *How to Entertain Small-Minded People*. Ruth and Will settled on a low bench and began to watch a video that was badly out of focus at first but then became clear. The video showed a man sitting in an armchair, reading the paper. In a sudden flourish of activity, he turned the page and carried on reading. Will and Ruth watched for a minute or so and nothing much seemed to be happening. After a while, Ruth nudged Will and they left.

'So, my dear Will, was the newspaper the method for entertaining the small-minded man in the armchair? Or was the video used to entertain small-minded people wandering around this gallery?'

'Mmm. I hadn't thought of the second option. I just thought it was a dull movie with no plot, no character development and no subplot. Certain to be up for an Oscar this year.'

And so Will and Ruth continued throughout the remainder of the exhibition. They found a small drawing entitled *Wisconsin without the Rest of the USA* most amusing. They also marvelled at the masterpiece, *White of Many Colours*, in which a single frame contained many squares of white with marginally different shades. Eventually they stumbled back into the daylight and stopped in the main square for a much-needed cuppa. Here they allowed themselves to giggle about the experience and to swap favourite moments. Will was glad about getting the day wrong and for not walking through several galleries of flags and pictures of foundries, steel and men working all designed to promote the cause of a communist Soviet Union. The funny thing was, while they took the piss mercilessly out of much of the artwork, in a way it did the job, as they found themselves discussing things like abstraction, conformity and creativity. In that way, the gallery had delivered. Most significantly they left with a lot of smiles.

Will took Ruth's hand which seemed to be becoming easier and more natural, and they wandered along Piccadilly towards Chinatown. They stopped briefly to have a look in Hatchards bookshop and browsed luxury cars and Persian carpets they could never afford.

They both agreed a Chinese would be good, not least because it was fairly quick as they had the theatre to get to as well. Will did wonder whether he had overplanned the day but it was too late to bail out now and sit in a bar over dinner.

Chinatown had a distinct aroma that hit the taste buds hard. It was busy at all times of the day, alive with colour and energy and a bewildering choice of restaurants. Ducks, marinated and glazed, lined the windows; lanterns lined the skyline; and menus lined the street, ready for inspection. The choice was bewildering and Will headed into a small establishment almost by accident.

Inside, the small space was full of tables, each lined with a cheap white cloth and a bottle of soy sauce. They sat down and within minutes a rather abrupt waitress arrived and threw menus on the table, along with a small supply of prawn crackers.

'I'm never really sure what these are,' said Will. 'Are they some kind of large rice crispy soaked with prawn juice?'

Ruth wasn't sure and they both scanned the menu.

Will now found a dilemma. Every Chinese restaurant has a range of set price menus that are designed for dumb tourists. They feature the blandest combination of dishes and one can only imagine the contempt held by the chef for slopping out yet another bowl of rice and sweet and sour chicken. The alternative is to go à la carte, and here there is yet another choice. There is the English menu full of things like chicken, duck, beef or prawns. Or the Chinese menu with an unintelligible range of soups and noodles. The choices are laid out over six pages of information and prices. When faced with such overwhelming choice, Will did the only thing he could.

'So Ruth, what do you fancy?'

Thank God for Ruth's decisiveness. A quarter of duck, Singapore noodles, and a couple of prawn and rice dishes. White wine and tap water on the side. The waitress made a few notes but visibly sighed at the predictability of the food ordered. She turned and shouted, 'Usual stuff for Table 12' to someone in the kitchen.

Barely two minutes had gone by when a young waiter arrived with the duck, a plate of sliced cucumber and spring onion and some dark sauce. Deftly he separated the flesh from the bone as the waitress brought a basket of steaming pancakes. Ruth crafted a pancake with a small line of sauce and all the other ingredients, and grinned as the flavours spun around the roof of her mouth. 'Surely one of the greatest tastes on earth,' she mumbled, and Will agreed. Barely had the first mouthful settled than the waitress was back, this time with the other dishes ordered. Four steaming bowls of food were deposited on the table, leaving no room for an elbow or even a wine glass.

'I think they like people to eat quickly in here,' said Will. 'In fact, I think they would be happier if we just shoved the whole lot down in one go or better still, asked for a doggie bag.'

During the meal Ruth discovered that Will was not as good with chopsticks as he liked to think. He tried to demonstrate his prowess with single grains of rice but came unstuck with those slippery mushrooms often found in Chinese food. Ruth, however, was a master. Able to name and pick up any given portion of meat, seafood or veg on demand. Will had met his match.

***

The modern ballet was due to start at 7:45 at the Jermyn Street Theatre. Will had bought discounted tickets through a website but wasn't quite prepared for the size of the venue once inside. The theatre had just seventy seats and, Will discovered, aimed 'to provide talented new actors, directors and writers with the opportunity to be recognised and given a platform in the best West End Studio Theatre'. A small stage area was surrounded on three sides with rows of red seats, and Will and Ruth found themselves in the front row on the stage right. They chatted while other people began to fill the remaining seats until the theatre became about two thirds full. Will explained that he thought some ballet would be a good thing for a date but confessed he had taken a bit of a gamble as this was a first night of a new production. The show was called *Animal Parts* and apparently the cast would allow the spirit of the animal kingdom to be absorbed into their bodies to create movement and emotion. 'Sounds a bit like a grown-up *Lion King*,' Will commented.

Mid conversation the lights went down and the audience was left in complete darkness. There was a sound of shuffling and a cinema screen flickered into life. The screen showed an abattoir and the death of a cow in graphic detail. Nothing was left to the imagination as blood flowed, innards were spilt and machines minced and ground. Three minutes into the animal gorefest a man in a black leotard uncurled from a foetal position and arched his back. The film froze and the man glared at the audience with a mixture of rage and hatred. He then moved his face within inches from Will and let out a scream that sounded like someone was removing his leg with a saw. With the scream, his arms flayed and legs stretched and he began running around the stage, confronting everyone with his anger. Next, a group of four other dancers, all similarly dressed, ran onto the set looking irate. The movie clicked back into life and the soundtrack of metal, machines and grinding was turned up to eleven. The five performers cavorted, jumped and pirouetted while screaming and yelling at the audience. On cue the screams turned to words. 'Bastards!', 'Animals!', 'Destroyers!', 'Evil!', 'Fuckers!' The cast were now hurling insults directly at the audience in a frenzy of noise and mayhem.

Will was mortified. He'd expected contemporary dance, not ritualistic abuse. Thank God the music eventually died down to just being rather annoying. Will noticed his whole body relax. This show was stressing him out. But it wasn't over. The cast began to tear at each other, ripping leotards and dragging each other around by the hair. Two small buckets appeared on stage and the lights and cinema screen all changed to a deep red. Hands reached into the buckets and began to smear and spread and splash. Faces cavorted as the supposed blood of animals was now dripping from torn black costumes.

Then all the noise stopped. All the dancers began to writhe on the floor apart from one, who rose slowly to his feet. He reminded Will of Kurtz from the movie *Apocalypse Now* and leered at the audience while breathing deeply.

'You are to blame!' he screamed. 'You are the blood on my hands. You are the blood on the floor. You are the death of my comrades. You are the death yet to come.' And then he closed his eyes briefly and his whole persona changed. His eyes opened and he spoke again. 'Thanks for coming to our show. There will be a short break while we clear the stage and get ready for *Animal Parts II*.'

With that Will seized the moment. He grabbed Ruth by the hand and quickly led her out of the theatre. The cold night air was a welcome relief, as was the smile on her face.

'Oh jeez, I hardly know what to say,' said Will. 'What the fuck was that?'

'That,' said Ruth, 'was an interpretation of man's abuse of the planet directed most clearly at us. Revenge for enjoying the duck.'

'Sorry, Ruth. I couldn't take any more of that. I felt so awful taking you there. Can we just go for a wander or something and I promise not to book any more dates? From now on we can just sit in a pub and go for a pizza.'

Ruth loved that he had tried. She loved the effort, the attention, the conversation. One day and so many stories. People often say that people create stories. She felt it was the other way round. She could return to a more interesting, more vibrant and more colourful person than the week before. It felt so good to be out and immersed in the mad creativity of this city. She clutched Will's arm as they strolled aimlessly towards Holborn.

'So, Will, let me get this right. You invite me to a working men's café and leave me stranded. You take me to a bizarre gallery where people present blank canvasses and call it art. You take me to a Chinese restaurant where I am ignored by the waiters. You then finish the day off with a gorefest and a whole bunch of people in black leotards hurling abuse at me, claiming I am personally responsible for the destruction of the planet. I do hope you are not expecting to see me again.'

Will looked a bit sheepish. 'Well … I was rather hoping to.'

'Good,' said Ruth.

***

A couple of days later, Will found himself at a job interview. He sat in reception texting Ruth and smiling at some of her suggestions for questions and answers. When invited in to meet the panel of three serious souls with the dubious job of spending company money on a new hire, Will felt so much more relaxed than usual. He had a spring in his step and a light in his eyes that was obvious to anyone who knew him and even those who didn't.

The panel had a pre-prepared list of questions for him and sat there with pens at the ready, waiting to put a tick or a cross on a form in front of them. 'So, Will, how was the journey?' they started.

Will rightly assumed this question was designed to relax him with safe territory and he could talk about buses and Tubes. On reflection he hoped they were not looking for some grand insights on his journey from infant to adult via puberty.

'Do you normally get on well with people?' they continued.

Well, most people apart from arrogant managers who know nothing and who pretend they know everything was the answer that ran through his head. Out loud, he spent a minute or two saying 'yes' and they seemed happy with that.

'This job can be quite pressured; do you think you could cope with pressure, Will?'

Honestly, what did they expect him to say? *No, I worry that I will go insane after a couple of days of true immersion into the reality of the role. Better take away my shoelaces*, he thought. Instead he offered a couple of examples of tight deadlines and sudden changes of priority that showed a man who could cope with anything.

'What do you see as your main weaknesses?'

Will had already given this some thought and prepared an honest answer and an interview one. The honest answer would be like this:

'I have a strong fixation with my phone. I can't stop looking at it and I worry that it is an addiction. I am very bad at keeping in touch with people; I forget all the key birthdays of even my closest friends and let them down terribly. I am untidy most of the time unless I have a purge, in which case I can be impossible to talk to while I sort out the crap in the house. I don't find things funny that other people find hilarious. I rarely laugh at Facebook posts, for example. My timekeeping is at best random. I live with a feeling that every journey takes about half an hour so I keep leaving late and apologising. I meander around with an overwhelming sense of failure about women. I fear that I am not attractive and even dull/ boring and no one will like me and I am doomed to a life alone. I don't enjoy parties or social occasions, although I like the idea of being invited. I go through life accepting invitations and then not looking forward to the events themselves. I am often confused in meetings at work and can't see the point of them. Rather than try and get involved, I check my phone a lot and nod at people. I can't cook that well so eat far too many instant dinners and if I invite people over for a meal, I have to cheat by using cook-in-sauces. I worry that my IT skills are rapidly becoming outdated and I will be replaced by a twenty-something enthusiast who humbles me with his current and up-to-date technical know-how. I don't like people using the word "jodhpurs". I don't understand or enjoy any American sport and distrust people who do. I have mood swings that correspond with the results of a football team, which I know is irrational but it's true. I dislike people who sing the first line of a song over and over. Oh, and peppers are awful and should never be served with any meal.'

Instead Will went for the interview option which was, 'Sometimes I work so hard, I forget to look after my own wellbeing and need to remind myself to relax from time to time.'

The panel nodded and ticked a series of boxes on their forms.

Then came the technical questions. These were often unpredictable and had the potential to trip him up. Normally Will would start bluffing his way through and attempt to disguise any lack of clarity on his part. But today his mood was different. He noticed something that wasn't confidence, exactly, but perhaps indifference. He searched around his mind when presented with a particularly tough question and wondered what Ruth would say. In this case, she would probably grin and say, 'No idea.' So that's what he did, albeit packaged well with some flattery: 'What a great question and a strong request for support … I would need some mentoring from you guys over the early stages of the project to help with that one.' To his amazement this was met by more nodding and ticking of more boxes.

Today Will didn't mind that he didn't know the answer and the panel seemed delighted that he had confessed. He couldn't help but wonder whether this approach would work with any profession. Could he, for example, bluff his way as a brain surgeon by being an all-round nice bloke who confessed to a lack of knowledge on all matters relating to incision but a keen desire to engage people to help him?

Forty-five minutes later, Will found himself back on the pavement and heading back towards the Tube. As he ambled along, window shopping, his phone buzzed. It was Greg Davis, offering him the job. He could start immediately.

Will rang Ruth immediately with the news and left a quick voicemail. 'Hi this is Will, Project Manager for DLS Systems, wondering if you would like to meet for dinner to celebrate my new position.'

Summary of Research into the Use of Affectionate Symbols to Convey Emotion

Excerpt from a study by Patterson and Lovejoy, published 2012 Psychology Today

Our research aimed to explore the addition of modern symbols of affection into common methods of correspondence and to review their impact on the perception of the message. We published a paper in 2001 on greetings, personal space, kissing and cultural differences. This research was inspired by the growth of messaging as a source of interaction and the replacement of words with symbols, aka emoticons or emojis. Readers are also advised to review the research paper published by Imogen and Preece on the impact of the 'like' symbol on self-image.

For our study we worked with fifty students at the University of Surrey and began corresponding with them. They were in the first year of study and were therefore receptive to messages from strangers. Our researchers created a persona and Facebook profile. The profile was designed to be impact neutral to create a limited lasting impression.

Soon after the first freshers' night out, we began to email our students from a google account. Each student in the sample received exactly the same content. For example, the first message read 'Great to meet you last night, I am liking it here already.' Another note read 'I am worried about all the work we might have to do once term kicks in.'

The study ensured:

• Everyone received the same message

• Whilst they may reply, we made sure not to engage in interaction of any sort. No questions were answered. Our emails were scripted to be standalone and free of any hint of personal emotion.

The only difference we made to the emails was over the sign off. We experimented with kisses, using the letter x. We wanted to see how this particular sign off would impact the perception of the person over time.

It should be noted that our university freshers seemed perfectly comfortable communicating with someone they had never met and who, in fact, didn't exist.

The trial ran for eight weeks from the start of the first term. At the end of the eight weeks our students were given a questionnaire to rate and rank their feelings about the person they had been chatting to. We then summarised the outcomes using a ten-point scale, with ten being incredibly close and intimate, and one being cold and distant. The findings were as follows:

No kisses, message ending with a formal sign off, such as 'Regards…'

Students rated this person as cold on our scale. The average score with a no-kiss sign off was 3.7. The descriptors included: nerd, dull, who, outsider.

One kiss
This rated 4.2 on our scale. Not a significant difference to the 'no-kiss' scale but the descriptors began to change. Words included: warm, cool, okay, yeah, fine.

Two kisses
This pushed people into the upper part of the scale. An average of 5.7 scored for this. It seems that two kisses suggested a stronger connection and a higher level of intimacy. Recorded descriptors included: schwing, decent, hot.

Three kisses
This created an interesting reaction. For some, the scale went up to 7.3. The descriptors associated with this included libidinous, carnal, hot, prurient. For a small number of students, however, the number dropped dramatically. The

score dropped to 2.5 and descriptors included: abhorrent, repugnant and loathsome.

Four kisses
This scored the highest at 7.9. The descriptors here were strongly intimate, suggesting carnal knowledge, copulation or the sharing of secrets or fluids.

Five kisses
This was deemed the drop-off point. The scores tumbled to 4.1 and in some cases, below that. Descriptors began to appear such as, creepy, desperate, OTT, slime.

Our conclusion for those signing-off emails in a professional context, especially in a work environment, are to be careful over subliminal signals in email or letter-writing sign off. One kiss seems to be the benchmark for professional behaviour. More than that and the writer is heading into hot water.

Chapter 5: Mad About You

The week had been busy. Will had started his new role so found himself launched into meetings about systems builds and systems architecture. He found his best bet was to nod sagely as he only had a vague idea of what they were doing on the project. He managed to impress early on by asking, 'How is the project plan linked to the strategic goals of the organisation?' His other favourite was, 'What would a customer make of these proposals?' These two questions seemed to carry considerable weight and generated much scurrying about by colleagues.

***

Ruth immersed herself in work but found the day had more smiles than usual. She was less irritated by the place and wondered if people could spot her sunnier disposition. Was there a big arrow following her round with a sign that said *Ruth has a boyfriend*?

The other thing that occupied her was texts to Will. How had people stayed in touch before social media and SMS? It would start with a *Morning x* and would end with a *Goodnight x*, and in between they would exchange a myriad of questions and useless bits of information.

Bloody Tube was mad this morning

Yep. Always is.

Fancy a coffee?

Sure, Americano would be gr8

Will get Deliveroo on it

Would rather it came in person … with a kiss

Will see if Deliveroo offers that as an option

Ha ha very funny

God this meeting is dull x

I bet mine is worse x

Try and liven it up!

What do u suggest?

Try disagreeing with everyone for 30 mins

OK I will do that – u agree with everyone for 30 mins

Deal

How did u get on?

I was praised for bringing some challenges to the project. U?

Seemed 2 go well. Boss asked me to take the lead on part of it.

Cool. For the next one u should pretend to be American from Texas

I don't have the hat for it

Coward

Just going into another meeting with the boss. Quiet for a bit

Enjoy!

U have been quiet. What u up to?

Planning world domination

Gr8 – b4 or after lunch?

B4 – don't think I can do world dom on a full stomach

What u doing 4 lunch?

Is that an offer?

Sadly no – too far to meet not enough time :-(

How was lunch?

Usual. Salad in a box – yours?

Lobster Thermidor was slightly tough. Chablis most excellent – Crème Brûlée melted on the tongue – Also had a chicken & bacon sarnie from Tesco Express

I am jealous. Wish we had a Tesco express.

Fancy dinner Sat?

Love to – any idea what u fancy?

Wonder if u fancy a place where u kill your own meat and grill it

Sounds great! Come to my place – I will cook

Love to

Is there anything u don't eat?

Well u know about my pepper theory

Thought I would do pepper soup & stuffed peppers

I will stop 4 McD on the way and tip food surreptitiously into plant pot

I will move them and see what u do then

U are cruel

Just amused

Will experienced a shudder of excitement and anticipation as Ruth invited him for dinner. The dates had been 'interesting' but they got on amazingly. He couldn't wait to see her again. They only lived three miles apart but so far Ruth had insisted on not being escorted home. The nights had concluded with tender kisses and all too brief moments of physical connection.

This felt like their relationship was moving to another level. Dinner at her place felt like an invitation to be closer. Eating out is easy and being surrounded by people means the rules of engagement are clear. Light touching of hands is allowed. Brief kisses on the cheek or lips are fine. But any lingering kisses or advanced fondling are frowned upon by fellow diners. Any attempt at intimacy is likely to result in eviction. But Ruth's place was her domain. She could change the rules.

***

Ruth got home from work and found a brown padded envelope on the floor. She didn't recognise the handwriting. She took off her coat and opened the package in the kitchen. There were small plastic objects inside. She tipped them out onto the table: eight red Lego bricks and a handwritten note in a small card with a flower.

Dear Ruth,

Each of these bricks represents a story, a moment or an emotion.

The first is for the moment I met you standing post robbery in Hammersmith.

The second is the fear of anticipation I felt as I picked up the phone and the joy I felt when you answered.

The third is for the glass of wine in Lancaster Court and how I noticed the rest of the world disappear and you become my focus.

The fourth is for discovering your sarcasm in the face of art that simply wasn't worthy.

The fifth is for ordering with confidence in the Chinese despite the fact that they wanted us to leave.

The sixth is for enduring abuse in the face of contemporary dance with class and grace despite the shouting and the blood.

The seventh is for the kisses we shared on the Tube train.

The eighth is for the look over your shoulder as you left me on the train.

I hope every time we go out we add to them in some way. Let's build a big tower of red bricks as a reminder of the rich colour and the wild stories behind them. As we experience them, they will become small red squares of memory that begin to fill in our magnolia walls.

Can't wait till Saturday.

Love, Will x

P.S. I looked everywhere for a card with a picture of a flower but without the flowers and couldn't find one. Perhaps you can rub these out when you have a moment or use Tipp-Ex.

Ruth smiled on the outside and on the inside. She reached for her phone.

Thanks for the Lego bricks and the card. What a lovely thought. I have put my bricks on the side in the kitchen and hope we build a tower xxx

And Ruth put up the card and stacked her little bricks next to them, wondering whether they would indeed be adding to them at the weekend.

***

The next day at work, Ruth began to think about the food she might prepare for Will. The menu needed to be classy, coherent and delicious. It was once said, 'we are what we eat' and so she was determined that her meal would be something memorable. Perhaps worthy of a brick. She was reminded of going over to a friend's house for supper recently and the whole meal had been constructed from Marks & Spencer's ready-made suppers. Fish pie, cooked in the oven in the foil for thirty-five minutes and served hardly equated to cooking. Plus her host had taken the packet instructions literally. 'Serves two,' it said so she had bought two boxes to feed four people. Surely everyone knows that all instant meals are marked 'serves two' so as not to embarrass single people at the checkout? The measly portions were dished out onto embarrassingly large plates. Ruth recalls leaving with a sense that her friend lived her life through shortcuts and other people's hard work, and was lacking in generosity.

So Ruth surrounded herself with a variety of cookbooks. What was it with master chefs that they seemed unable to cook normal things? She was determined to avoid the roast pigeon with Pernod and grapefruit served on a couscous bed flavoured with anchovy. Flicking through Jamie Oliver's latest instalment, she didn't fancy anything. Or more to the point, the food just wasn't her. Jamie was all for throwing in bits of veg into a giant pan and mashing it up and roasting it and overusing the word 'beautiful'. But the food didn't seem right for the occasion.

She spent a few moments thinking about curry. Everyone likes that but Ruth figured the volume of garlic, ginger and cumin required would poison the average visitor. Thank God for *LEITHS Cookery Bible*. A haven of common sense and culinary excellence. Here things were simply laid out and every page listed the sort of thing you might find in a French bistro. And then she had a theme: French bistro. She settled on onion soup, beef bourguignon, crème brûlée and a cheeseboard. With red wine, of course. She figured much could be done in advance so that she could find time to spend with Will and not be trapped in the kitchen all night.

A couple of days early she headed to the local Waitrose and, after buying the right sort of wine, beef, button mushrooms, bacon lardons, button onions, herbs, cream, vanilla, cheese and vegetables to steam, she had spent at least the price of a decent meal at a local restaurant. She enjoyed the shopping, and it felt good to be buying food with someone else in mind. She was purposely cooking for four to six people rather than two, as all the recipes were for larger numbers and she didn't want to risk anything going wrong. Once all the ingredients were safely stored until needed, she began to plan what to wear. This also required some thought. Something casual – she was at home after all – and yet sexy/attractive. Something that would look okay stirring a casserole and look equally okay being torn off in a moment of sublime passion. She struggled making these two images connect. It was one or the other. What do men want, a chef in the kitchen and a whore in the bedroom? This wasn't a problem Ruth had wrestled with that often.

***

Will spent the evening with Steve over a pint.

'So, what's she like then?'

'Yeah, really nice Steve, I like her a lot.'

'Pretty?'

'Yes, I think so.'

'Nice hair?'

'Yep.'

'Previous boyfriend, husband or lover?'

'None for a while.'

'Tits okay?'

'Um, they seem fine…'

'You mean you have yet to have a look?'

'Well, we are taking things nice and slow, mustn't rush these things.'

'You didn't say that with whatever-her-name-was at that party in Brixton we went to.'

'True, but this is different.'

'Different?'

'Yeah, different.'

'Bloody hell. You're in love!'

'Give me a break, Steve, I hardly know her.'

'I know that look, young Will – you can't pull the wool over my eyes. What team does she support?'

'We haven't really talked about footb –'

'What do mean you haven't talked about football? What in God's name have you been talking about?'

'Well, I didn't want to put her off by appearing too much of a typical bloke. So I kinda missed that out of the conversation.'

'And replaced it with what?'

'Contemporary dance and abstract art.'

'Fuck! You are joking, right? I have known you how long and you and I have never gone through an evening without some reference to football!'

'Or politics, Steve.'

'Okay, I grant you. Politics and resolving world issues is also our thing.'

'I plan to gradually unveil my love of the beautiful game over time.'

'This doesn't bode well. You are already suppressing your true self. A few steps away from marriage and the Disappearing Man Syndrome.'

'What's that?'

'It's what will happen to you. Your opinions will disappear and you will ask the wife what to think.'

'Hardly!'

'Well, if and when I meet her, I plan to tell her a few home truths about you. And don't think I won't tell her about that incident with the asthma inhaler and where you put it.'

'Thanks Steve, I knew I could rely on you to open up about my love life.'

'You are most welcome.'

'She's invited me to her place for dinner on Saturday, actually.'

'Really! That sounds like progress. At least for checking out the breasts.'

'That's not what the evening is about, Steve.'

'Bollocks, Will. You and I know 100 per cent that the evening is exactly about that. I bet you think about what will happen all the time.'

'No, I don't.'

'Bollocks.'

'Well, just a bit … okay, okay, a lot. It's been a while.'

'Just saying, mate, that if you have been invited over for "dinner" it's worth doing some preparation.'

'What advice do you offer, oh Steve the great seducer?'

'Okay. For a start, take flowers. Not roses! Roses are for people who are trying to prove something. Not a big bouquet, either. It looks ridiculous. A small bunch of white something or others will be fine with a bit of greenery in there. Enough to fit in a small vase. In fact, if you can get some that are in a bag of water already, so much the better.'

'Shall I take notes?'

'Yeah, if you like. Next take some classy chocolates. Not and I repeat *not* a bar of Galaxy or anything made by Cadbury. Nor should they be shaped into a pink heart or in a heart-shaped box. It's not Valentine's Day. Be classy and go to somewhere like Fortnums and spend enough money that you wince at the checkout. Bits of orange or violet in them are good. Ginger or bits of chilli are bad.'

'Okay, not chocolate hearts.'

'Under no circumstances should you buy anything furry either living or dead and take it with you. No fluffy bunnies, pandas, bears, dogs or orangutans. They make you seem like a right wimp.'

'I wasn't going to.'

'Oh, you'd be surprised. You go into a shop and spy a cuddly animal. Next thing you know, you're bringing it home and ready to hand it over. Just … *don't*. Now, let's not forget the obvious. Contraception.'

'Steve, I seriously don't need your pearls of wisdom on that.'

'As long as it is in hand, Will. Just making sure you have thought of everything.'

'It has crossed my mind.'

'Are you getting any practice in?'

'Steve!'

'Okay, okay. When you get there, don't forget to say how nice she looks.'

'What if she doesn't?'

'Then two things. One: what are you doing there if she doesn't; and two: what does it matter? No one looks at the mantelpiece while they are poking the fire, as they say.'

'Okay, but I do intend to look at the mantelpiece.'

'Up to you – oh, compliment the shoes.'

'I'm good at that. That went down well the other day, in fact.'

'Yeah, girls spend a lot of time on shoes, so say something nice. Oh, and polish your own. Women look at your feet a lot, apparently.'

'What, even trainers?'

'We are not wearing trainers, Will.'

'No?'

'No. Nice shoes, good quality shirt, casual jacket, nice belt and some killer aftershave.'

'Does killer aftershave actually exist?'

'No, but the thing is, it is part of the whole package. It shows you have thought of these things. Women take ages getting ready and they like to think you have bothered as well. The fact that you threw on your one good outfit in a couple of minutes should not enter conversation.'

'Have you finished?'

'Yeah, maybe. Oh, tell her it smells delicious.'

'What if we're having salad?'

'If she has made just a salad, apologise and say, "Sorry, I meant to say it smells delicious at the curry house around the corner," and leave. No woman in her right mind would subject you to an evening of radishes and lettuce on a first date. Get out of there fast.'

'Okay, I will. Especially if she prepares a salad with lots of peppers. I hate peppers.'

'Well, there you go. All sorted apart from the wine. Officially, the host is not supposed to use the wine that guests bring. They are supposed to have already thought about it. But you never know…'

'Champagne?'

'Not a bad idea, but expensive and a bit over the top. Get some French or Spanish sparkling wine and spend more than a tenner on it.'

'Okay, I will. Anything else?'

'No, you should be fine. As long as you get that facelift in and the personality transplant.'

***

Ruth's recipe for French Onion soup required 8 lbs of onions and five hours of cooking. She wondered whether prawn cocktail would have been a better idea. On Saturday lunchtime she found herself peeling a huge pile of onions and she cried as if her own mother had just been run over by a bus. Eventually she emerged from the pile of onion peel with a mighty pot and began to simmer the sliced onions until caramelised, as the recipe said. They needed stirring every twenty minutes, so that was her rooted to the kitchen for the day. The beef was fairly straightforward and at least she could throw everything into a pot and forget it. Having started the cooking, the next thing was house tidying. Whenever she expected visitors, Ruth liked a good tidy up. You never know which rooms they might enter. So, Ruth spent a good couple of hours polishing every surface and hoovering every crevice. Had the queen been coming she might have painted the hall as well, but Will would have to put up with things the way they were, despite the poor standard of painting.

Then Ruth wondered about which books or magazines to have scattered around. Which music to have playing? So many tough decisions on how to create the right impression. She opened a new Jo Malone room fragrance and hoped that the pomegranate noir would defeat the scent of caramelised onions. Sadly, a battle it was destined to lose. She fluffed the cushions. Left her copy of the Hilary Mantel book that she had yet to finish despite her best intentions on the side, put her iPod on shuffle and hoped for the best.

She sometimes wondered whether the iPod contained a

small person with a brain, a heart and who knew her well and was listening in on the conversation. It was amazing how often, when chatting with friends about an artist, their song would randomly start playing. Only the other day, a brief conversation about Madonna was accompanied by a burst of 'Vogue', surely one of her best songs. With 15,653 songs to choose from, there was something more than random happening here. At other times, it set the mood just right. When she felt melancholic, the iPod would shuffle away and find something incredibly fitting. Perhaps some Nick Cave or Nick Drake. In fact, anyone called Nick would be melancholic.

***

And so it was that on Saturday evening, the table was laid for two. The best glasses sparkled. The soup decanted into a smaller saucepan, ready to heat. Croutons and Gruyère cheese at the ready. Beef tender and vegetables ready to steam. Crème brûlée out of the M&S packet (Ruth ran out of time for cracking eggs and adding vanilla pods). A nice selection of cheeses, ready to place in a spiral pattern on an olive wood board. Grapes washed and chilled, ready to accompany the cheese. Red wine open and white wine in the fridge. A tasteful bouquet of flowers on the table. Lights down low but not too low. The room tidy, polished, hoovered and dusted, and giving off a hint of Mr Sheen, mingling subtly with Jo Malone and the multiple smells of cooking.

Ruth was wearing black trousers with casual but stylish shoes. Her white top had been protected from potential cooking stains by an apron with classic blue stripes. Her hair, simply washed and clipped to one side. Makeup applied to look sexy but a few stages of application away from street hooker. Around her neck hung her favourite oval silver pendant that she could proudly say she'd bought herself. No point running the gauntlet with any ex-boyfriend attire.

The doorbell rang. On cue the music changed to a rather cool song by the xx. Surely a sign.

'Ruth! How great to see you!'

'Oh, er, hi Ange, haven't seen you in ages.'

'No, I know, and I was working nearby and you always said I should call in for a cuppa. I did try to call but no one answered, so I figured I would just pop round.'

'Come in, come in.' Ruth silently cursed her bloody phone. Damn the silence. Damn the vibration being turned off. 'What can I get you, coffee? Wine?'

'A wine would be great, it has been such a crappy old day. It looks lovely in here, Ruth, are you expecting company?'

'To be honest, yes. I have a friend coming round for dinner. A guy called Will.' Ruth now found herself in an unusual dilemma. Ruth had always told Ange she should pop round. Mostly it would be fine. Mostly she would enjoy her company. Ange could talk for England, always had stories to tell and could drink most people under the table. But not tonight of all nights. She handed over a glass of wine with a smile while secretly screaming, *Can you drink that fast and please fuck off?*

'I won't stop if you have company, Ruth.'

'Honestly, Ange, it's nice to see you. Will will be here in a minute; I think you'll like him.'

'I promise to give an honest opinion. If he isn't good enough for you, I will use subtle hand signals like pointing at the door and waving goodbye to him.'

The doorbell rang.

'That will be him, Ange.' Ruth moved round her friend towards the door. On cue, the iPod selected 'I Wish It

Could Be Christmas Everyday' by Wizzard. Ruth was now panicking as this wasn't what she had in mind at all.

'Hi Ruth,' said Will, leaning in for a kiss and noticing a slight reticence in her approach.

'Will, great to see you,' said Ruth in a voice that had a slightly louder volume and hint of the dramatic about it. 'Come on in. Will, meet Ange, my old friend.'

And so began the commencement of polite formalities. Will played the part well. He handed over the wine, the chocolates and the flowers, which all seemed a perfect choice. He said all the right things about the room, the decor, the table and even managed a surreptitious 'You smell delicious' under his breath.

Of course, Ruth asked Ange if she fancied a bite to eat and of course, Ange accepted. What is it with some people? You would think she would notice the room setting, the cooking and the ambience, and work out she needed to go. But Ange was one of those thick-skinned individuals who seemed oblivious to such matters. Ange was also a smoker, or these days, a vaper.

'Do you mind if I vape, Ruth?'

Now cigarettes would clearly have been banned but Ruth wasn't sure how she felt about vaping. So she mumbled an okay, and Ange took out a silver contraption with a vial of brown liquid.

'It keeps me going. I don't like the tobacco-flavoured ones, funnily enough. Tastes wrong somehow but some are quite nice.' She inhaled and puffed out a plume of white cloud.

'Oh, that's interesting,' said Will. 'What's that smell?'

'Monkey Fart,' said Ange, 'and no, I am not joking.'

Will smiled with a smile that was invented to placate people. It wasn't a smile he meant. But it was the right thing to do.

'So how long have you two known each other?' said Ange.

'About three weeks,' Will replied. 'Ruth came to my hour of need when someone nicked my phone.'

'That sounds like Ruth, she is always there when you need her. A bloody good friend, I have to say.'

Will then reached into the recesses of his mind and remembered the FORD formula. He began to pepper Ange with questions about her family, her job and her dreams. Ange liked him immediately. Meanwhile, Ruth heated the croutons with the cheese under the grill and added an extra place setting at the table.

Ange was not stupid. As soon as she saw they were having starters, a red light flashed above her head and she realised it was a date. Let's face it, you only have starters at dates or dinner parties. The rest of life is a one-course experience. Pizza and salad. Pasta and garlic bread. Steak and chips. But the second you add something to the front of the menu – prawns in Marie Rose sauce, perhaps – you are in date territory. It even sounds romantic. You can match wine to the food. Ange cornered Ruth in the kitchen.

'Ruth, why didn't you bloody tell me this was a fucking date? Blimey! You and I have known each other long enough. You just needed to tell me and I would have gone. It wasn't till the onion soup came out that I realised…'

'Ange, I wouldn't do that to you. And anyway, you would have been offended and it's fine. It's good for Will to meet my friends.'

'So, are you like an item now?'

'Well, we are getting that way. It depends whether I pass the cooking test.'

'Of course you'll pass that. It's the other test that matters.'

'Other test?'

'The how do you look in the morning test, Ruth. I will eat my beef and then I am going to make my excuses.'

'You don't have to, Ange.'

'Yes, I do.'

***

A woman of her word, Ange demolished her main course and made her excuses. No one believed them but that wasn't the point. Will and Ruth were together at last. Alone.

'Will, I am so sorry! I had no idea she was coming. She never pops in.'

'It's fine. I must admit it was a bit of a surprise. I thought you might have arranged a gang of girly protectors for the night. The Christmas music was also a nice touch, by the way.'

'What Christmas music?'

'The sound of Wizzard wishing it could be Christmas every day as I came in.'

'Yes, well obviously I chose that especially to create the right mood. Would you like some more wine? Oh, and we have desert and cheese yet.'

'Yes please. Nice place, by the way. I like it. Much cosier than mine.'

'It will do, sorry it's such a mess.'

'Mess? I am definitely not inviting you round if you describe this as messy. My place isn't exactly piled high with beer and pizza boxes but I do have to tidy up before I can even think about cleaning anything. Just stuff in the way. Are you reading this?' Will pointed to the Hilary Mantel book. 'Someone bought this for me and I couldn't get on with it. Seems that once you put down one of her books you can't pick it up again.'

'I'm part way through,' fibbed Ruth. Her response suggested that she would finish it but in reality, she too had put the book down.

***

There comes a point during a meal when you know you have had enough food. Well, for most people, that is. Will had a couple of mates who seemingly could keep eating ad infinitum. *But what is food, anyway?* he wondered. Food can be seen as something that keeps a person alive, involving the process of ingestion, digestion and the absorption of fats and protein. But that's not really it, is it? We have turned food, the art of eating, into an event. Food is prepared and produced with a flourish. We work out what sort of people we are dealing with by the food that they serve. Food becomes a show, a demonstration and a backdrop to conversation.

Tonight, food had been the surface reason for getting together. Food had provided a haven and had enabled safe and welcome conversation. Food was a facilitator of human interaction. Did Will want anything more to eat? No, of course not. He was impressed by Ruth's cooking and more than that, her evident effort. Even someone with a rudimentary understanding of cooking could see that Ruth had spent the day in the kitchen.

But now the food had served its purpose. No other flavours were needed. Not even the luxury chocolates were necessary. Will sat on his chair, debating his next move. He didn't want to be forward, inappropriate of disrespectful, but Steve was right. He didn't really come round for dinner. But he found himself engaged in random small talk while his head considered what he should do. He even thought about saying he had to leave. Now that may seem crazy, but what do you do when you leave? You kiss people goodbye. And that's the excuse you need. This gave Will an idea.

'Ruth, can I ask you a question?'

'Yeah, sure.'

'Can we pretend I am about to go home at the end of the evening?'

'Will, why would you do that?'

'Trust me.'

'Oh … okay. Well, thanks for coming, Will, it's been great to see you.'

'Thank you for a lovely meal, Ruth, it's been amazing. See you next week.'

Will stood up and Ruth met him in the middle of the room.

Will leaned forward and kissed her goodbye. Except it wasn't a kiss goodbye. They both knew it.

'Bye, then.' Ruth grinned.

'Yeah. See you later,' said Will.

Minutes later, Ruth led Will by the hand up the stairs and to the darkened seclusion of her bedroom. Seducing a new lover is rarely as it appears in the movies. Will had seen many great lovers on celluloid and admired their charm and sophistication with seduction. His favourite was a Bond movie where Bond had a magnetic watch. With a flick of the wrist, 007 magnetised his watch and moved his wrist to the back of the neck of his beautiful conquest. Then, with a slow, deliberate movement he lowered his hand down the small of her back and as he did so, the zip from the tight-fitting dress followed his movement, setting his conquest free from her outfit. Bond had obviously never encountered a bra with a hook at the front.

After several moments of searching around the back in the dark, Ruth had to point out he was trying to unlock from the wrong side. Now that's all very well, but this only prompted yet more fumbling. Bond would never find himself in such a position. He would have had some sort of laser for this kind of situation.

Will then encountered his next challenge. Why, oh why did he wear trainers and why did he double knot the laces? He tried to remove his trousers and felt a bit of an idiot with them hanging around his ankles. Not to mention the severe restricted movement this offered at a time like this. He tried subtly kicking them off but only succeeded in a hefty kick into the dresser followed by the sound of various bottles falling from their perch.

'Hold on a minute,' he said.

'Will, what are you doing?'

'Taking my shoes off. This could take some time.'

Now undoing trainers in daylight can be difficult but, in the gloom, Will succeeded in pulling hard on the wrong section of the lace, thus tightening them so they would never again come free. Ruth flicked on a bedside light and grinned. 'Is this one of your killer moves, Will?'

'It's not funny. I won't be a minute…'

With that, Ruth slipped to the floor and pushed Will out of the way. 'Let me try, I have nails.' She kneeled at his feet working his white laces with strong fingernails and a fixed grin. She then loosened a trainer, repositioned herself and pulled gently to remove it. She glanced up at Will and smiled. One shoe down she started on the second, which offered less resistance as Will began to relax. Ruth finally removed Will's trousers and threw them into a small heap on the floor. Will watched her graceful movements and concluded he had never seen a more erotic sight in his entire life.

Four minutes later, Will found himself lying on his back. Ruth had disappeared into the bathroom. She returned with a handful of tissues and handed them over.

'Thanks,' said Will. 'That was lovely. A bit quick, and I am blaming you for that by the way, but lovely.'

'What are you blaming me for?'

'Well, if you weren't the sexiest woman on planet earth, my entire body would not shudder and explode at your every touch. And we might last a bit longer.'

'It was lovely,' agreed Ruth and then added after a long pause, 'Again?'

'Give me a minute…'

***

At 2:00 in the morning Will and Ruth were still wrapped around each other. This is where Will disagreed with the movies. Apparently, men have a strong desire to clear off quickly after sex. Or at least to turn over and go to sleep. Will had no such thoughts. Under the moonlight that peeked through the curtain, Will whispered, 'Ruth, this may be crazy but it's true. I'm mad about you.'

Love and states of madness: Is it possible for overwhelming love to bring about temporary paralysis of common sensibility?

Transcript excerpt from a TED talk by Alexander Shelvick, broadcast September 2012

You may have come across a theory by the great intellectual and author, Will Self. He wrote about an interesting idea based on what he called the Quantity Theory of Insanity. The idea is roughly this: There is only the capacity for so much sanity in the world and this is balanced by people we would classify as unhinged or insane to various degrees. Thus, when one person is cured from a dark place, another person will go off the rails. Some of you might have read that.

This may have been a work of fiction subject to studies, although looking at this audience there may be some truth in it.

[Ripple of amusement in the hall.]

Anyway, our research into brain activity and the capacity for problem solving suggested that whilst Will Self may be wide of the mark at a collective level, when it comes to an individual, he may have a point.

Let's take Dave here, whom we chose from a dating agency site where he was looking for love.

[A picture of a man in a suit appears on the screen.]

Let's put him to work. Let's give him some simple, rudimentary tasks that require close attention and some cognitive skill. Okay. Now let's give Dave an IQ test and see what he is capable of mentally, and a personality test to see what sort of person he is. We'll also interview him to get as close to the real Dave as possible. This provides us with a clear picture of an average Dave and how he can function under reasonable pressure.

We then found thirty-seven other people to help us with our studies, all bound by a common thread. They were all single and active on dating sites.

Our research tested them at various points in the dating cycle. We wanted to see whether there was a correlation between cognitive and behavioural skill, and stages of romance. We had data on pre-courtship, first meetings, early stage intimacy, advanced stage intimacy, engagement and commitment to a wedding.

So this is what we found.

All of our subjects gave clear results pre-courtship. They were bright, intelligent and focussed.

As soon as courtship commenced, there was an interesting drop in tasks requiring mental attention to detail. Error rates went up and there were some behavioural fluctuations.

Early-stage intimacy began to present some fascinating variables. We encountered errors on cognitive and problem-solving tests. Most interesting were the reported changes in personality type. We noticed the extreme traits of personality being smoothed and our subjects reported greater neutrality.

Once we hit advanced-stage intimacy, results went off the scale. Quality and accuracy of all tests declined to a significant degree. Strange spikes appeared in our personality tests that demonstrated a strong desire to be liked. All the social indicators rose and any indicators of conflict were reduced. Some of the interviews we conducted during this phase made no sense. Take a look at this guy.

[A video clip is played on the screen. The sound of an interviewee is heard.]

'I just think about her all day. I find myself wandering around in a daze and thinking, what can I do now to make her happy? Yesterday I put my shoes in the refrigerator without even noticing. Now why would I do that? I have started eating olives. I hate olives, so why would I eat them? Well she loves olives, so get me. I am joining in. I read the paper but have no

memory of the words on the page. I am feeling quite pathetic. Am I happy? No, not really. With romance comes stress and I am worried the whole time that something might go wrong. I catch myself doing things I don't agree with. For instance, I will drive miles just to look at her house. I sit there knowing that this is a totally dumb idea. But there you are. Love makes you crazy, huh?'

[The TED talk resumes.]

What we discovered through these studies is that the true experience of love and romance can have a strong and disruptive impact on people's ability to function as normal. We recorded mood swings, a drop in IQ, suppression of natural personality traits and, in some cases, extreme irrational behaviour.

Now I know what question you are asking. What about later on, as the early stages of love become a distant memory? Well, as soon as those dates for the wedding get put in the diary, ladies and gentlemen, back come the extreme personally traits and cognitive skills, and the problem-solving ability returns. Effectively people become their old self. Whether or not that's good enough for the bride or groom to be remains to be seen.

Revisiting Will Self's research, we believe that people have a limited capacity for rational thought and what seems to be happening is that dating takes so much focus and attention, it reduces the capacity for common sense and objective problem solving. Our message to any employers out there: Don't interview anyone for a job who has recently found love. And if you do employ them, keep a close eye on them. Chances are they will be distracted and may screw up.

Thank you very much.

Chapter 6: Jealousy

And so it was that Ruth and Will entered a territory known as Advanced Dating. Such a strange experience when you reflect on it. Two people arrange to meet, connect and intertwine over a series of set pieces and to see how they get on. TV shows try to recreate this experience with shows like *Love Island* or *Big Brother* but reality TV is a long way from reality in life. If they get on well, they might forge the start of a long-term relationship, but everything still has the potential to go badly wrong.

The trouble is that, on the first couple of dates, people are adept at acting the part. They can smile in the right places, present a face alive with interest and empathy. They can prepare food, demonstrate common courtesy, be present, be attentive, show affection and kindness. There is, of course, a 'but' and this comes in many forms.

Firstly, it is difficult to act the part consistently for any length of time. People's personalities have a tendency to break through, especially if stressed or under pressure. What was Rita Hayworth's famous quote? 'They go to bed with Gilda and wake up with me.' So, whilst Will and Ruth got on famously at first, they soon had to deal with the darker side with all their habits, mannerisms and peculiar ways.

Secondly, there are many external forces that come into play that are outside the control of the new couple. Friends, and worse still, relatives, have a habit of arriving on the scene and causing havoc with any couple that seems to be enjoying its own company.

Will and Ruth were pretty good at being on their own. This was a good sign. They quickly reached an assumptive phase of the relationship. Not much was said out loud but they began to assume they were seeing each other at the weekend. They developed a pattern of behaviour whereby they connected over dinner every other day during the week, sometimes more. There was an assumption that they would update each other at regular intervals on the phone.

Date Number 1
A weekend in York. This was Will's idea. He liked the idea of getting a train to York, finding a boutique hotel, getting lost in the back streets and smiling over candlelit dinners for two followed by long lie-ins. His plan was sound apart from a couple of things. They decided to travel up on a Friday evening and underestimated the mass of commuters heading the same way. They found two seats situated some distance apart and did their best to communicate by text and semaphore.

The hotel was found on booking.com and was supposed to be 'centrally located with modern amenities'. This was all well and good but the hotel stopped serving food at 8:30 p.m. and Will found himself searching the web for nice places to eat. So, the first night was sadly a Chinese called the Duck Palace. Will hadn't expected chopsticks and Chinese music to set the scene for the evening.

The other strange thing they needed to get around was the hotel toilet. What is it with modern designers that decide to put a thin smoked glass door on the toilet with a clear section at the top and bottom so it is quite obvious what the inhabitant is doing? Will and Ruth arrived with detailed knowledge of each other's bodies but now they were presented with a new challenge: levels of intimacy and toilet behaviour. At home, Will would wake reasonably early, head to the loo and happily sit there for twenty minutes reading his phone and stewing in his own aroma. With Ruth the other side of the smoked glass, this took on a different perspective. He didn't want Ruth to experience the embarrassing sight, sounds and smells of his early morning motions, so he found himself avoiding any significant toilet action. Some blokes would happily wander into the loo, do their business and exit with a loud proclamation recommending everyone give the room a wide berth for some time. Will was not that kind of guy. The other problem he encountered was that the hotel had a non-flushing toilet. Oh, it had a handle to press and vast quantities of water would gush with Niagara Falls enthusiasm towards the toilet bowl. But once the noise and spray had subsided, whatever Will had left in the toilet was still sitting there. It didn't seem possible but he now faced the problem of Ruth coming in only to be confronted by something Will had deposited. Will wondered if a guide to modern romance explained the best course of etiquette to follow when you get thrown together into a small room with a loo attached.

Fortunately, York offered a perfect escape from the chaos of London and Will and Ruth soon found themselves lost in the maze of back streets as well as the company of each other. In doing so, they began to develop new ways of being together, little habits that seemed natural and relaxed, if at times a little immature. They began to find comfort in holding hands, sometimes the whole hand, sometimes little fingers, or the alternative, which was the arm-in-arm grab. They developed an ability to move through even crowded streets as one. Neither wanted to be the one to let go. Sweet kisses were exchanged under the shade of trees in the park, moments of passion and longing were muttered between the trivial moments of conversation. If one of them needed to nip to the loo, their eyes would meet with a grin and a 'miss you already' look of affection. They may as well have wandered around with a sign labelled 'Happy Loving

Couple' so that those nearby could give them a wide berth or make allowances for their obvious public displays of affection.

They even began to find strange shops interesting. Will would normally never be seen dead in a craft shop but here he browsed displays of small wooden animals, gaudily printed silk scarves and a plethora of candle holders. There seemed no limit to the imagination of those in the craft industry to create and shape objects designed to hold and display candles. Will had no idea this was such an expansive profession and he found himself expressing a preference for one style over another. Four shops later he took the plunge by investing in an olive wood tea light holder, which was wrapped neatly in paper and handed over in a plastic bag. Ruth complimented him on his choice and mentioned they should look out for some fragranced tea lights to pop into it. Will agreed so off they set towards yet more craft shops, especially those offering the very best aromas captured from exotic plants.

And so it was that Will caught himself wondering if it were possible to capture customised scents. Perhaps beef casserole simmering in Mum's kitchen would sell well. Or hot dogs sizzling on a cold day. But then he had a moment. He was now a man who bought things in craft shops. *Is this what romance does to a man?* he wondered. He vowed never to tell Steve he had been shopping and comparing white musk and oud with citrus and frangipani.

Date Number 2

A night out with Ruth's workmates hardly sounded compelling, but that's one of the things that happens early in a relationship. Either party will accept absurd suggestions for evenings out when the whole idea is the very last thing you would want to do. Ruth's firm was having an off-site conference and for some reason decided to hold a black-tie dinner and to invite partners. Apparently, this was designed to 'celebrate the progress made over the last twelve months and to connect with those outside the company who have played a part in their own special way of helping and supporting'. In actual fact this made the whole evening feel rather depressing. Work colleagues are an interesting collection at the best of times but at least they share the same employer in common. They have the chance to drink too much, gossip too loudly, embarrass themselves on the dancefloor and perhaps be shocked by the random coupling of two unlikely people in the procurement team.

Ruth and Will arrived looking suitably well dressed. Ruth began to introduce Will to a variety of colleagues. Samantha from HR and her husband, Daniel, who worked for a City law firm. Jenny from Marketing who actually started work the same week as Ruth and her partner Aaron (or was it Darren? It was hard to make out). Robert and his new girlfriend also popped over to say hello. Before he could say, 'I'm a computer analyst, get me out of here,' Will found himself surrounded by colleagues and partners and he did his best with small talk. In reality, he watched the clock and smiled and nodded his head in all the right places.

Questions on how they met, where he lived, the traffic, the weather were easy. But it is hard to gauge the temperature of the room when just about everyone is a stranger. Will wasn't sure how much to drink at such events. On the one hand, he was tempted to drink to excess to reduce the impact of the banal conversation, but he was worried about letting Ruth down with inappropriate comments or gossip. Instead he paced himself and mastered the art of neutral responding and enquiry. This required an attentive stance on his part and he kept himself awake with occasional trips to the bar and the loo.

He also discovered and mastered the essential art of agreeing with Ruth's assessment of everyone afterwards.

Date Number 3

Cinema trip to see the latest Jennifer Lawrence movie. Will didn't know much about the movie but spending time with Jennifer was always reason enough. They went through the commonly observed ritual of movie going as follows:

1) Buy tickets online.

2) Arrive at cinema to collect tickets to find that, no matter how hard you press the screen on the ticket collection machine, nothing happens. You can swipe random credit and debit cards and press and thump the area on the screen designated for confirming things, but the machine will not release any confirmatory bits of paper.

3) Queue for tickets at a desk with a bored member of staff.

4) Go the refreshment kiosk and get conned into buying a 'value bucket' meal which includes enough popcorn to expand the stomach lining of five people and a five-gallon container of Coke with two straws.

5) Wander towards Screen 37 and hand over recently purchased ticket only for someone to tear it up.

6) Find seats in darkened cinema that seem smaller and stickier than expected. This involves climbing over the knees of four other people, all the while muttering apologies.

7) Take coats off and put them on the seat next to you. Kick over the popcorn, spreading a nice layer over the floor and behind the seat in front.

8) Tut and glower as a bunch of teenagers come in to show off to each other rather than watch the film. Move your coats as said teenagers settle in right next to you.

9) Put on 3D glasses, look around the cinema and declare they work really well in a loud voice.

10) Sit back for ten minutes of adverts for other films you are unlikely to see and then ten mins of adverts for items you don't want.

11) Think of Spinal Tap as soon as the advert for Dolby appears.

12) Watch with amusement as the screen seems to resize for the main feature.

13) Sigh with annoyance as 6 ft 7 in man sits in front of you wearing a large hat.

14) Ten minutes into the film realise you should have gone to the loo before the film started. Convince yourself that this is not pressing and can wait.

15) Fifteen minutes in, go to the loo based on an assurance from some bloke at work that all movies are designed to be dull between fifteen and twenty minutes in to accommodate emergency escapes from the theatre.

16) Return to seat midway through a car chase involving people you don't recognise.

17) Spend five minutes mighty confused by plot developments.

18) Leave Screen 36 and return to Screen 37 but don't admit to partner that you have been an idiot.

19) Spend remainder of movie wondering what is now going on. Hope partner is enjoying it.

20) Hold hands for five minutes longer than is enjoyable/comfortable/romantic.

21) Leave movie during the credits.

22) Mutter 'Hello' to Jason Isaac under your breath as you leave.

Will and Ruth made their way to an Italian restaurant after the movie and spent a few minutes dissecting what they had seen. The verdict was 7/10 for Will and 6/10 for Ruth. Plot a bit thin, special effects obviously made on a laptop and the last ten minutes involved large machines hitting each other. That was an objective verdict but of course, people in love are not objective. They are not really rating the movie at all. They are saying a number that would seem appealing to their partner. It is not the movie that matters as much as the ritual and the experience.

Date Number 4
Eventually Will owned up to his love of the 'beautiful game' and his adoration of West Ham United. He was warned by Steve not to overdo the football discussion but his obsession became clear when Ruth found him obsessively checking his phone and muttering 'bollocks' and 'fuck' under his breath. It turned out that this was not some life-changing event involving his nearest and dearest but a last-minute equaliser robbing the Hammers of a much-needed three points to help them escape the

clutches of relegation. Will tried to explain the meaning of football but Ruth just looked on, aghast. She pointed out that his emotional state was being dictated by people who had no idea he was even alive. At which point, Will launched into a defence of his obsession and discovered that Ruth had never been to a match.

And so it was that he convinced Ruth to go to a game. He figured an England International at Wembley would be a good place to cut her footballing teeth. The national stadium was an impressive building and there was always the chance to spot a few famous people pottering about. Plus he could avoid the less savoury aspects of West Ham at home. She needed to build up to that one.

So Ruth found herself on the Tube, exiting at Wembley Park to be immersed in the sway and song of thousands of fans. Apparently 'Football is Coming Home' and this needs to be sung in a low register with guttural and primitive overtones.

Ruth was quite overcome with the pure volume of people and the sight and sound and colour. She was amused with the number of selfies being taken against the backdrop of the great arch as a seething mass of humanity surged down Wembley Way. Hidden among the England Fans was a smattering of supporters carrying Swiss flags. Apparently, this was a friendly as part of preparation for a tournament the following year. In other words, Ruth pointed out, the match didn't matter. Although this seemed not to have dawned on the many thousands who had come along to watch.

'We have Club Wembley seats,' Will announced with some pride.

'And that means?'

'That means we get a good view, it feels less chaotic, and the queues for drinks and toilets should be much shorter.'

'Okay, well that all sounds fine,' replied Ruth. 'Do we

get to meet Gary Lineker?'

'I can't guarantee it but I will keep a look out for him just in case.'

They completed their long walk to the stadium and entered a series of escalators that elevated them from ground level to the Club Wembley concourse. Here Ruth was surprised to see many beautiful women with well-fitting red dresses and air hostess smiles offering directions and support. Will took Ruth to the Champagne and Seafood bar with a nice seat by the window.

'Welcome to Wembley,' he said with a flourish.

'It is much nicer than expected,' Ruth conceded. 'I am sure this is not normal, though.'

'Oh, you'd be surprised. Although I am pretty sure last time we went to Millwall, they didn't serve the gravlax on the menu and sadly the espresso machines had insufficient pressure, which resulted in a rather disappointing cappuccino.'

'How tragic for the poor fans of Millwall FC.'

'Yes. Apparently, they were so annoyed that some left the stadium and kicked the shit out of a few random people.'

'Wow, I never knew they had such passion for their coffee.'

A nice young man in a freshly pressed uniform and a pleasing smile stood beside them, holding a small electronic device and a plastic pen. 'Hi, my name is Jamie and I will be serving you today. What can I get you?'

'Hi Jamie, we will have the seafood sharing platter and a nice cold Sancerre,' said Will with the easy assertion of someone who knew the menu well.

Minutes later Jamie returned with a bowl of warm bread and an impressive display of salmon, prawns and smoked fish topped with a side order of salads and mayonnaise.

'Well, this is a nice surprise,' said Ruth. 'I was figuring we would be on beer and pies.'

'Oh, you can get those for sure. In fact, go down that corridor and every need for trash food is catered for. You can't keep the football fan away from burgers and pies. Except here they will cost you the price of a decent meal in a bistro.'

'I see. Anyway, tell me about today's game. What do I need to know?'

'Well, it's a friendly.'

'Does that mean players are politer on the pitch? Do they make pen friends or something?'

Will was about to take this comment seriously when he realised Ruth was playing with him and smiled.

'I'm not stupid, Will, I get the idea of the game but I do struggle with people's obsession with it.'

'It's hard to explain but I think it involves some sort of mass hypnosis. The crowd get on the side of the players, the atmosphere soaks into the bloodstream and by some peculiar process, if the team does well, you believe somehow inside that you are a better person. So, when your team wins the FA cup, for example, as a fan you feel that you are rising above other mortals to take a more superior plinth on the platforms of life. Win the World Cup and the whole country moves up a significant number of notches in the world order.'

'Blimey. So if, say, we lose to Switzerland today, it represents a dent in our national pride and they benefit from a rise in tourism, investment and an economic boom?'

'Well, I wouldn't track the correlation between football results and prosperity but I do think, if the team does well, the days will be sunnier.'

'So, if you follow a team like Sunderland or Newcastle, does that mean you walk around in a constant state of depression?'

'Now you're getting it. That's why so many Northerners are miserable. If their team does well it can be transformational for the town's sense of wellbeing.'

'Does that then mean if you are from Manchester, you are constantly happy?'

'Not really. Some cultures have misery woven into the very fabric of their being and are miserable even if they win.'

'Mmm. It's complicated being a fan, by the sounds of it.'

Ruth enjoyed the banter and the feel of being in the heart of the stadium. She was amused when Will suggested to Jamie the waiter that the price of the meal must surely include a night's stay in the Hilton over the road. Apparently not. The wine settled nicely and Will and Ruth wandered arm in arm through the crowd towards their seat.

And so it was that the great nations of Switzerland and England came to realise they were in fact on an economic par. For a long while it looked like Switzerland would end the evening ahead in the world order but our great nation was saved by a last gasp winner, headed in by a young man with plenty of tattoos and a shaved head. According to Will, the referee clearly had Swiss ancestry for denying two clear penalty claims and for allowing a dubious goal in the first half. It seemed a nation's wellbeing rested on the whim of a man in black with a whistle and the dexterity and timing of the England number 10.

***

Over time it becomes clear that dates are nothing more than hurdles and jumps put in the way of a courting couple. Some will fall at the first fence by getting into arguments over which film or which restaurant or whose house. Others experience a gradual decline in enthusiasm as the reality of each other's true character becomes apparent. People can break up over the simplest of things, not over the things themselves but because they represent a much wider sense of incompatibility.

Will and Ruth discussed this and knew people personally who had split up over things as trivial and diverse as:

- how long to cook pasta

- the ideal colour for a living room carpet

- whether cats are friends

- real or artificial Christmas trees

- walk to the shops or get a cab

- Motown or modern definitions of R&B

- ex-girlfriends/boyfriends, even though they are not around any more

And so it was after a few weeks of dating and romancing, they received their first invitation as a couple. They made the transition from being known separately as Will and Ruth, to becoming collectively Ruth and Will.

***

Weddings are such strange affairs. They become topics of conversation and the planning and preparation can be all-consuming. As a guest, a wedding can be something of a mystery or even an irritation. Will had been invited to the wedding of Bryn, an old university friend, and Bella at the Marriott Golf & Country Club in Virginia Water. He had, of course, invited Ruth as his guest and instantly felt better about having to go along.

The trouble was that Will didn't like weddings. He felt that deep down inside, no one else liked them either. Well, apart from the bride and groom, and even then he doubted they were convinced. Before the event itself, Will was also invited to the stag weekend. The stag night has somehow transitioned from a few hours in a dodgy bar with a curry to a whole weekend in a beer-swilling paradise, in this case, Prague. Will announced that he was busy the weekend of the Prague trip, and much as he would love to attend, he couldn't make it. In reality, he didn't want to spend a whole weekend with people he hardly knew, drinking beer he couldn't pronounce.

A few weeks later, he picked Ruth up at 10:30 for a wedding that was due to last just over thirteen hours. And therein lies the problem. How come it takes so long to celebrate a wedding? The ceremony itself lasts twenty minutes, thirty minutes at most. And yet he found himself arriving at Ruth's for a marathon day of mingling and waiting. Will didn't much fancy mingling and the constant waiting would drive him nuts.

Ruth looked lovely. A red dress with a crossover fabric on the back that looped over her shoulders to form a perfect V, which was sexy without being too revealing. Pretty shoes with a small red bow that were impossible to walk in as usual and a small clutch bag that wasn't quite Chanel (actually Walthamstow Market). Will wore a dark suit, black shoes and a tie that all matched and he figured they looked a pretty handsome couple for meeting people and photographs.

The wedding started in a small church not far from the hotel. Will amused himself by looking at the range of fashions on offer. Women squeezed into dresses a size too small. Fascinators perched on starched hair. Men looked uncomfortable in suits that only came out of the wardrobe for special occasions. Children ran between legs and were chastised by parents who wanted to preserve the clean lines for at least the photographs. There was the inevitable awkwardness outside the church where complete strangers congregated and exchanged the smallest of small talk. Here the British excel at discussing the weather, the motorway, the weather, the bride and groom and, last but no means least, the weather. Will recognised a couple of old mates from uni and introduced Ruth to them. He reflected that time changes our connection to people. At uni a couple of these guys were his life. They were drinking buddies, partners in crime, brothers in arms. But a few years and a few jobs later, not to mention the addition of wives and partners, and the connection seemed slight at best. Meanwhile, Ruth nodded, smiled, shook hands and added a few air kisses whilst promptly forgetting most of the names she had just learnt.

Will and Ruth made their way over to the groom's side, said a quick hello to Bryn and muttered an appreciation of his white carnation and small display of greenery pinned to the lapel of his charcoal grey suit. They took their seats towards the back while the rest of the congregation filed in.

'All weddings are the same,' whispered Will.

'Well, they usually involve two people exchanging vows in front of their nearest and dearest,' replied Ruth.

'It's not just that. The space to sit down is always too small; the chairs are too hard. If there is singing, it's always 'Love Divine' sung in a key only suitable for a soprano or someone with overly tight trousers. Then someone will stand up and read the bit from the Bible about love being clanging bells –'

'I think you mean Corinthians,' interrupted Ruth.

'Whatever. They read that out, nip over the back to sign a few bits of paper and emerge to smiles and people throwing suitably chosen rice and environmentally friendly paper in time to commands from a pretentious photographer while some old dear plays a large organ as loud as possible.'

"Well, what would you do?"

'I like the idea of a Vegas-style wedding but somewhere else. And rather than an Elvis Presley impersonator as the vicar, maybe something more English. Someone like Jarvis Cocker who would marry you and then wave his arse in your face.'

'Remind me never to marry you, Will.'

Their exchange was interrupted by the sound of Wagner's 'Bridal Chorus'. All guests strained to get a look at the bride as she walked slowly down the aisle. Bella looked lovely in white. Very traditional with a medium-length train sweeping behind her. She carried a small bouquet with white and light blue petals that matched a delicate sweep of flowers in her headdress. They also happened to match the outfits worn by the five bridesmaids following behind. It seems that choosing a bridesmaid is difficult these days. So instead of one or two sweet girls aged between six and ten, here there were five twenty-somethings. In fairness, one of them looked fabulous. The chief bridesmaid was tall, slender and elegant. Her dress clung in all the right places and she looked a vision of bridesmaid loveliness. The others Will referred to as the 'Blue Minions', despite Ruth's objections. It was pretty clear who'd chosen the dress and who was forced to wear it.

The service was mercifully short and although no one mentioned the clanging bells, 'Love Divine' was sung at an even higher register than usual. All the guests were ushered outside, where the sun shone and the birds in the trees chirped in harmony to celebrate the happy couple. Well, that was what Will said happened in the movies. The reality was that this wedding was about to be hijacked by the photographer. Rewind the clock a few hundred years and the wedding ceremony used to be a lot longer. It was common for the priest to take around two hours to build the required level of religious fervour for a proper service. But members of ye olde photographic union in 1746 changed things to allow time for the portrait painters to capture the moment. In the 1700s, the happy couple would emerge from the chapel to be greeted by a man with a canvas, oils and a variety of brushes and would have to stand still for five hours while he mixed and splashed and dabbed until he had rendered a fair likeness. According to records, you can evidence that the wedding ceremony timing was reduced to allow the portrait painters sufficient time and light to do their work. This tradition remains to this very day.

And so it was that a man with a variety of lenses, tripods and bits of lighting took charge. He started with a bit of audience participation. He got everyone into a quick shot, fooling them into thinking this would soon be over with minimal fuss. He then began to whittle things down. Bride's family, groom's family, bride's friends, groom's friends, bride's mother, bride's stepmother, people who knew the bride between April 2009 and May 2017, gay friends of the groom, people who walked with a limp and who had been out drinking with the bride and groom over the last twelve months, bridesmaids who had yet to have sex, bridesmaids who didn't look like a Minion, children who had no idea whose wedding it was but were forced to come by their parents, friends of the bride's father's stepson, and so on.

'Any minute now, they are going to ask for people "losing the will to live and in desperate need of a drink" and I will be right there,' said Will.

Thinking there could be no more possible combinations of people, the photographer announced he was taking the happy couple down to the local river to take a few shots and would be back shortly. An hour later he returned to a dwindling number of guests and announced in a loud voice, 'We need the bride, groom and their parents.' By now, of course, they had all gone to the reception.

And so ninety minutes and 3,871 photos later, the guests arrived at the Marriott to be greeted by a nice man holding a tray of Prosecco and orange juice. At some point over the last decade, Prosecco had become a popular choice for all things celebratory. In the olden days of weddings, the rich would serve champagne while the poor would go for some kind of sparkling wine. Now it seems that everyone has been persuaded that Prosecco is sophisticated when in fact it is just Babycham in a bigger bottle. Fizzy grape juice served cold in a glass that makes it look more expensive than it is. Will and Ruth grabbed a glass each with some enthusiasm as the last drink was a while ago and they were not sure when the next one would arrive. They were then subjected to an hour of pre-wedding breakfast mingling. This involved wandering around and chatting to yet more random strangers. They eventually found the few people that Will knew from the old days at uni. Scott and his wife, Ella, now lived in Milton Keynes, Scott doing interesting things with computers and Ella, a teacher. Grayson and his partner, Miles, both worked for one of the big banks with suits to match. Finally, Ian and his girlfriend of four weeks, Hannah, who ran her own fashion business in London and Ian, clearly 'punching above his weight', working for ASDA as a buyer.

'We met when some bloke decided to rob Will of his phone and left him alone and broken on a pavement in Hammersmith and I took pity on him. I haven't managed to get rid of him yet,' said Ruth in reply to the inevitable question. 'What about you guys?' she asked of Ian and Hannah.

'Oh, we met on Tinder,' replied Hannah. 'I swiped a few pictures and here we are.'

'We have both deleted our profiles now, though,' Ian added enthusiastically.

'Er, yes, of course,' said Hannah in a way that no one quite believed.

Miles and Grayson met in a supermarket reaching for the same brand of coffee. It seems that this mutual love of a certain brand opened the door to many other areas of common ground.

'Well, Bella seems like a lovely girl, I've not met her before.'

'Oh she is: I think she will keep Bryn in his place.'

'I'm not sure he needs keeping in his place, to be honest. We spent several college summers together and apart from him spilling a pint over a freshly laundered shirt, I can't remember any moments of controversy. God knows what the Best Man will find to say.'

Through all the small talk, Will couldn't help but smile. Not an outward smile, but an inward one. Something he would keep to himself. He loved introducing Ruth to friends and acquaintances and even people he didn't know. It felt so much better being with someone at an occasion like this. He loved the way Ruth and he were developing an almost subliminal level of conversation. A nod, a wink, a slight shake of the head, a grin, a small grimace, a flick of the hair. Small signs between them that meant a myriad of things. He loved the way they worked a room together. Sometimes together and never quite apart. At any given time, they would know roughly where each other was in the room. Will was proud of her looks, her intelligence and the way Ruth found it so easy to connect with people. He would introduce her to someone and within minutes, Ruth would seemingly know all about them. She had an endless supply of questions and a face that glowed with authentic attention. The more impressive he found Ruth to be in company, the more he wanted them to be alone. It was a conundrum. At one point he noticed that Ruth had even made the wedding tolerable. He hated to admit it but he was quite enjoying himself.

***

Ruth navigated the wedding reception with a finely tuned sense of paranoia. Her first concern as ever was her outfit. Her dress, courtesy of Reiss, felt and looked great. But her confidence could easily be shattered by spotting the same or similar on someone else. So far so good on that front. Her new shoes from Russell & Bromley were just showing signs of pain around the heels but as usual, she would grin and bear it. She found it awkward meeting so many new people at once. She knew so little about them but was also surprised to find that, when she asked Will some obvious or simple questions, he didn't know much about them either. For example, Will knew that Ian was a lifelong Chelsea fan. He didn't know how long his mother had been ill or what job his sister had taken in Germany. It amused Ruth to reflect that Will seemed able to spend years in the company of someone else, followed by years of keeping in touch via updates on social media, without really knowing anything about someone. It was perhaps a 'bloke thing'. He seemed to have the ability to meet up and exist in a landscape of superficial conversation where anything was open for discussion apart from the lives, trials and tribulations of the people talking. It was pretty certain that Will knew more about Boris Johnson than he did about his friends.

Ruth smiled and shook hands and exchanged more air kisses. Held plenty of discussions about the bride's dress, the service and the weather. ('Yes, how lucky, it is such a beautiful day.')

Finally, they found themselves at the wedding breakfast table.

'Ruth, how often, when laying the table, do you think, "Let's put guests in a line facing away from each other"? I mean, what is the point of a top table layout like that?' Will was observing the ritual of a top table in a wedding. A long line of people who barely knew each other were sitting facing outwards towards an assembled mass of relatives, friends and hangers-on. 'I must say, I am bloody relieved that the flowers match the bridesmaid's dresses. God forbid they would have been a different colour.'

'Shh,' whispered Ruth, 'it's what people do.'

'And a vote of thanks has to go to the people who covered the chairs,' Will continued. 'God forbid that we would sit on a chair that doesn't also match the flowers, and the bridesmaids' dresses. Still at least they provided this nice bag of chocolate mints – I am starving.'

'Will, you are being embarrassing,' replied Ruth. But with a tone that signalled agreement and a hint of mischief.

Will examined the cutlery. 'Okay, let me guess the menu before looking at the nice card in the middle of the table. I am thinking soup – probably broccoli and blue stilton with a hint of anchovy – granary bread with unsalted butter. Then some sort of chicken. Or lamb. I think it is written somewhere that it is compulsory under statute to serve chicken or lamb at a wedding breakfast. With insufficient potatoes. On the side we will have some green leaves with flecks of almonds in them and a single carrot. For desert I am thinking a chocolate mousse with flecks of orange peel followed by stewed coffee poured from a large flask. Wine will be a light Pinot Grigio or a merlot, followed by a splash more of that delicious Prosecco. Okay, now look at the menu and tell me how many points I get. I think one point for every right answer.'

Ruth picked up the menu that was printed in fake handwritten font. 'Okay, you were right about the soup but not the flavour: cream of tomato with a hint of basil and cream.'

'That's Heinz with a sprinkle and a swirl, then.'

'For the main course we can choose between salmon or chicken.'

'They will of course be served with peppers,' Will observed.

'It doesn't say they are.'

'Trust me, there are always peppers.'

'For dessert we have lemon mousse or ice cream – you were right about the wine though, so I'm not sure how many points you should get.'

The food came eventually and the meal was efficient, at least. The bread was indeed granary and Will did wish for more potatoes. The wine slipped down nicely until a tapping of a fork on a glass announced the commencement of speeches. The bride's father began with a worryingly large pad of paper. He had obviously spent a lot of time preparing this but clearly hadn't read it out to anyone. Otherwise he would have been told to trim it, slice it, cap it, delete it. For forty minutes he droned on about Bella's life story. No detail was missing. Her cute smile as a child, how she refused to wear nappies on holiday, her accident in the swimming pool aged five, her first tooth, her first book, her school reports, her friends, her achievements, her first job. It didn't get interesting until guests heard about the first boyfriend. That was, until they discovered he was ten years old. All through this Bella watched, embarrassed and attentive. This was a father's adoration of his daughter but the longer it went on, the less sincere it sounded.

Will had been on one of those presentation skills courses at work and learnt that over a twenty-minute period, you are likely to capture your audience's attention at the start and again at the end. The middle needs some damn good stories or visuals to keep people interested. The course didn't warn him how to behave during forty minutes of turgid self-indulgence. The first couple of minutes were okay but twenty-five minutes in, Will began to question his own sanity. He caught Ruth's eye and flicked his own upwards in a style of which Donald Trump himself would be proud. He played with his watch, checked his phone, gave a few work problems some thought and kept checking in with Ruth. It was pretty clear, she was bored rigid too. With this realisation Will began to communicate with sign language. The trouble was, he wasn't that good at it. Then he had an idea. His phone had an app where he could type a short word or phrase and it would turn it into a red LED scrolling sign. He worked out that he could type something and show it under the table so that only Ruth would see it.

I hope he doesn't forget the years 2010-2011

The LED scrolled and Ruth smiled. She grabbed the phone.

I am loving the detail about her work experience at BAE systems

You look lovely BTW

Will had grabbed the phone back, prompting an exchange of swapping and typing.

Why thank you

Shall we escape for wild sex?

Do you think they will notice?

No, everyone is too interested in this speech

118

Maybe later – just nod and look interested

Can I just look at you instead?

Yes, you can

Eventually the speeches were done. Glasses were raised. The best man had done the best job he could in finding stories for the groom. Will leaned back and reflected that being with Ruth made even the dullest of moments bearable. The smiles, sneaking a phone under the table, flirtation and innuendo meant that Will's face held a grin, not a grimace. He was working out for himself that a great relationship was one in which you could survive even something as dull as a wedding. And there were only another six hours to go!

The DJ seemed to be on a mission to play songs that no one liked, no one owned or no one wanted to hear again. He was brilliant at misjudging the crowd, their preferences, their song choice. Either that or Bryn had given him the worst possible playlist to work with. Something like 'Now That's What I Call A Shit Song You Have No Desire To Hear Again Volume 187' or 'Embarrassing Singalong and Dance Move Songs Volume 23'. And so it was that Will found himself watching twelve tortured souls performing a badly timed Macarena. Will had been reading in the *Evening Standard* about a kid in Saudi who had been arrested for performing the Macarena in a public place. He felt the Saudis had got this about right. This was followed by the sound of 'Oops Up Side Your Head' by The Gap Band where the same enthusiastic folk sat on the floor while moving from side to side and clapping. Will knew what was coming next. This DJ was on a roll and Will and Ruth made their escape outside just as the Black Lace selection started.

'God save us from that awful music!'

'Oh Will, I know you are just hiding a secret desire to "comb your hair, swim and do macho man" to this song.'

'I could think of ways to spice it up. They could try "rub your tits, smack your neighbour's arse, give me the finger" to at least make it amusing.'

'Now that is not politically correct.'

'Yeah, I know, but really.'

'Will. Are there any songs the DJ could play that would get you on the dancefloor?'

'One or two I guess. Depends if you were with me. I have never been much of a fan of blokes dancing together. It's alright when women do it for some reason.'

'We don't actually have a song, do we?'

'No, now you mention it. What would you like it to be?'

'I'm not sure you can actually decide on a song. I think they have to find you. Certain moments become wrapped up in sound and before you know it, you connect the song with the emotion and, whenever you hear it, you are taken back to that time. I think choosing a song as a soundtrack feels a bit contrived. In fact, my friend Michelle married a guy called Harry and their song was "Walking In The Air" by Aled Jones. Apparently, they first kissed when *The Snowman* was on TV, so that song takes them back to the first time their lips met.'

'At least you only get to hear it at Christmas.'

'Oh, it's quite romantic … What would you choose if you could pick our song?'

'Now there is a challenge. I will give it some thought.'

'Do you have any songs with anyone else?'

'No, of course not!' exclaimed Will. 'The only soundtrack to any encounters I can remember is the sound of glasses being clinked and the word "Time" at the bar. What about you?'

'Mmm, well there is one. It's crap though and an old boyfriend used to send me the lyrics in cards.'

'What is it?'

'"Wonderful Tonight" by Eric Clapton. I don't even love the song that much but when it comes on I spare a few seconds' thought for Neville Delaney.'

Will hadn't experienced the emotion that came next. He knew Ruth was just answering a question, and he knew Neville was probably a distant memory. But he resented the fact that somewhere in Ruth's brain was a small compartment with his name on it. Open the door to that section and there were memories of Eric Clapton, first kisses, first fumblings, sounds, smells, moments and perhaps love. Will noticed a brief flash of emotion spin around his head that wasn't at all pleasant. He disguised this with a smile and a nod and by trying to appear disinterested and aloof. Inside, he was reminded that some other bloke existed on the planet who shared knowledge of Ruth.

The trouble is that, in the absence of information, the brain gets all creative. It replaces reality with conjecture, fact with fiction and certainty with suspicion. In that brief moment, Will could see Neville as a successful businessman, with a nice car and a smooth line in banter. He was tall (taller than Will) and had a broad smile that could seduce a woman at thirty paces. Oh, and funny too. Women love a funny and amusing guy and Neville had it all. Will knew that deep inside, Neville's motives were purely physical and there was no depth or honour to his intentions. He was a user and a seducer and Will didn't like him already. Neville was also a guitar player and had learnt how to play 'Wonderful Tonight' and had sent Ruth homemade but artfully-produced recordings of it. He could see the glint in Ruth's eyes as he played it to her. And so it was that moments ago, Will did not know Neville Delaney existed and moments later, he knew all about him and despised him in equal measure.

'And where is Neville now?' asked Will while hiding his inner turmoil.

'Oh God knows, I haven't seen him since college.'

Will felt good about this reply but found himself wondering whether Neville might one day reappear armed with a copy of the song and bad intentions. 'Shall we go back inside?' he asked.

'Well now that "Y.M.C.A." has started, what's to stop us!'

'I'll get you a drink.'

'Same again, yes, but see if you can get them to include more than one ice cube this time.'

'Will do but I overheard one of the staff saying they had lost the recipe and the guy who knows how to do it is on holiday.'

'Very funny.'

'If you want ice, Ruth, you need to go to America.'

He was about to leave for the bar when Ruth pulled him closer and kissed him tenderly. 'I am glad I found you, Will. I would go to America to get the ice for your drink.'

Will smiled inside just as the music blurted out, 'You get to hang out with all the boys!'

'Oh fucking hell,' cried Will. 'Why did you do that? You could at least have waited for that Van Morrison song or something.' But deep inside he knew that the Village People, Ruth and himself were now firmly joined at the hip.

Ruth found a chair and a quiet table away from the sound of Diana Ross singing 'Chain Reaction' while elderly and not-so-elderly relatives shuffled around the dancefloor. The lights from the DJ pulsed and span and occasional burst from a small smoke machine providing a focal point for them to shine onto. In the old days this job was done by Benson & Hedges, Old Holborn and Sobranie

Cocktail cigarettes (whatever happened to them?).

Ruth was happy people watching or playing with bits of gold confetti that were sprinkled on the tables. She found she could stack them into small piles before scattering them with a flick of her finger onto the floor to join the other discarded symbols of matrimony.

The room was busy now. More people had joined the party. The second division guests had arrived. Her dad used to call them that. At most weddings there are close family and friends and certain relatives who have to come to the wedding. They get to watch the service and they get fed. The second division guests arrive in the evening. They get a buffet of rather tired sandwiches, miscellaneous pastry objects and chips (if they are lucky). They don't get free drinks but they do get to watch the cake being cut and they can bring a gift or vouchers.

Even with the extra people, the room seemed too big for the number of guests. Ruth estimated there were about ninety people there in total and the room could easily hold a couple of hundred. The good news was that there was space to escape the godawful DJ and she could sit back in reasonable anonymity and just watch the evening pass by.

The DJ switched the song to something more bearable at last. You can't go wrong with classic Motown, even the DJ had worked that out. Ruth looked over to the bar where Will had taken rather a long time buying a drink. She could just make him out near his old uni buddies. Of course, he was spending a bit of time catching up. Finally, he wandered over with gin, tonic, lemon and three cubes of ice (apparently this is how the barman defined the word 'lots').

'Just catching up with the gang, Ruth, sorry.'

'Oh God, that's fine.'

'Come on over and join us.'

'I will in a minute. Right now, I am enjoying the view

and my feet are breathing a sigh of relief. I will see you on the dancefloor the second they play "The Birdie Song" or "The Ketchup Song".'

'Deal,' said Will.

Ruth felt quite content. Well aware she wouldn't know anyone, she had been quietly dreading this day. Not knowing the bride and groom or their parents, she'd worried whether she would get the outfit right. She'd worried that the day would drag on and she would be left for large chunks of time by herself. But she shouldn't have worried. Will had been sweet and attentive and kind. She didn't mind sitting on her own for a while, sipping her G&T.

It is funny how things change. There is a subliminal level of communication enjoyed by people in love that means they connect on a different level. Ruth couldn't pin it down but she glanced over to the uni lads and noticed a small change in them. Perhaps their smiles were a little wider, they were standing slightly taller. Had the stomachs been sucked in a little more? It was only a slight difference but enough to make her look up. There was one obvious conclusion. A woman had joined them.

***

Jenny arrived fashionably late. The invitation mentioned 7:30 start for the evening reception but she arrived closer to 8:00. She hadn't seen Bryn in ages and a lot had happened since university.

She walked into the main bar and began to scan the groups of people. Some were slumped in armchairs, others were propping up the wall, yet others were seemingly being propped up by the wall. Some were near the buffet table displaying a selection of crisps and increasingly curling sandwiches. And then she spotted the uni crew.

'Oh my God! Scott, Grayson, Ian, Will!' She launched herself at them.

'Jen,' exclaimed Ian, 'bloody hell, we didn't know you were coming!'

'When I got the invite from Bryn I wasn't sure I could make it. To be honest, I didn't know who else was coming and you don't like to ask in case your friends aren't invited.' She turned to Grayson. 'However, you can always rely on Grayson, who puts his whole life on Facebook. I even know what you had for lunch for Christ's sake. In fact, you don't need to tell me much about today as Grayson has been posting a minute-by-minute update on his Instagram story. I feel like I know the bride already. Nice dress, probably slightly too much makeup. Seems okay. Where is Bryn? Is he looking like a henpecked husband yet?' Jenny hardly paused for breath. Words and exclamations flowed from her like a damaged fire hydrant and no one could stop her. The whole group exchanged greetings, hugs and air kisses.

Amongst the hugs and air kisses, Will felt some mixed emotions about Jen. The two of them had been 'not quite an item' at uni. They met, they shared a lot of good times. They drunk cheap beer, poor quality wine, strange blue concoctions mixed with vodka. Shared late night kebabs and laughed till the early hours. They walked the streets looking for lost shoes, bought coffee and offered sympathy to get them through the tough times. In fact, if pressed, Will would confess that Jen was his 'if only'. 'If only' meant that if things had been different, if Will had been braver, if Jen hadn't linked up with some bloke called Rory who was far too good looking for his own good, if they had lived closer together, if the New Year's Eve kisses had been replicated over more months of the year. If they had said hello in the same way they said goodbye to each other. If Will had listened to Grayson and done something about his obvious crush.

Well, that was then and Will was different now. The last time Will had seen Jen, she was arm-in-arm with some bloke and she gave a quick wave and she was gone. Since then they had been at different ends of the country and connected with a few comments on Instagram and Facebook with a regular commitment to meet up soon. A commitment that carried less and less weight over time. And here she was. Time had been kind to her. She looked radiant in an expensive-looking dress with large pink flower prints. Everything matched; her hair, shoes, bag and her wide smile completed the package.

'So, Jen, what's the news?' said Will.

'Oh, Will, you follow Facebook. You know I've moved house and moved jobs. Oh, and dumped Alistair for good. I had enough being messed around by him so I am back in the land of being single. And not sure how to deal with it. So, filling my time with work and in danger of becoming a 'woman who lunches'. Did you ever meet Alistair? No, I don't think you did now I think about it. He had two characteristics: charm and selfishness. I spent most of our relationship falling for one and resenting the other.'

'I saw you change your status to "single" and did wonder, but didn't like to say anything. Sorry if it's been tough.' Will passed Jen a gin and tonic which apparently she was in desperate need of.

'What about you, Will? Haven't read much lately which can either mean your life is so exciting that you don't have time to post anything, or you have a dull as ditchwater existence and have nothing to say, which I can't believe by the way.'

'Mmm, well a few new things. New job, started recently but I won't bore you with that. New girlfriend who is here actually, you must meet her,' said Will.

'God yeah, do introduce me to the woman who is lucky enough to be on your arm tonight. Does she like football?'

'No.'

'PlayStation?'

'No.'

'Blue drinks with random amounts of vodka or gin in them?'

'Not that I am aware of.'

'Well, she sounds bloody perfect. Can't wait to meet her.'

Grayson interrupted. 'Does anyone want a sandwich? The buffet is open.'

'Oh God yes, bring on the sausage rolls and crisps immediately,' said Jen. 'Oh and Will, where is this woman of yours? You can't hide her away all evening.'

Will wandered over to Ruth and handed her a new glass.

'Looks like you have company.'

'Yeah, an old uni friend has turned up. No one was sure she was coming. Jenny was an honorary bloke at uni. She was out late and good at drinking games. It's nice to see her. She hasn't changed much at all. She still speaks at 100 mph and seems not to need to breathe while doing so. Come over and meet her.'

And so Ruth joined Will at the bar. The noise from the disco pulsed and then silenced slightly as the L-shape of the room diverted some of the sound.

Will did the introductions and Ruth observed a smile and familiarity that seemed to go beyond an old mate at uni. Ruth found herself feeling on her guard. There was something about being in the middle of a group of old friends that she found unnerving. People with a connected past, shared stories, jokes, anecdotes and who had even generated their own language. Funnily enough, she hadn't felt that all day. She had been part of a moment of awkwardness amongst strangers. But now the dynamic had changed. She, of course, knew why. The blokes were all trying to impress. The arrival of Jenny had prompted an outpouring of competitive behaviour and they were all keen to drag through the memories and pull out the most humorous gems they could find.

Ruth listened carefully to the language. She knew little of Will's past and now she found herself a voyeuse, as those who'd witnessed his growth and development through university life could now provide testament to Will's history. Inevitably there were exaggerations and expansions of the truth. Simple moments collided for comic effect. Emotions were amplified but there were three words that came to the fore more than others. Will and Jen. Jen and Will. Will/Jen.

***

There is an old adage that you find what you seek. If you were to count the number of red cars driving through a town centre, you would focus on the red cars. Cars of many colours could pass you by but your focus on red would blind you to everything else. Ruth caught herself and wondered if she was doing that. Her break-up with Dan had been painful and he'd accused her of looking for things to complain about. Was she doing that now? Was she filtering the conversation and focussing on the few elements where Will and Jen were at the forefront of the story at the exclusion of all others? She didn't think so. Amidst the group of friends and with the buzz of the DJ in the background, Ruth became wary of Jen. Perhaps she had no right to. Perhaps she was creating a problem or concern where none existed. But there was something beneath this conversation. Her intuition was on red alert. She put on a brave face, obviously. She smiled and managed to laugh along with those who had true memories of the shared stories. But inside she felt uncomfortable and wanted to leave. She wanted to remove herself from the forced imprisonment of conversation and being sociable. She looked at her watch briefly and sighed when she figured she had another two hours to go. At least.

The DJ put on a Black Eyed Peas song and of course Jen loved it.

'Come on you lot, time to show what you are made of,' she cried, grabbing Grayson by the hand. He beckoned the others, who followed with a mixture of reluctance and resignation.

Will and Ruth hadn't danced together before although technically they were dancing in close proximity rather than together. Dancing had become a predominantly solo activity and people were connected by roughly facing each other and establishing only occasional eye contact.

'I've got a feeling, that tonight's gonna be a good night,' sang Jen with her hands raised high above her head.

Ruth clearly had great rhythm and could shape her body to match the beats. Will, on the other hand, was able to demonstrate the move that he learnt at his first school disco. This move had been fine-tuned over college nights out. It had been further developed and enhanced through his university years and was now demonstrated for all to see. He slightly raised his arms and moved his weight from one leg to the other.

Jen seemed to decide that she was dancing with everyone. She twirled and flexed and flitted from one person to another in what appeared to be a demonstration of inclusivity. She flicked her attention from person to person and each bloke responded with a smile and perhaps a touch more enthusiasm with their rudimentary dance moves.

The bride and groom joined them, which prompted the photographer to leer at everyone and take multiple photos, the camera flash joining the pulse from the lights to illuminate the gathering in the centre of the floor.

Finally, it was time for the bride and groom to leave. A strange wedding ritual in which the guests form a line and the newlyweds are ushered into a waiting car adorned with tin cans and wedding paraphernalia. Oh, and on this occasion a bit of smoked kipper tied onto the engine block courtesy of one of the ushers.

Bryn apologised for hardly talking to anyone. Bella hugged everyone and waved enthusiastically. The assembled wedding party waved back with enthusiasm, half wishing them well and half delighted that they could now leave and go home.

The university crew went through a lengthy farewell with promises to keep in touch, promises to write more emails, and enthusiastic agreement on how great it was to see each other.

Will and Ruth were the first to actually leave the building, a move partly inspired by Ruth's desire to get out of there. She was especially attentive when Will and Jen said their goodbyes, her radar attuned to any sign of intimacy.

'Great to see you, Will,' said Jen.

'Oh, fantastic,' Will replied. 'It's been too long.'

'Yeah, let's stay in touch and don't be a bloody stranger.' With that, Jen leant forward for the obligatory peck on the cheek but a casual observer might have spotted a quick squeeze of Will's bottom. A move that was, of course, spotted by anyone paying attention.

'Well, for a wedding, that wasn't too bad,' said Will from the back of a pre-booked taxi.

'Yeah, it was fine,' Ruth replied. 'Nice to meet a few of your old uni buddies.'

'They haven't changed much. Ian has put on a bit of weight but other than that they are wearing pretty well.

Why does everything take so long? Even the cake cutting has to pause for a million bloody photos. And, while I think of it, what happened to some cake to take home?'

'Jen seems nice,' said Ruth with a false level of moderation in her voice.

'God, I wasn't expecting to see her there. Didn't realise she was that close to Bryn, to be honest.'

'She seemed pretty close to everyone.'

'Actually, that was the odd thing about Jen. We all knew her, used to go out together and in some cases shared the same lecture theatre. But she was kind of one of the lads. No one seemed to fancy her, I don't remember anyone chatting her up or flirting with her. But after a year of uni life she met this bloke called Rory who no one liked that much. But they became an item. One night we went to an end of year ball and she turned up with Rory and we nearly fell over. She looked incredible. I remember standing at the bar with Ian and debating how the hell we had missed her. In all our nights where girls were a genuine quest, we didn't think of her. But when she turned up with Rory looking like that, en masse we all could not believe it. Ian and I spent ages wondering why we hadn't asked her out before.'

'You don't know what you've got till it's gone,' said Ruth.

'Exactly! Anyway, it was nice to see her. She hasn't changed either.'

And so it was that Ruth found herself in the back of a cab while Will waxed lyrical about a woman from his past. She wondered how much she was hearing was a story. She wondered how much was said to appease her. She wondered if she should be careful.

Definitions of Jealousy by Marcus Wright, published in the NY Medical Journal, 1836

Level 1: Neutral state – not jealous at all

Comfortable with the current situation and low drive to change or improve oneself.

Level 2: Aspirational jealousy

Triggered by objects possessed by others.

Example: I am jealous; I would love to acquire that string of pearls.

This level is often about desire rather than reality. The jealous person knows that the pearls are unattainable and therefore jealousy at this level tends to be a spoken word rather than a genuine ambition to change.

Remedy: leeches, bleeding.

Level 3: Personal jealousy

Triggered by the desire or compulsion for authentic possession.

Example: Note how affectionate he is towards her. How I wish his heart were mine.

This manifests in spending time and energy on emotions such as regret, contempt, personal review of ownership, reward or status.

Remedy: leeches, bleeding, religious chanting.

Level 4: Romantic jealousy

Triggered by threat to personal status, romantic connections, sense of belonging. Can be a challenge to status and place in society.

Example: We are betrothed and I resent the clear betrayal in his eyes as he covets your time, your affection.

Can result in a punitive response. Withdrawal of favours. Quid pro quo punishment. Threats and demands for compliance. Evidence that actions are driven by intuition and compulsion rather than objective reason.

Remedy: leeches, bleeding, religious chanting, monastic studies.

Level 5: Italian Jealousy

So named after the concept in Italian law where a crime of passion is an acceptable defence for homicide or grievous bodily harm.

Example: You are my love, my wife and he dared to cross the threshold defined by respect and honour. For that he deserves to die.

Likely to result in complete loss of control and disregard for statute and the legal process. Unable to listen to reason, the jealous subject is capable of anything regardless of whether this repairs his emotions or builds his self-esteem.

Remedy: monastic studies, solitary confinement, imprisonment.

Level 6: Suicidal jealousy

Authentic desire to end life rather than confront the reality. Subjects at this level are convinced that all emotions are irreversible and the outcome will be negative and pre-ordained with no alternative.

Example: There is no point going on. I will take my own life.

Often seen as a cry for help until action is taken to hold good the promise. Symptoms include withdrawal, self-absorption, obsessive rambling, crying for help, howling and death.

Remedy: monastic studies, bleeding, imprisonment, sanatorium.

Chapter 7: See You Again

Will was early so he pottered around Trafalgar Square, people watching. He had thirty minutes to kill before his lunch appointment and found himself being amused by buskers, street performers and artists. He was confused by the predominance of people dressed as strange statues and whose only talent seemed to be the ability to stay still for ages and to move in a creepy robotic way whenever anyone passed by. There was one guy who looked like he had been made from papier mâché. He was covered in white fabric. The small amount of face that was uncovered was painted an emulsion white. He perched on a small box and as people passed, he would move like a confused mime artist – an effect that made him look like a poorly wound clockwork statue. At his feet lay a small tin collecting coins and he hoped that people would donate more money if they took a photo with him. Will wondered how much he made and whether the rate of pay was better than his own.

Next to him was one of two Yodas. The Yoda guys had perfected the art of appearing to hover in mid-air when in reality they were held up by a bit of metal and some simple engineering. Unless one of them really was Yoda and was in fact using the force to suspend them both above the ground. If this was the case, it would be certainly worth more than the 50p someone had just dropped into the tip box. In fact, someone might be prepared to pay good money for that. Although Will doubted the real Yoda would choose to spend a day perched like a budgie in Trafalgar Square.

He wandered up past the National Portrait Gallery where lines of tourists waited patiently in line to buy half-price tickets to a West End Show.

On the north side of the Square some street musicians were warming up. One guy was beat boxing. His microphone fed into a small amplifier that was turned up to full distortion to try and make an impact on the hordes of people. In front were four lean, trim and energetic guys all dressed in black. They had perfected a number of choreographed dance moves in time to the sounds coming out of their friend at the back. They spun and twirled with incredible energy. Meanwhile, a man with a hat moved through the assembled crowd hoping for folding money to be deposited inside.

As a tourist, it is easy to get trapped into these shows. The performers take an age getting a large crowd together. They then convince the crowd to clap loudly for no reason whatsoever (apart from attracting other people). Next, they build up the tension before unleashing forty-five seconds in which some bloke hops on a unicycle whilst juggling three blunt knives that have been stolen from the *Aladdin* prop box. For this forty-five seconds of uninspired wonder, the buskers hope for multiple donations of £5 notes before setting off to perform the show elsewhere.

Will managed to perfect the art of looking without being too bothered. If you are a regular visitor to these places, then you mentally decide that buskers are for tourists and are not your chosen charity. The challenge is to stand a healthy distance away and look as if you are still moving forward. Most importantly, you need to be aware of the location of the bloke with the hat and to keep out of his way. Will wondered how all these people travelled around the City. Do mini Yodas get on the Tube carrying large pieces of steel pipe? He didn't remember seeing a bloke dressed all in white on the public transport system.

Will looked at his watch. He was fifteen minutes early but that was good timing. He headed towards Leicester Square Tube, past yet more half-price booking offices, past the slices of pizza on display in the local café. Past the man advertising today's 'Golf Sale' by drifting about with a large sign – *Surely a job at the lower end of the employment competence ladder,* thought Will – and to the Cork & Bottle.

The Cork & Bottle was a haven of calm amid the chaos that was Leicester Square. A small entrance was difficult to spot but a glass door opened and led to a spiral staircase that wound down to the underground wine bar. The bar was cosy and bathed in candlelight. Couples were scattered throughout, some deep in conversation, others peering at the menu in the gloom. Will looked for a table but was distracted by a hand waving at him from a darkened corner. He made his way over.

'Hi Jen. Blimey, you beat me here.'

'Hi Will, yeah my meetings finished earlier than I expected and I couldn't be bothered to hang around on the square, listening to those godawful buskers.'

'Have you ordered anything?'

'Just sparking water, but I could murder a glass of wine.'

***

Ruth staggered home from work having practised the art of shopping bag juggling. Not that long ago, shopping bags were free and so it was easy to spread the weight of a few items amongst them. Since the introduction of a charge for carrier bags, Ruth had joined many people who resented spending money on them. Most of the time she would take bags with her but now she was being penalised for spontaneous shopping. Arriving at a till with a trolley full of food, she was now being accused of being an anti-environmentalist simply because she needed a few bags to carry the stuff home in. So when asked how many bags she needed, she replied that two would suffice and then proceeded to cram them to the brim with food. The implication being that a third bag would result in a 5° centigrade rise in the temperature of Brighton, which would enable pineapples and cactus to be grown on the seafront and would signal the arrival of basking whales. Meanwhile, monsoons would ravage the Eastern Seaboard. Or something like that.

She gratefully dumped the bags on the kitchen floor and began to sort the content. Tonight was curry night and she had offered to make Will one of her specials. Within minutes she was chopping onions and spooning a variety of spices into different pots. She followed a favourite recipe and soon the apartment was flooded with the aroma of cumin, coriander, turmeric, garlic, ginger and onion. Ruth added some lime, basil and mandarin from a Jo Malone candle and wondered if the candle could cut through the overpowering scent of her frying pan.

With chicken sizzling, she popped a bottle of Chablis in the fridge along with four bottles of Tiger beer. She could give Will the choice. She did a quick whizz round with a hoover, tidied away a rogue magazine and set the table for two. She also flicked a couple of artificial candles into life on the windowsill so that the house looked inviting from the moment Will arrived.

With the curry simmering nicely and Will not due to arrive for an hour, she went upstairs to tidy the bedroom and get changed. An easy choice of what to wear given that this was a night in. Underwear was important, as was the careful layering of body cream and L'Eau D'Issey perfume. Finally, she selected some music from an Apple playlist entitled *Music For Seducing Your Boyfriend*, which she carefully checked to ensure it contained no songs by Ed 'bores the arse off me' Sheeran.

***

Will arrived ten minutes late, carrying a couple of bottles of wine and some After Eight mints.

'Smells amazing, Ruth,' he said as he held her close by way of greeting.

'Well, I hope you like it.'

'You can't beat a good curry on a Friday night, you know that.' Will reluctantly let go. 'How was your day?'

'Oh, it was okay. Actually, I was bored and distracted. Found myself in meetings thinking about what I would cook tonight and then lost the plot about what they were talking about. At one point I agreed to do something and I have no idea what it is. What about you?'

'Same old stuff, really. A few project meetings and people explaining in detail what they haven't managed to achieve this week. I did manage to stay awake during a thirty-five-slide PowerPoint presentation by one of the dullest members of the team.'

Ruth disappeared into the kitchen and called, 'I hope you're hungry?'

'I haven't eaten all day. Can I help with anything?'

'You can choose some music, if you like.'

'What, you mean, you haven't spent as long on the playlist as you have on the cooking?'

'Very funny.'

There was a pause. 'Ruth? You have bloody Ed Sheeran on your iPod! And I thought you might be the girl for me...'

'Well, you don't have to play it.'

Will found a War on Drugs album and set the volume to audible but unobtrusive. They sat down to eat and Ruth produced a selection of Indian snacks served with a homemade raita and some crisp poppadoms.

'I didn't make the snacks,' she said. 'I mean, who has time to actually make an onion bhaji? I did slice the cucumber and added the garlic to the yoghurt, though.'

Will settled into a relaxed conversation and loved the food. Ruth was a great cook and he ate more than he'd expected, washing it down with a chilled Tiger. Just as he finished, his phone buzzed and he reached for the message app.

'Steve asking what I am up to tomorrow,' he explained. 'Sorry mate. Intend on taking Ruth out,' he said as he typed.

Together they tidied the table and rinsed plates and loaded the dishwasher. At least, Will loaded it and Ruth moved everything to its proper place. 'It washes better like this. If you leave all the plates touching each other, all the food sticks on.'

'Wow,' said Will, 'our first domestic. I can see the headlines now: *Couple Split Over Plate-Stacking Disagreement*.'

'I can't help being tidy,' said Ruth, 'and a bit particular. You'll have to get used to it.'

'Yeah, but do you have to stop and fold my clothes just after we have thrown them on the floor in gay abandon?'

Ruth threw a cushion. 'I'm not that bad!' Returning to the table, she picked up the last condiments as well as a serviette on the floor with a scrap of paper. She headed to the bin and checked what she was throwing away. 'Will?'

'Yeah?' Will called back from the lounge.

'Why is there a receipt for the Cork & Bottle on my floor dated today?'

Will had only split seconds to answer and Ruth would now witness what she would later discover to be the 'sports commentator effect'. When the starter gun is fired for the 100 meters in the Olympics or when all the swimmers dive into the pool, it is impossible to make sense of what is going on. There is a lot of energy, a lot of movement but no one can say anything objective about what is happening. So instead, commentators learn to fill the air with meaningless chat. They continue with this until they can think of something to say and to give their brain time to absorb the scene and to make sense of it.

On realising the receipt must have fallen out of his pocket with the phone, Will was mortified. A brain scanner at that point would have observed the following tortured calculations:

Option 1

Deny the receipt is yours. Claim it must have been someone else's or been stuck to the shoe on arrival.

Pros: This demonstrates no betrayal or hiding of the truth has taken place. If believed, integrity is maintained.

Cons: This feels pretty implausible and can lead to more challenge and the potential to be called a liar at a later date.

Option 2

Admit going to the wine bar but suggest it was someone from work called Colin.

Pros: This is clearly not a date and Ruth doesn't actually know who went to lunch so is difficult to challenge.

Cons: You made no mention of lunch today when asked earlier and you have never mentioned Colin. Plus the Cork & Bottle is hardly the land of the bloke lunch.

Option 3

Tell the truth. Admit a meeting with Jen.

Pros: This is honest, and honesty may surprise her. You can certainly make it sound like an innocuous meeting and play the whole thing down.

Cons: Who are you kidding? A meeting with Jen in a wine bar reeks of intimacy and she won't buy it.

Option 4

Fake illness, perhaps choking. Get Ruth to perform the

Heimlich manoeuvre and use this as an opportunity to kiss her.

Cons: Who are you kidding?

Option 5
Refuse to talk about it and hope it goes away. As if…

'What did you say?' said Will.

'Receipt,' said Ruth. 'One bottle of Pinot, two coffees, cheeseboard and a shepherd's pie. Today's date at 14:30.'

'Oh, I had lunch with Colin.' *Option 2 it is then.*

'You never said?'

Now at this stage Will should have learnt something important. When fabricating information, less is more. People who are lying often go into far too much detail in an attempt to paint an authentic picture. It is better to keep things short and simple. Instead, Will launched into a long, convoluted story.

'Yeah, Colin is working with a client on Shaftesbury Avenue and needed some support with the project management and configuring the SAP user interface. So, I went along to the meeting with him, which is where we both sat through the presentation. Finished at lunchtime and then fancied a bite to eat. The pubs were all rammed so we wandered along to the Square and Colin suggested the C&B as a good alternative. In fact, it wasn't busy at all and they do a wicked cheeseboard. I paid but I can claim some of it back on expenses, apparently. Then we went back to the office and worked on the checking schedule, which reminds me, I must remember to tell the others about the slippage on the midpoint timelines.'

'And you didn't mention this because…'

'Because I knew you had put a lot of effort into cooking and I didn't want you to think badly of me for having a late lunch. The first thing you asked me was if I was hungry and I hardly felt like confessing to a business lunch not four hours ago. I am so sorry, Ruth, I should have mentioned it.'

'Likes his Pinot, does Colin?'

'Turns out, he is more of a wine than a beer man. He knows his wines, does our Colin.'

'It's a bit odd, Will.'

***

This is how it starts, thought Ruth as she wiped the kitchen surfaces with a blue cloth. Dan had done this. It started with a few 'business lunches'. Then work needed later nights. Then the conference calendar had become more and more congested. At first, Ruth had been loyal, trusting and a believer. After a while, she became suspicious, angry and betrayed. Dan was so convincing. He had stories to tell, many plausible reasons and an endless supply of what sounded like authentic work-related pressures. In reality, the pressures were called Emma and she worked in Purchasing. Ruth never discovered the affair but one day Dan announced he was unhappy. She knew that, of course, and had spent months agonising over her own self-worth. Dan said he needed time. It wasn't her, it was him, he told her and he moved out to 'get his head together.' Finally, after a serious row about what the hell was happening to their relationship, Dan confessed to having met someone else. It's funny but Dan had been under the impression that trust has many levels and personal pain is relative to time and frequency. So, Dan admitted to one month and a couple of occasions where he had met Emma, under the illusion that it was better for Ruth to hear this than the reality of fourteen months and countless meetings and nights away. Over time, Ruth learnt the truth. Mutual friends confessed to the loyalty dilemma and it seemed that everyone knew he was shagging Emma but her.

Her intuition regarding Will was now on red alert. This was how Dan had treated her.

***

Will breathed a sigh of relief that the conversation was at last over. He had got away with it. Just.

***

And so to bed. It is hard to define the date that relationships transition from the 'I wonder if she will sleep with me' phase to the point where you leave a toothbrush and change of clothes and expect to stay for breakfast. Ruth loved the feel of Will beside her and they were in that place where there was still a profound thrill as soon as the bedroom door closed.

Tonight felt different, however. Will was keen to get close and to prove through excessive cuddling and affection that the lunch really had been with Colin. Ruth felt strange and, where normally she would turn over and burrow her head into Will's outstretched arm, tonight she turned on her iPad and flicked through random Facebook pages and items of news. Will knew he was being punished and did his best to sound interested in the small lives of others.

***

Ruth woke early and decided to busy herself in the kitchen. The sun was attempting to cut through the gloom of an early Saturday and looked like it might succeed. She began by clearing up the remnants of last night's meal and then settled down with her iPad. Deep down inside she felt a sense of discomfort about the conversation over dinner. Perhaps she was being irrational, but her self-protection radar was now well and truly activated.

Opening the Facebook app, Ruth resumed where she had left off last night. She couldn't get suspicious thoughts out of her mind so she quickly typed in *Cork & Bottle*. A few clicks and she found a dedicated page full of reviews and comments. It seems that Melissa was unhappy about her meal on Tuesday. The steak was smaller and tougher than she'd expected. Hans, on the other hand, couldn't speak highly enough of the cheeseboard he was served although he would rather see a few more grapes. The Cork & Bottle made no comments on either of these pearls of customer feedback but that didn't stop other people leaving similar reports. On the main page, Ruth spotted a couple of links and found herself on the TripAdvisor page. A healthy selection of reviews but none from the last couple of days. The only words that sprung from the page were 'cosy', 'candles', 'romantic', 'dinner for two' and 'celebration'. She was yet to see any words about business lunches.

She then clicked on Will's Facebook page and clicked on his list of friends. Some she knew, some she had heard about in detail, some were mentioned in occasional stories and some she doubted Will would even know who they were anymore. Her cursor hovered over a picture of Jen and she clicked on the link. It seems our Jen was quite a private person and had locked her Facebook down only to be viewed by friends. Ruth debated sending a friend request but decided against it. The only thing she could click on was a button listing her friends and Ruth clicked on that. A column of names appeared and it seemed they shared three friends in common.

Next stop, Twitter. Ruth typed Cork & Bottle into the search bar. Seconds later, a list of options opened and she found herself staring at a range of tweets from the previous couple of days. One struck her as interesting. 'Lovely lunch @cork_bottle today. So good to catch up with an old friend.' It was posted by 'Cafegirl390'. A click on the link opened an account and a range of photos and there she was. Jen, complete with many selfies and proclamations all summarised within the Twitter character limit.

Ruth's heart sank. She could feel her stomach churn and her blood pressure begin to rise. She had no proof that Jen was talking about a lunch with Will. But they were both at the same place and 'lunch' was a narrow space of time. She paged through the Twitter feed, searching for any other clues, but merely confirmed that Jen was a woman who liked taking pictures of food and wine glasses. She clearly never cooked; judging by the Twitter feed she existed on £40 lunches washed down with something sparkling in a tall glass. It seemed her every day was full of restaurants, recommendations and some disappointments. Ruth also noticed the absence of anything else. No mention of theatre, culture, music, arts, politics or philosophy. It appeared that lunch with Jen would mean sitting down to discuss places she had been for lunch and deciding where to go next. Most tweets contained a link to someone else and Ruth could easily trace her associations and relationships. Plenty of meetings with the girls and regular correspondence with a guy called Dom who seemed to be an 'honorary girl' at most of the gatherings. Within a few clicks, Ruth had amassed a fairly clear picture of Jen's life. She was a girl who liked to broadcast her every move and was keen to expand her impressive list of followers.

Ruth heard the toilet door upstairs close and she began to contemplate what do to and what to say. One option would be to ignore her findings. She had done that in the past with Dan, trying to lock the emotions away and carry on. Ruth had never considered herself a confrontational person. She was alright once a subject had been raised on her behalf, but she found herself holding back from presenting people with tough opinions.

Will arrived in the kitchen, padded over to Ruth and landed a sweet kiss on her shoulder which shivered down her arm where she rubbed it away with her fingertips.

'Morning and how are you today?' said Will with perhaps an artificial brightness in his tone.

'Yeah fine, just a lot to do, that's all.'

'Oh? I thought this weekend was going to be pretty chilled.'

'It was but I have to get some work done for Monday which is a bloody pain but essential, and I promised Megan I would see her this afternoon for some shopping and a bite to eat.'

'I thought we could spend the day together?'

'Don't be so presumptuous – you may have entered my world but that doesn't mean all else stops for you. Anyway, don't you have anyone you need to catch up with over the weekend?'

'Ouch. Er, not really.' Will tried to figure out her tone. Was this real or was this punishment?

Ruth stood spooning Greek yoghurt into a glass bowl and reached for a packet of Waitrose Essential Exotic Fruit Selection.

'Typical Waitrose,' said Will. 'Only they would come up with the idea that exotic fruits can be part of an essential range. Most supermarkets will have bread, milk, butter and bacon as essentials. Go to Waitrose and you get essential asparagus, anchovies, kiwi fruit and Peruvian cured meats.'

'I have never seen any Peruvian meats at Waitrose.'

'Then that's their next untapped market. All they need

is Delia or Nigella or Jamie O to feature something in a recipe and the next thing you know, the stuff will be flying off the shelves faster than the ready meals for two. Mind you, most of the recipes are disgusting. Have you ever tried making anything they put on the cards they leave by the entrance? You pick up a card which says something like Chicken with Red Cabbage and Black Bean Sauce, spend more on the ingredients than you would on a decent meal at a restaurant and end up with something that can only be described as both interesting and inedible in equal measure.'

'Well, I have tried a couple and they're not always that bad. Dan and I used to love the Seafood Pasta, which we found on a card. I still have it somewhere, tucked inside a recipe book.'

'You don't mention him that often.'

Ruth's eyes met his. 'You know what it's like. You get to know someone well. You get close, closer and then completely intimate and share everything. You exchange secrets, you taste and touch in the most intimate of ways … and then it's over. The closeness disappears and you are left with a host of memories that occasionally surface through the recipe cards at the entrance to Waitrose.'

'Is … is that what's going to happen to us?' said Will.

Ruth heard the comment but chose to say nothing. She allowed the words to fester and shower the kitchen with question marks. Instead she began to wash up her bowl and spoon and tidied a few surface things away.

***

An hour later and Will found himself leaving the flat and heading off into a much bleaker Saturday than he'd anticipated. He had showered, changed, packed in relative silence as Ruth busied herself with laptops and dusters.

Nothing specifically was said but Will could feel a cold front descend on him and chill the air. As Will kissed Ruth goodbye, he noticed a lack of conviction over the 'speak to you later' promise. They agreed to be in touch once Megan and the shopping was over and either meet up later or see each other on Sunday. At least, that was the nature of the conversation but Will wondered what was left unspoken. He was desperate to bring some light and warmth back into the room but he felt like he was shining a torch into a cold cellar. He illuminated the room briefly but the room was still cold.

Will arrived home and looked through his cupboards for a spot of lunch. He was always uninspired by the food inside, it was almost as if someone else had bought it. A box of Cup-a-Soup never really seemed inviting, dried straight-to-wok noodles looked sad and tired in their plastic wrapping. Tins of tuna in a variety of oils and water waited be drained whilst leaving the impossible-to-remove smell of fish on the fingers. A tin of carrots in water (what on earth possessed him to buy this?). Eight months past their best before date but too early to give up on completely. Some tinned sweetcorn, tins of beans and a tin of ham in jelly (yuk). In the bread bin was half a loaf of dried out granary and a single muffin. The fridge revealed cheddar cheese, as yet unopened, a bag of wilting salad, half a cucumber and a selection of dips. He checked out the last remaining cupboard and found the ever-expanding supply of almost finished bags of dried pasta. Why was it that all pasta recipes always meant you had a bit left over, but never enough for another recipe so Will would have to buy some more? But usually a different brand and a different shape. This would go on for some months until Will could hardly open the cupboard without navigating the multiple shapes and sizes all in their own bag. He either needed a multiple pasta experience in which he tipped the remnants of each packet into a giant saucepan and purged the lot. Or he bought some of the same brand once in a while and merged new with old. The trouble was, he could never remember what he needed in a supermarket. And even if he did, when he got around to cooking, he would forget to check the remaining pasta selection before tipping the required quantity into the pot.

Will sat down to cheese on toast accompanied by a chicken and vegetable soup in a mug that, no matter how hard he stirred, still contained a worrying residue of dried animals and veg in the bottom of his cup, whilst small portions of croutons tried to stay buoyant on top of the sludge. Will wondered if he was alone in always throwing away half the soup to avoid the granules of monosodium glutamate eating away at his china cup.

Soup and cheese over, Will flicked through some Facebook pages and the competition for the best weekend was in full swing. As usual, the pages were populated with clips proclaiming: *I can't stop watching this – funniest thing ever!* A quick click revealed a man in a forklift truck misjudging the distance and knocking over a warehouse full of beer. No sooner had this clip finished than the screen cut to a man on a swing who would predictably fall off in spectacular fashion. Will couldn't help but wonder if these posts could be prosecuted under the Trade Descriptions Act since they were not remotely as funny as claimed. It was like going to a comedy film at the cinema and not laughing at all. He wondered if Facebook had a responsibility to the general public and should not support people who do this.

Will closed his laptop and surveyed his surroundings and felt consumed by an overwhelming sense of Saturday sadness. He was used to spending time alone, but this weekend was different and unexpected. He had been expecting to do not much with Ruth and instead he found himself doing not much alone. This may seem the same but was in fact a world apart.

Will didn't want to do nothing alone. He was reminded of his A-level studies of *Far From The Madding Crowd* where farmer Gabriel Oak defined success in a relationship by being able to look up and see his beloved a few feet away (although whether this would indeed be sufficient for the feisty Bathsheba Everdene, only time would tell). But that was Will's reality. He wanted company and the comfort that companionship brings. It is so much better surfing the internet when there is someone close by to share things with.

Will wasn't sure but the colours and light in his apartment seemed dulled this afternoon. Greys and magnolia predominated and the windows seemed in need of a good clean. He reached for his phone.

Hi Ruth how are U? Thinking of you x he typed and then pressed Send.

He then watched the phone for several minutes and even tried shaking it to spark it into life.

No worries, hope you are having a fab afternoon x he typed twelve minutes later.

Next, he flicked on his Find Friends app and began to search. He felt a bit clandestine about this but he had showed Ruth this function and they had previously found it fun to find each other on a map. The app sprang to life and announced 'Ruth … searching.' And there she was. Still at home. Will felt marginally better. He figured she must be in the bath or something.

***

Ruth was glad of some space. People often use this as an excuse for temporary break-ups but the reality is that any relationship can be claustrophobic at times. When you are used to your own company, the arrival of someone else into your life can feel oppressive. Things start off amusingly enough. Flirting, exploring, laughing, sharing and chatting are all part of the early days of courtship. There is, however, a line that everyone knows is there. It is a line called Love & Commitment and represents the transition from casual to serious. The line may be invisible but everyone knows when they cross it. Ruth had crossed that line for Will. It wasn't just what she said, words were incredibly easy. It was how she viewed the space in her diary, the key to her domain and the openness of her conversation. She began to share inner secrets, fears, desires. She had allowed Will into the hallowed ground of her bedroom where he had seen her naked, not only because of the removal of her clothes but through the way she cast away her reservations and opened up to him. They had reached a level of intimacy and both noticed their assumptions change. They now assumed they were spending time in each other's company. People they knew would begin to invite both of them to an event and they began to be seen as a couple. Ruth admitted a wry smile the first time she signed a birthday card, *Love from Ruth and Will.*

Determined not to spend the whole day moping, Ruth sent a quick text to Ange.

Hi – in need of spontaneous female therapy

Always ready for that – what do u fancy? came the reply.

Window shopping and wine

Great! Meet at Bond Street

Perfect

Ruth and Ange met at 2:00 and strolled along an inevitably packed Regent Street. Hordes of shoppers and tourists in a wave of humanity drifted along the small pavements, stopping only for selfies or to peer into store windows. Ruth and Ange entered the hallowed ground of Selfridges where they could indulge in what can only be described as handbag pornography.

'The trouble with this place is that my level of desire for products is far higher than my ability to pay,' said Ange. 'I mean, look at this bag: a thing of beauty if ever I've seen it. It would go perfectly with at least three of my outfits and I want it more than I want my own relatives. But I don't think I should throw away £1,399 on it, do you? I don't even have a sucker of a boyfriend to buy it for me, or a rich Arab.'

'Yeah, madness I know. Oh, I love this one,' said Ruth holding a small red leather clutch against her midriff.

'Can't you get Will to buy you one?'

'Mmm, well, I need a chat about him,' said Ruth.

Ten minutes later they were settled in one of Selfridges' many small corners of luxury where attentive waiters offered over-priced drinks and nibbles. With chilled white wine and a selection of snacks spread over a wooden board in front of them, Ange adopted her best listening expression.

'Come on then, Ruth, what's going on?'

'So, all going well and happy until we went to a wedding. One of Will's old mates was getting married and he bumped into an old college friend called Jenny. The sort of girl my mum warned me about years ago. Too attractive, too enthusiastic and too loud. Fast forward a couple of weeks and Will came round for dinner and a receipt dropped out of his pocket. Cosy lunch for two. When I asked him, he told me it was with a bloke called Colin. But Detective Ruth leapt into action and after a few clicks I discovered Jenny had checked in to the same place at the same time.'

'Blimey. So Will is sneaking around with her? What did he say when you asked him?'

'I haven't confronted him with it. I hoped he might confess and be straight with me.'

'Well, of course, he met her. Where did they meet?'

'Cork & Bottle.'

'Oh, that well-known venue for blokey lunches. I don't think so.'

'Exactly. And now I don't know what to do. I don't want to hear the truth, Ange, but I am driving myself crazy thinking about the lies. I am wondering how many other times they have met. What has happened. I have visions of them kissing and worse.'

'Ruth, I am so sorry, what a shit thing to happen. So, what *have* you said?'

'Nothing really, but I cancelled any plans to see each other today. I couldn't stand the tension and needed a break from him. He looked and sounded disappointed but I am wondering if right now he has taken the opportunity to do lunch with her highness.'

'Well, taking a break today sounds like a good thing to do. The trouble is, I don't think he is going to confess to this unless you confront him. Blokes hate to be seen as liars, so if they tell you something that isn't true, they will stick to that story unless cornered with no way out. What have things been like apart from that?'

'Things seemed great. Lots of time together, a lot of fun. I had no idea anything was wrong.'

'You know what they say, Ruth, women need a reason to make love, blokes just need a place.'

'Thanks for that, Ange.'

'Sorry, don't mean to piss you off but, in my experience, you can't trust them. You think everything is fine and then one day you find that your lover has been given the Oscar for pretending to like you when all the time he has been shagging some blonde at the office.'

'Don't remind me. I don't need to revisit the Dan saga.'

'It's not just you, Ruth. A girl from work was due to get married next month to a childhood sweetheart. Inseparable, they were. Then last month she discovered by pure chance a tag on his Facebook account. Seems her adoring fiancé was already living with someone else with two kids. Turns out his demanding job that took him away for nights on end was actually a cover for living with some other girl and starting a family. Incredible, when you think about it. So what are you going to do?'

'I think I will have to become a lesbian, Ange. That way I can ignore blokes altogether and have many hours of intimacy with women who won't cheat on me and who will be honest and loving and kind.'

'Yeah, but you will be doomed to cut your hair short, and wear purple and green clothes and join Greenpeace.'

'That's not all lesbians, Ange.'

'Granted, but you don't strike me as the lesbian type.'

'Okay, well, maybe not a lesbian, then. Maybe a nun. I could sign up for a life of celibacy and prayer.'

'Could you exist on a diet of gruel and penitence?'

'Maybe not. Although, those girls in *Sister Act* seemed to have a great time. Maybe I could be like one of them?'

'It helps if you can sing, Ruth.'

'True. Fuck. I don't know what to do.' As Ruth took a sip of her wine, a tear slipped unexpectedly down her cheek.

'You have to tell him Ruth,' Ange said, reaching over to squeeze her hand. 'You can't go on wondering what has happened.'

'Yes, I know. But part of me is scared of the answer.'

'Well,' replied Ange, deep in thought, 'the truth can't be any worse than your imagination, can it?'

'No, I guess not.'

Ruth's phone buzzed on the table. 'It's from Will,' she announced. '"Hope you are okay. Fancy dinner tonight?"' She began to type a response.

I am busy. Why don't you see if Jenny is free?

'Shall I send this?' She showed Ange the draft.

'Well, that certainly is direct, Ruth. Doesn't sound like you. I had you down as more of a "quiet discussion over a coffee in the kitchen" girl rather than a "take that, you bastard" kind of texter.'

'I know, you're right. Must be the wine at lunch talking. I should invite him over and chat this through. I am sure there is a rational explanation for this. I mean, there must be a good reason for him to be wining and dining Jen at the Cork & Bottle and hiding it from me. I am sure an open and honest conversation will clear everything up.'

'Yeah, right,' said Ange.

'Mmm,' said Ruth and she pressed the Send button.

***

Will was on his way to the local corner shop to buy some milk. The trouble was that he always came home with far more stuff than he expected. There was always some buy-one-get-one-free offer on chocolate biscuits or crisps. Coffee or tea would be massively discounted. So instead of spending £1 he found himself spending considerably more plus the price of a carrier bag on things he didn't want. He would then go home and start demolishing the biscuits. His corner shop had become a feeder, he concluded.

His phone buzzed and Will was rocked by Ruth's response. His stomach lurched. It was the first time Ruth had been so brutal and her meaning was clear. He had been found out.

Will started to type a response while juggling carrier

bags but decided he needed a moment to think. He rushed back to his place, dumped the stuff on the floor and sat down in the lounge, staring at his phone.

It was obvious Ruth knew about his meeting with Jen but how that had happened was beyond him. He couldn't fathom it at all. Was she guessing? There could have been no proof. He thought about a reply and concluded that the best thing to do was to admit nothing and to suggest a meeting. After a couple of drafts, he replied:

Blimey, wasn't expecting that. We need to talk. Miss you x

He figured this acknowledged the text from Ruth, didn't admit to anything and displayed signs of ongoing affection.

His phone buzzed within seconds.

Busy right now. Out to lunch with a friend who doesn't lie to me.

Will sat in his lounge feeling sick to the core. How could a weekend go so badly when it started with such promise? He was truly shocked by the tone of Ruth's texts. The walls of his domain seemed to close in on him and he was struck by an overwhelming sense of claustrophobia and sadness. That and a feeling of anger. He was pissed off that Ruth was treating him so badly. Why hadn't she said anything? Why could they not meet and talk about this? He felt like he was being punished.

***

Meanwhile in Selfridges, Ange and Ruth were on glass number three.

'Wow, Ruth, that told him.'

'No more Mrs Nice Guy,' said Ruth. 'I am not being given the runaround.'

'So are you going to meet him? Maybe you should let him sweat for a couple of days. Don't make it too easy for him.'

'Good idea. I will be unavailable for reconciliation and will spend my time shopping and drinking wine.'

Ruth's phone burst into life with an incoming call from Will. She stared at his face on the screen. His lovely, lying face.

'Are you going to answer that?' asked Ange.

'No, not today.' Ruth pressed the Decline button.

***

There are few things more depressing than rejection. It might have been easier to deal with during the week when surrounded by colleagues and a busy schedule. But sitting alone on a damp and gloomy Saturday created an overwhelming sense of loss. Will picked up his phone and typed.

So sorry you feel like that. I would do anything to see that smile of yours this weekend.

He pressed Send.
Ruth's response was instant.

I am sure you would. I'm also sure you have other options.

And with that Will sank into his chair.

The Creation of Reality

Summary of the paper published by Doctor Margaret Daniels – Philadelphia Press, 2012

My research explored human brain activity when dealing with an absence of known facts and clear information. There are many research papers on problem solving and creativity, and they tend to rely on three things:

a) There is a clearly defined problem.

b) There are at least some known facts to work with.

c) As human beings we have the capacity for creativity and can bring this talent into a problem-solving equation should we command it.

I wanted to delve into the neural processing present when people are dealing with a lack of information. Our hypothesis was that a creative brain and a capacity to invent explanations could be more compelling in relationship building and problem solving than the facts themselves. We conducted a three-stage experiment:

Experiment stage one
A number of test subjects were brought into a room with simple furniture and told they would be part of a research project into neural activity. They were told the experiment would commence shortly and that a research scientist would be with them soon. We had previously asked them to make arrangements to be picked up at a specific time and driven home by somebody else. They were then left alone for twenty-five minutes. After this time, they were interviewed by a member of our team who gathered data on their expectations, fears and concerns.

Through detailed questioning we discovered evidence of elaborate invention in the absence of objective data.

Many of our test subjects had seen science fiction movies and had clearly used these images as part of their own creative process. They were expecting to be linked to scanners, to have wires and probes attached to their body. Some were worried about the use of electric shocks to stimulate reactions in the brain. Eighty per cent expected a degree of discomfort but justified this by the privilege of contributing to scientific development. They expected to feel disoriented by the process (this feeling was raised significantly by the need to be picked and driven home by somebody else). Some reported feeling nauseous.

All of them were surprised when, at the end of the interview, we thanked them for their time and asked them to leave.

Experiment stage two

As our test subjects were leaving the research lab, we led them to a waiting/reception area. We made sure that the people who were there to meet and collect them were taken to a separate area. We blocked the mobile phone signals in both rooms and left them for thirty minutes. At the end of this time, a research assistant entered the room with a list of questions to explore the stories, hopes, fears and concerns created in the subjects' minds during this time. The results were fascinating.

All the test subjects admitted a change of emotions over time. Once the agreed meeting time had lapsed, they reported the following range of responses:

• The traffic must be bad – here our subjects found a plausible reason for lateness (other people)

• They are always late – reinforcing a stereotypical view of personal characteristics

- They must have had something better to do – this puts our subject as a low priority

- They got lost – making allowances based on their own experience

Once 25 minutes had passed, the stories and concerns became more dramatic:

- Road accidents – fear of dramatic events with catastrophic extrapolation

- Abandonment – fear of being left alone, deserted

- Betrayal – wondering if the person picking them up had given loyalty elsewhere

- Personal impact – thinking about the long-term impact of the worst-case scenario and the impact on life thereafter

Experiment stage three
We conducted phone interviews with those who were picking up our test subjects. We wanted to explore their experience of the mood and disposition when they reconnected. Here are some of the key observations:

a) Anxiety – the feeling of anxiety continued through the journey home and beyond. It only took thirty minutes to create a dramatic shift in mood and temperament.

b) The facts didn't matter – clearly there was a perfect excuse for being late but this was not sufficient to change the atmosphere. It became apparent that the stories and problems created in the minds of our subjects while waiting to be collected were more persuasive than the subsequent reality.

c) Long tail impact – the stories and emotions were sufficiently strong to create a lasting impact on the relationship and levels of connection thereafter.

d) People make unfair conclusions about others based on minimal/no information.

Chapter 8: The Last Goodnight

Will needed to keep busy and decided to balance his time between worrying, grovelling and entertaining himself. He logged into Interflora and decided some flowers would be a good idea. A nice, simple bouquet of sunny and bright carnations with a couple of yellow roses and some random greenery. All wrapped with a bow and presented in a plastic bowl filled with damp tissues. The biggest problem with flowers is not the flowers, but the card. So hard to decide what to say. It's like those cards at work that are circulated when people leave. Will always found himself staring at leaving cards for ages, reading the heartfelt, amusing or trivial comments from others, determined to say something profound and memorable but instead ending with 'Good luck and best wishes from Will.'

Will found the Interflora greeting card presented the self same dilemma. First, he typed 'Miss you like the stars above', which was a quote he vaguely remembered. But soon he dismissed this as too retro. Then, he tried, 'Bed's too big without you', but felt this was perhaps too selfish. She might think that all she was to him was an object of sexual desire. He then attempted some ancient Chinese philosophy: 'Man without woman is like fish without bicycle', which amused him but again was deleted. How about, 'I Love You But I Don't Know What To Say', a classic Ryan Adams song? Perhaps that only landed well if someone had the song playing at the same time.

Movie quotes sprang to mind. 'You complete me' (perhaps). Or, 'No one puts Baby in the corner' (no, definitely not). 'You can't handle the truth, yes I ordered a code red' (irrelevant and too strong). 'Here's looking at you, kid' (too old fashioned). 'How can I tell you I love you when you are sitting on my face' appealed for some strange reason but she might not get the Pythonesque references and be offended.

Will amused himself for a while and dismissed many quotes and songs. He looked up 'love songs' on the laptop as a source of inspiration and in so doing surfaced the ghost of the Carpenters. The trouble was, as soon as he read the following words, they get stuck in his head and it was almost impossible to rid the brain of them.

Why do birds suddenly appear

Every time, you are near?

Will read the words and instantly created the melody in his head. Somehow, he even knew the next verse. Within minutes he was singing 'Wow, wow, wow, wow, wow … close to you' at the top of his voice. *Damn this song*, he thought. He went to make a coffee.

How come Richard and Karen Carpenter had now entered his brain and were controlling his thoughts? This did not seem rational.

Will dismissed the idea of quoting the Carpenters on his card but struggled to get past the sound of the song.

That is why, all the boys in town (boys in town) …

Jesus, he was singing the damn harmonies. He was now getting annoyed by Richard Carpenter and so did a quick search on Google to find a way to rid himself of the tune buzzing round his head. He discovered there was a name for his problem. Apparently, he had an earworm.

He logged onto the site which claimed that the best cure for an earworm was to replace it with another one. Something not as annoying. With great confidence the website presented him with a large button that bore the title, *Random Earworm Destroyer*. Will clicked on it and the website spun into action.

I'm coming home, I've done my time

Oh Jesus, not that bloody song, thought Will and quickly shut down the link, but not before he found himself singing:

So tie a yellow ribbon round the old oak tree

And just like me, they long to be

Close to you

Will had now created an earworm medley. Which was not helping him with the Interflora card problem.

What does one write to the love of your life when they are pissed off with you for seeing another girl? He debated how other people might handle this. Russell Crowe, for example, would probably write, 'Tough shit, babe. You want me, I'll be in the bar.' Eric Cantona would write, 'The birds that sing above me, are mere shadows of the corners of my tortured soul and I remain obtuse,' or some other such bollocks. Wayne Rooney would write, 'Well, erm, like, well, erm, do you fancy going for a drive, like?' Indiana Jones, on the other hand, would likely get out a long whip and lasso the love of his life.

In the end he did the only thing that seemed okay. He deleted the flowers from the online basket and contemplated his next move, somewhat concerned that he couldn't even construct a small card with the emotions he was currently feeling.

He reached for his phone and simply typed.

Thinking of you and hope you are OK xxx

With no reply, Will opened his Find My Friends app and checked to see where Ruth was. He was delighted to see the app still in operation and a little icon popped into the screen. Ruth was home.

In that moment Will became all decisive, grabbed a coat

from the back of the chair, slammed the front door behind him and headed out towards the Tube.

***

Ruth was keeping busy but not busy enough. When something is on your mind and troubling you, your day needs a full dose of activity and preoccupation to leave no space for intrusive and destructive thoughts to enter the brain. The trouble is that being not quite busy means lots of time for reflection and contemplation. Ruth felt sad, a little confused, but overall, pessimistic. She was pessimistic about romance in general and disappointed that her romance seemed so fragile. Ruth was a great believer in the concept of an emotional bank account. The relationship between two people depends upon lots of romantic moments and gestures that create memories. Over time these add up and so if a partner does something wrong, stupid or inconsiderate, there are sufficient deposits to compensate. If they forget a significant anniversary, for example, you can eventually forgive them because they have been pretty good at depositing love and goodwill over time, so that makes it okay.

Ruth knew that not everyone was like this. She could recall an old work colleague called Janet, who had an arrogant bastard as a husband who treated her with apparent contempt. He wouldn't go anywhere, never took her out, expected his food to be on the table. Was prone to fits of rage over the smallest things. He called her horrible names when in the company of others, which she shrugged off with a false grin. He would only buy Christmas or birthday presents from a local convenience store (if she was lucky) and he would joke about this to everyone as if being inconsiderate was a badge of honour to display to friends and family. Ruth was one of many who would try and coax Janet into a better life with a better person, but the pleading fell on deaf ears. For whatever reason, Janet put up with him. Ruth never really understood why, as she figured being alone would be better than being with such a negative presence in her life. But Janet hung on in there and seemed resigned to a life full of sloping shoulders and false grins.

Ruth didn't feel like that at all. Maybe it was a consequence of her previous failed relationships but she wasn't about to bow to indiscretions so early in the relationship. It was time to set the stall out from the start. She also knew that she wanted Will back. She didn't plan her days to feel like this. She trusted her intuition and felt she was a pretty good reader of people. Deep down, she knew something wasn't right, but for now she didn't feel completely betrayed. Not yet anyway.

Ruth turned on the radio to create some background noise in an attempt to fill the silence in the room. Much to her disgust, she had recently become a BBC Radio 2 person, having abandoned the noise of Radio 1 with its over-reliance on grime, garage, drum and bass and RnB, and instead tuned into the morning sounds of Chris Evans and his ability to sound happy, even if the sky was falling. The trouble was she hated roughly one in four of the songs they played. This meant either turning down the volume until the music was barely audible, putting up with some awful music, or grinning and bearing it. Today was clearly worse than normal. The bloody Carpenters singing 'Goodbye To Love'. Why was it when she felt miserable about relationships, every damn song acted as a reminder and a soundtrack to the day? It was almost as if they were playing songs just for her. The song changed to 'Love Is A Losing Game' by Amy Winehouse.

'For you I was a flame, love is a losing game,' sang Amy.

'Bloody hell!' Ruth shouted at the radio and turned it off.

Ruth needed to pop out for groceries. She also needed to escape the confines of the kitchen and breathe some air, so she took a quick stroll to the local minimart and picked up some of life's essentials. Some milk, a small loaf of bread and chocolate. Well, actually, two bars of chocolate as inevitably there was a deal on if you brought two bars.

'Hi Ruth.'

'Will!' Ruth had left the shop and was daydreaming on her way home when the sight of Will brought her down to earth with a bump. 'What the bloody hell are you doing here?'

'Well, I could say I was shopping, but that's not strictly true. The truth is, I followed you.'

'What? You followed me here on the train?'

'No, I just had to see you.'

'How did you work out where I was?'

'I was tracking you on my phone – you left the Find My Friends app open and I was on the Tube to your place when you re-emerged here. So I sat myself over there and waited.' Will pointed to some seats near a coffee bar that would be ideal for people watching. 'Ruth, I am so sorry, this is so shit. Can we have a coffee or something?'

'I guess so … but that is kind of creepy, Will. I'm not sure I like being spied on.'

'Yeah, sorry, desperate times and all that.'

They made their way from the minimart where a line of restaurants and bars awaited. They headed towards a discreet Greek taverna and sat outside, filling the air with stilted and irrelevant chat that just absorbed the time and space until the serious conversation started. After a brief discussion about olive oil, rosemary and garlic, Ruth signalled that it was time to get down to business.

'So, anyway,' she started, 'Jen or Colin. That is the question.'

'Hey look, I am sorry about this,' said Will. 'I should

have been straight with you over something so trivial but I wasn't. Yes, I had lunch with Jen. Although how you found that out is bewildering, I have to say.'

It seemed Ruth also had a confession to make, but all in good time. 'Well, perhaps you had better explain the secrecy, lies and the cover-up.'

'She got in touch with me after the wedding. I hadn't heard from her in ages but then a couple of texts came through.'

'And how did she get your number?'

'I gave it to her and to everyone else we met there.'

'And?'

'And she mentioned that we had hardly had any time to chat, so we should meet. And without thinking it through I said yes and we made arrangements. We had lunch and that was it. The lunch was nice, as it went. We caught up on old times and had a glass of wine, as you know.'

'A *bottle* of Pinot if I remember rightly, in the cosy Cork & Bottle.'

'Well, it didn't feel cosy. It was just a convenient place we both knew. We were there no more than ninety minutes then went our separate ways. Haven't heard from her since.'

'So, then you come over to me for dinner and don't mention it.'

'I didn't know what to say, to be honest. I did think about that briefly but I didn't know what to say. I didn't know how you would feel about it. In the end I said nothing and was just pleased to see you. I was bloody mortified when you found that receipt.'

'And Colin?'

Will looked at the floor. 'I do work with a bloke called Colin but his was the first name I could think of. I thought you would be okay with me meeting Colin, and worried about the reaction to the Jen thing.'

'So it's okay to lie to me, then?'

'God no, I would never do that.'

'Well, you did!'

'But that wasn't lying as such. It was more about protecting people. Well, you, actually. Er, no … it was more about self-protection, I guess. I didn't want to upset you.'

'And how did you get on with that ambition, I wonder?'

'Oh, just crap. I am so sorry.'

Ruth took a sip of her coffee, then stared directly into his eyes. 'Will, the trouble is that I have been messed about before. I have had blokes sit in chairs like this and they have looked me in the eye with sworn affidavits proclaiming a range of emotions from surprise, misery and innocence. And I have believed them. One bloke accounted for his actions by telling me that he had been out buying me a birthday present. He then gave me the aforementioned present a couple of days later. Except, I found the receipt which stated he clearly bought it the day after our discussion. He then said he had kept the other present as a surprise and wanted to give that to me another time. And do you know what? The whole lot was total crap. He was seeing someone else and was handing out scraps of affection in small boxes as if that would serve to placate me. So, forgive me for listening to your emphatic statements with a sense of suspicion. The idea that you met for ninety minutes could easily be missing the part where you spent the morning or the night together.'

'Ruth! Nothing like that happened.'

'Maybe not. But the thing is, how do I know? You are not that good a liar, Will. You see, you have replaced certainty with doubt. Last week, I was certain everything was fine. I was certain you were loyal and loving. I felt I could trust you with so many things. Today, doubt has crept in. I found myself waking up this morning, wondering what you have been up to. How many times you have "met for lunch".' Ruth added sign language to the inverted commas.

'Hey Ruth, this isn't fair, nothing happened!'

'Oh, but it did, Will. Not in the restaurant, maybe, but over dinner at my place. What happened was your decision in the moment to create stories that were untrue.'

'I didn't know what to say.'

'Okay, so let me ask you this. How long was it between getting a text suggesting you meet for lunch and actually meeting?'

'I don't know … maybe three days or so.'

'And how many times did we see each other during those three days?'

'I guess most days we met up.'

'You see, that's what's so crap. You talk to me as if you were cornered and made spontaneous poor decisions. In truth, you had days to think of this and you chose not to talk to me about it all that time. You could have told me you were meeting her, or refused to meet or even taken me with you but no, you decided to be Mr Clandestine.'

'Would you rather have come too?' said Will.

'Oh fuck off, Will, as if I would. You know bloody well what I am saying. It wasn't a one-second lie, it was several days of conceit and fabrication.'

Will was silent for a moment. That wasn't how he saw it, but he could see her point. 'So now what?' he said eventually. 'Where does that leave us?'

'It leaves me not very happy and you apparently grovelling.'

'How am I doing?'

'You're not exactly showering yourself in glory right now.'

'Okay. Ruth, I am sorry. I really do mean that. How can I make it up to you?'

'You can explain your relationship at uni.'

'Oh … well, we were just part of a group of people who went to pubs and clubs.'

'So never officially an item, then?'

'Not as such, no.'

'And that means?'

'A few kisses at New Year and slow dances at the end of drunken nights out.'

'So why did she single you out to meet after the wedding?'

Will frowned. 'Dunno, to be honest. Maybe she had seen the others more recently. I can't answer that.'

'Will, I don't know what to say.'

'How about I buy you dinner tonight?'

'I can't do tonight, I have promised the girls I would meet them in order to drink wine and moan about you.'

Will allowed an invisible smile to creep across his face. She could have said many things to that request but she didn't say no. 'Then how about tomorrow, somewhere nice?'

'Yeah … okay.'

And so they parted. Ruth wanted to finish her shopping, get ready and go out. Will pretended he had things to do and breathed a sigh of relief that it looked like he had made a good recovery. As soon as he was alone, he fired off a quick text.

Free tonight, what are you up to?

***

Ruth met up with Megan and Helen for early evening cocktails. A two-for-one offer at the Gem Bar in Beak Street in the centre of Soho. The bar was busy and the girls sank into a corner booth of leather armchairs and glass tables. The waiter brought over a tray of multi-coloured and well-decorated glasses. A rainbow selection of alcohol and mixers at pre-evening out prices.

'I hate the way they name these drinks,' Helen complained. 'Surely there is a better and less sexist name than "Slow Comfortable Screw" or "Slippery Nipple". I bet the first person to think of it thought it was hilarious but it feels like a sad joke which not even the waiter finds funny.'

'I know what you mean,' said Ruth. 'I won't order them myself. I am a Mojito girl, anyway. You can't go wrong with that.'

'Oh, try this,' said Helen, licking her lips as she removed a straw. 'Peach Schnapps, Blue Curaçao and Advocaat with a dash of lemon juice and Angostura bitters topped up with tonic.'

'Not bad, what's it called?' asked Ruth.

'Come In My Mouth,' said Helen.

'Surely not!' giggled Ruth.

'No, but it could be called that. A similar consistency…'

'Must be the Advocaat,' said Megan. 'Anyway, come on Ruth, what's up?'

'Oh, usual story. Maybe something, maybe nothing. You know I have been seeing Will? Well, it all seemed to be going so well but he met a girl from uni for lunch and it was all rather clandestine. He came over to dinner but not until he had been wining and dining her in a cosy wine bar.'

'Bloody typical,' said Helen. In fairness, Helen was anti-men since her last two disastrous relationships. She had met a guy called Pete who seemed the perfect man. Incredibly loving and attentive but with a problem she later found out was labelled OCPD (Obsessive-

Compulsive Personality Disorder). 'Does he come round and rearrange your cutlery drawer or the food in the cupboards? Does he check through your list of contacts and appointments and start deleting the details from people he doesn't approve of? Does he insist on the removal of a small butterfly tattoo just because it appeared while you were seeing someone else and was therefore a visible symbol of past love? Does he spend more time tidying the kitchen than eating in it? Does he refuse to have visitors as they will untidy the place so gradually bans all friends from coming round?'

'Not really,' said Ruth. 'That's not Will.'

'Well,' Helen continued, 'that was Pete, who drove me insane for eighteen months. Before that I had Gavin, who had Dependent Personality Disorder or something like that. His self-esteem was so low he would get depressed by adverts for Saga Holidays, thinking they reminded him of his inevitable decline and pending death. Gavin, who would agree with everything you said and responded to the question, 'What shall we do this weekend?' with 'I don't mind.' Jesus, the man was void of opinions and yet it was bloody clear that he often agreed to do things he hated. We would go out and he would sit on the periphery looking glum. And when I confronted him, he would argue that he was in fact enjoying himself. The only thing he liked was long walks along the seafront and stroking my hand with his thumb.'

'What's wrong with that?' said Megan.

'Have you ever sat through a movie with a man stroking your hand the whole time? The first few seconds are nice; a minute is okay. Once you are into twenty-five minutes you feel like stuffing his face with popcorn to prevent breathing. Instead, you move your hand by finding some excuse and he carries on stroking your leg where your hand once was.'

'Sounds creepy.'

'It was. I eventually told him to stop and he was mortified and took it as a major rejection. You could see him shrink inside himself until his head disappeared.'

'Sounds gross,' said Helen. 'Anyway, Ruth, what are you going to do?'

'I'll tell you what you should do,' Megan interrupted. She was never one to miss an opportunity to hand out random advice to people whether they needed it or not. 'Invite him over and then a few hours before he would be setting off, send him a text to say that you can't make it after all and that you will call next week.'

'And why would I do that?'

'Because essentially everyone in a relationship is a masochist. They need to be treated badly.'

'That makes no sense,' said Helen.

'It does. Remember Adam?' They all nodded. 'Well, I was lovely to him. I was attentive and loving and kind and generous and always there for him. He treated me like shit. Anyway, when I started seeing Rob, I wasn't that bothered, to be honest. He was okay and a bit desperate and that's when I learnt the secret of romance.'

'Which is?'

'You have to find the dividing line between misery and abandonment. You treat them bad enough so that they keep coming back. You dish out occasional moments of love and goodwill to remind them of why they started seeing you in the first place, but mostly you give them a hard time. So if they want to meet up with their mates on a Saturday, do lots of sighing around the house and accuse them of favouring their friends over you. This can easily result in flowers or jewellery or just affection in general. I have come to the conclusion that people are basically masochists at heart. They like to be treated badly, as this generates a feeling of being wanted. It also makes them work harder for love and attention. You need to be careful, mind you. If you are too horrible they eventually crack and leave. The trick is to keep them just desperate enough to keep grovelling.'

'And is that how things are with Rob and you?' enquired Ruth.

'Yep. I keep him on his toes, that's for sure.'

'So Ruth, what are you going to do?' Helen persisted.

'Well, truthfully I don't want to turn him into a miserable servant. I guess I will see how things go but I am going to be wary, that's for sure.'

***

Will was early in the pub. He sat nursing a pint whilst checking through his phone. Funny how he no longer took much notice of his surroundings. He didn't notice the stunning old architecture that framed the doors and ceilings. He didn't spot the couple having an argument in the corner in hushed tones but broadcasting everything through expressions and sign language. He didn't spot the two girls who came in looking for love. Nor did he spot the spider weaving a delicate web on the window beside him. He was equally immune to the old table supporting his pint with many shades of beer and wine varnished and polished into its ageing frame. Nor did he spot Steve when he came in.

'Hi Will.'

'Steve. How you doing?'

'Good mate, yourself?'

'Yeah, not bad.'

'So how come I get the pleasure of your company tonight?'

'I was at a loose end and didn't fancy a night in with the TV.'

'Glad to see I am top of your priority list. When you have nothing better to do, ring Steve.'

'Sorry mate, I didn't mean it like that.'

'It was a joke, Will. Relax. What you been up to?'

'Not much.'

The two then shared a couple of beers and put the world to rights. Had they taken minutes of their meeting, they would have looked like this:

1. Agreed that the manager of the England football team be replaced forthwith. His team is clearly as dull as he is and he should be replaced by Michael McIntyre. MM knows nothing about football but he could at least provide the crowd with a damn good laugh as the penalty shoot-out goes to the Germans.

2. Motion carried that the pub needs faster broadband. Will was unable to watch the YouTube clip of a Russian shot put champion demolishing a parked car with a wayward throw without excessive buffering.

3. Agreed that the Prime Minister needs to liven up speeches in the House of Commons. In future the PM is to be connected to jump leads. Whenever the speech becomes too full of monotonous clichés and vapid statements of policy, a short electronic shock will be administered. The aim is to achieve a temporary reminder of the need for inspired spontaneity and the temporary infliction of Tourette's syndrome. This will liven up Prime Minister's Question Time no end.

4. Approval given for the re-opening of the Makashi Kebab shop on Shepherds Bush Green. The owner is to be reinstated with direct orders to produce vast quantities of lamb kebab with chilli sauce. This will

necessitate the destruction of the Subway store that replaced it with recipes containing too much bread and too little flavour. This decision being taken on the basis of taste but also with due consideration to environmental issues. It has been noted that the shops and stores around Tube stations are becoming homogenous and it is almost impossible to tell locations apart, especially after a couple of pints. There is a need to preserve familiar landmarks and cultural icons so that people know where they are.

5. Agreed that the Monty Python film, Life Of Brian, be a core part of religious education in schools. It is clear that religion is corrupting young people and most Christians are now in their seventies. It is hoped to replace religious fanaticism with a healthy dose of humour and cynicism.

6. With immediate effect, all 'grab bag'-size packets of crisps and snacks are to be banned in garage forecourts. It is clear that this is a money-grabbing exercise and the increased prices do not compensate for the measly increase in snack volumes.

7. Approval given to the removal of all covered areas for smokers to gather outside. It is deemed funny to watch them in huddles puffing away but it would be even more amusing watching them get rained on.

8. Related to (7): a ban on all vape ingredients that smell like fruit, vegetables or sweets. They all smell gross and tobacco should at least smell right.

9. There has been a rise in junk emails which is cluttering up life. It is hereby passed that a person writing to you offering vast amounts of money to

transfer to your bank account is immediately liable for the debt. And failure to pay aforementioned debt within fourteen days will result in the FBI tracking down the spammer and sending them to Guantanamo Bay. Here they will be able to open a new email address and will be waterboarded every time a piece of junk mail arrives.

10. Agreed that all passwords for Netflix and Amazon Prime to be removed since no one can remember them, and that these services should be available on the TV without having to do any typing.

'Anyway,' said Steve. How's things with Ruth?

'Oh, okay I guess. She was a bit pissed off the other day.'

'Women are always pissed off. That's what they do. Do you want another pint?'

Thus concluded the discussion on the state of Will and Ruth's relationship.

Steve returned with two beers and some pork scratchings.

'Ah, the famous pork scratchings. What exactly is in there, do you think?' asked Will.

'Inside this bag, mate, is the taste of Britain. You won't get any of that in bars across Europe, I can tell you. Nor in America. Oh no, they will sell you bits of "jerky", which is your conventional dried beef. In Asia, they will sell you a bag of dried scorpions and crunchy beetles. Only in Britain can you enjoy the hallowed pork scratching with a pint of flat beer. I think they scrape the skin off the pig, stretch it, dry it, bake it at a hot temperature and then turn the heat down for about three days until it is crisp and brittle. Then they put salt all over it and seal it in a little bag. That, my friend, is the wonder of the pork scratching.'

'But they are a bit gross,' said Will.

'Yes, indeed they are, but with a pint and a traditional pub we are reminded of the spirit of England and are ready to fight anyone on the beaches.'

'Do we need to fight anyone on the beaches?'

'Only in Brighton on a Saturday night. It's a metaphor, Will, get stuck in. Oh, and I was thinking about you and women…'

'And?'

'I think you seem too desperate, mate.'

'How so?'

'Okay. I bet that when you didn't have a girlfriend, it was almost impossible to find one. Girls not interested. Do you know why?'

'I think you're going to tell me.'

'Because you are desperate. You meet girls and start to evaluate their potential for long-term love and romance. You try too hard, smile too often and girls can sense this a mile away. All your behaviour screams of being a desperate fucking loser to be avoided at all costs.' Steve took a gulp of his beer, warming to his subject. 'Then by some miracle you meet someone. In this case you met Ruth when your guard was down. You didn't have the time or the mental capacity to create an image or anything and you were just yourself. Suddenly you are vulnerable and attractive.'

'You don't say.'

'I do say. And then a couple of things happen. Firstly, because you are now attached so to speak, you are less bothered about other women and by definition you become more attractive to them. You become more interesting and more of a challenge. Now they need to fight for your attention and you hardly notice it. You need to ignore women or offer them subtle insults if you want to get through to them and without realising it, you are doing that all the time. For example, see those two girls at the bar?'

'Er, where?'

'Exactly. The ones on the right over there.'

'Yeah, nice girls.'

'You have avoided them all evening and they have barely looked over.'

'And that means?'

'It means there is a lot of potential there, Will. They are ripe for the picking.'

'I had no idea that the girls seeming to ignore me were in fact incredibly attracted to me.'

'Well, there you have it. They have probably been discussing us all night. And for my next observation, you now move your desperation onto Ruth. You are so pleased to have a girlfriend at last that you behave like a servant not a bloke. Always available, saying yes a lot, dishing out compliments, buying flowers, arranging things and doing a lot of apologising.'

'But surely that's just courtship, Steve. That's what you do.'

'Granted, the first few days you need to show enthusiasm but you need to put your foot down once in a while. Before you know it, she will have you running to the Co-Op to buy nail polish remover and you'll walk past your mates on the way to watch the football in the pub. It is a slippery slope. Just saying.'

'And you think that's me, do you? Puppy dog Will who does whatever he is bid?'

'Yep, she rings a bell and you come running, mate. Okay, here is a test. How often do you check your phone to see if she has sent you a text?'

'Pretty often.'

'Pretty often? Mate, you never stop. Imagine, if you can, we are sitting in your house watching TV or something. And then you get up to see if the post has come. So you wander to the hall for a quick look. Then sit down again. Then five minutes later you repeat the same movements. Then again, every five minutes. By the end of an episode of *The Walking Dead*, we would declare you insane for doing that. That's what you are like with your phone. I bet from the time you receive a text from Ruth to the time you reply, we are on average thirty seconds apart. You are a slave, mate. Not just to the phone but to the sender of the text. You can't bear the thought of not being at her beck and call.'

'So what are you saying, Steve?'

'Women love a man who makes them wait.'

***

Will and Ruth met for a Curry on Thursday night. It was a busy and chaotic restaurant with an aroma that would soak into clothes and hair within minutes. Eating here would guarantee curry impregnation for the whole of the next day. Will made a rather disgusting observation about wiping the heat away with toilet paper which Ruth found amusing, if gross.

They scanned the menu without needing to since all Indian restaurants sell the same things. There is always a list of rice and sundries. The starters always contain prawn puri, onion bhaji and pakora. Then a range of curries which includes things that no one ever orders. They all list fish, either trout or sea bass, or something in curry sauce. No one ever orders them. In fact, what everyone does in an Indian is to scan the list until they find the thing that they always order. They then order it and compare it to other dishes that are called the same thing in other establishments.

In reality, a chef out the back gets the order, stirs a variety of ingredients into a well-used frying pan and adds a small selection of dish-defining spices and herbs.

So Ruth and Will were served the usual things. Korai Chicken Tikka and a Chicken Tikka Dhansak with mushroom rice and a side of Sag Aloo.

'Not bad. Although I prefer the Bombay Spice Island Dhansak for heat, I think,' said Will, proving the theory about curry house menu ordering.

'Will, you have spilt something on your shirt,' said Ruth.

'Dammit. It's only a grain of rice but it has been soaked in sauce that contains turmeric. This will stain for a thousand years and won't even come out with industrial bleach.'

'Put some water on it,' said Ruth, dabbing his shirt with a napkin dunked in water.

'Now I have a stained shirt and I am also wet and soggy,' said Will. 'Water is no match for this, I can tell you. I am not sure a substance has been made that will get this off.'

'What about one of those pre-wash Vanish things you always see on the TV? You know, where the little kid goes out, rolls in grease, oil and mud, and with a quick spray and forty degrees of washing they come out clean and fresh and smelling of honeysuckle and lemon.'

'I would be better off buying some clothes dye and colouring this shirt a shade of yellow and brown and making it smell of coriander and cumin.'

'Well, do that then.'

'Maybe I will,' said Will. 'I will ask the waiter where he orders his clothes and see if they have any. Hey Ruth, I have been thinking. I want to make things up to you and wonder if you fancy a weekend away. Somewhere nice.'

'Dunno, what were you thinking?'

'Somewhere romantic. Venice, Prague, Paris, Istanbul, maybe.'

'Not Istanbul, they are likely to blow you up there. And

they have been running people over in Paris recently.'

'Then maybe Venice. I can't imagine a terrorist attempting to steer a requisitioned gondola over St Mark's Square.' Will was smiling inside. They were already discussing where. Not if, or maybe but where. This was a good sign.

'I've not been there but have always fancied it.'

'I went there years ago with a school trip. I don't remember it that well as we were taken around en masse and subjected to museums I thought were deadly boring.'

'You must have gone to a good school. We went to the local museum, which housed a small fragment of roman mosaic, three Roman helmets and a bit of old cloth. We were there for three hours looking at that while a man showed a slideshow on how to build a road.'

'We went there as part of a Latin trip. I think it was an excuse for the teachers to get a free holiday. I am pretty sure they were all hungover in the morning after a night on the Venetian tiles. Shall I have a look for some ideas? Maybe at the end of next month or something. I could find a hotel or an Airbnb somewhere nice and central. We could wander out and eat pasta, drink red wine and you could sponge Bolognese sauce out of my shirt.'

Ruth nodded and smiled. 'Okay but let me know how much it will cost and the dates you are thinking about. I can't just spontaneously leave the country. I will need some time off work and will need to do some shopping.'

'Shopping? What for?'

'Weekend holiday clothes, of course. We are going to Italy where scruffy jeans and trainers are banned. Everyone looks so stylish there. You can always spot the Brits abroad. The only ones wearing Nirvana T-shirts and jeans with random holes in them.'

'Or tracksuits and hoodies,' added Will.

'Exactly,' said Ruth.

'But don't you have enough clothes and shoes already?' asked Will naively.

Ruth looked up from her place at the table and delivered the 'you have no idea what you are talking about. Of course, a girl can't have too many shoes, too many clothes or too many handbags' stare.

Will got the message and shut up.

***

In relationships, timing is often everything. Sometimes it works for you and sometimes it works against you. Will was about to fall victim of some bad timing courtesy of his bladder. When he looked back on this moment he would wonder why he left his phone on the table. He would wonder why a message would be sent at that precise moment. He would curse the phone manufacturer for enabling someone with an inquisitive mind and a swipe of the finger the ability to read the incoming WhatsApp message.

Will returned from the gents and could tell all was not well.

'Will, you just had a message arrive. It was from "Colin" saying, "Are we still okay for lunch tomorrow. Same place? xxx"' Ruth's expression was impenetrable.

Will stumbled. 'Oh yeah, I am meeting Colin tomorrow lunch.'

'And he is a three kisses kind of guy, is he?'

'Not normally, I must say.'

'Show me the rest of the messages, then.'

'Ruth, I'm not showing you all my messages. That reeks of lack of trust.'

'That's because when texts like that turn up, I don't trust you. You honestly expect me to believe that you are meeting three-kiss Colin tomorrow? Let's get the bill. I need to get out of here.'

'Hey, I'll get it,' said Will hoping his generosity would help calm things down. It didn't. With that Ruth stood up, collected her bag and her jacket, and walked out. Will was too embarrassed in the busy restaurant to say anything so he motioned for the bill. He wanted to rush out and talk things through. He wanted to offer words of reassurance but of course on this occasion, the bill was even longer than usual. It was delivered with two hot towels, two mints and two glasses of fake Baileys. Will left them all on the table, entered his PIN and rushed outside. There was no sign of Ruth anywhere, so he sent a text.

Where are u?

There was no reply. He sent another.

I will wait here so u can find me

And so he waited. He waited for forty-five minutes, straining at faces emerging from the gloom of the streetlights but none bore even a passing resemblance to Ruth. Finally, he typed:

Looks like you've gone. I will head home but text me if you want to come over.

***

It is funny how important text messages have become in relationship building. They are a sign of true connection and they remind people that you are thinking of them. In some cases, they can be a ping of reassurance. For others, they become virtual handcuffs that tie the user to the phone and subject them to a constant pressure to be in touch. There is a whole host of emoticons to choose from to add colour and flavour to words. But all seem better placed in a cartoon than in real life.

Ruth scanned through the list of emoticons to see if any

summed up how she felt. She skipped through the round yellow faces with limited facial expressions. Then glanced at the hand gestures but failed to find the single middle finger she thought might be appropriate. She scrolled past all the mini people and professionals with a variety of hats and props. Ignored all the cute animals, moons, suns, stars, vegetables, boats, cars, other modes of transport, buildings, signs, arrows, clocks and flags. Where was the emoticon that symbolised, 'How could you do that, you bastard?'

Ruth was hurting and she wasn't stupid. The WhatsApp message was clearly not from Colin. No self-respecting businessman would be scheduling a cosy lunch and would be signing off with such affection. She wasn't sure who it was but enough was enough.

Her phone pinged at regular intervals. Each text trying a different approach to find something to coax a response. He tried concern:

Where are you? Are you OK?

He tried even more concern:

So worried about you. Ring me xxx

He tried light-touch enquiry:

I assume you are home. Just checking you got home OK xx

He tried testing the future:

Can we meet tomorrow xx

He tried grovelling:

Ruth I love u so much, please talk to me

He even tried a confessional:

I can see you are upset and I am sorry I failed you so much

186

He tried the 'at least' text:

Ruth please talk to me. At least we will have Venice

None of Will's messages elicited a response. Finally, he sent a goodnight with three kisses and put his phone down. Even Will knew when he was getting nowhere. He turned off his bedside lamp and stared at the light creeping past the curtains in his room.

Will's phone pinged and the screen burst into life. He leapt at it and scrolled to a message from Ruth.

I am hurting so much, Will. I can't go on with lack of trust. This is the last goodnight you will get from me. I have too many doubts and my head is overwhelmed with suspicion. I can't hang onto the threads of this anymore. Please don't reply x

When It Is Over It Is Never Over

A conversation on BBC Radio 5 Live between Professor G Smale from Durham University and Mike Asterley

The game lasts ninety minutes, said the referee.
Agreed, but there is always extra time.

And how long is extra time?
Well, extra time is infinite. We can always find small moments.

How small?
Okay, well, let's take the concept of one second.

Okay, got that.
Now let's divide it in half into one half of a second. Let's use that time.

Not long, half a second.
Granted but time available nonetheless. Now let's take the half second we have yet to use and divide that in half. And let's use that, shall we?

Okay, again a small amount of time.
Yes it is, but it is still time available.

Granted. How long do you think we can keep doing this? Will we ever run out of time?
Well, no. You end up dealing with microscopic moments, but that can be long enough. In the same way, if I was to ask you to step towards that wall over there by walking half the distance between you and the bricks and to keep repeating that instruction, how long would it take you to reach the wall? The answer is, you would never reach it. You would get close as per our common definition, but you would never meet it.

So you are saying we always have enough time?

We have long enough for many things. Long enough to score a goal, for example. Long enough to change our mind on something. You see, we often look at time as a finite measure. We have a week to do something, or a month, or a year or indeed, ninety minutes. We get trapped into whole numbers and they are unreliable. In reality within, say, a one-week timescale, we have millions and millions of opportunities to progress something or change something.

What are the implications of this research?

My main advice is that things are not over until they are over. For example, if a lecturer gives you a deadline for a piece of work, there is always massive scope to meet the target or indeed massive scope to extend the target. The deadline date isn't real. It is often a random number designed to provide some momentum. The other implication is in relationships. Have you ever been given the cold shoulder by a partner? Or finished a book that you wished would continue? My theory suggests that there is no such thing as the end, per se. There may be a moment in which people pause and reflect. But never take the words 'The end' at face value.

Because there is always more time?

Exactly.

Thank you very much, Professor. I was going to wrap this up because we have run out of time but by the sounds of it, we have plenty left. I guess it depends how quickly we can talk and how well we use it.

Chapter 9: Four In The Morning

Breaking up is a mighty strange experience. You go from being with someone to being alone in an instant. Not in itself a huge transformation. If someone were to observe you from afar and the two people concerned were to stand next to each other, all would appear to be well. Arms, legs, feet, body and faces would all seem to be in the right place and doing what they were supposed to be doing. The human body is quite capable of getting up, walking about, eating, sleeping and functioning as usual. But on an emotional level, things are not the same at all. In this case, Will went through a mixture of anger and rage at himself and an overwhelming sadness. He was desperate to do something to repair the damage. He was fuming over the text from Jen. It was just like her to send something when she should have known he would be busy and with company.

All these emotions buzzing around his head and nowhere to put them. All he could do was to distract himself for a few moments. Simple household chores didn't work as they were not taxing enough to divert his complex brain and its dive into the depths of misery. Cleaning his teeth, for example, would only result in him thinking of the toothbrush he had left at Ruth's house. Putting on socks would remind him of the way Ruth could pull them off in a moment of passion. Dusting the furniture would remind him that Ruth would always make her place spotless for his arrival. He tried the radio but the sound of music was just a blur and his thoughts began to drift.

Nothing would get in the way of him checking his phone. He had developed an obsession with refreshing Facebook, checking WhatsApp and hunting for any form of text message. Every four or five minutes he found himself paging through trivia just to make sure he hadn't missed a text or any sort of sign. His phone did ping at one point but to his disgust is was nothing more than advertising from his phone contract provider. It seems O2 were hoping he would spend the weekend buying tickets to gigs he had no desire to see … unless, of course, Ruth were to go with him.

He promised himself he would leave her alone and not become some sort of crazed obsessive ex-boyfriend. He had seen movies where the ex became so desperate it only resulted in driving a deeper wedge between them. He certainly had no desire to do that. He would remain cool, in control and ride out at least day one of being single again. He knew that he needed to give Ruth some space and to allow her to come round to wanting to see him again. There was no point in being all pushy and trying to convince her she was wrong about him.

Five minutes later he rang her. The phone went to voicemail.

'Hi this is Ruth, sorry I can't pick up but leave a message and I will ring you back.'

'Hi Ruth, it's me. I woke up and decided to leave you in peace. Not because I wanted to but because I thought it was the right thing to do. But actually, I don't want to leave you in peace. Anyway, *please* call me back.'

With that, Will determined to leave her alone and to respect her need for silence. He was pretty sure he sounded as miserable and desperate as he felt inside and this was bound to stir up some sort of sympathy and a need to connect. He now needed to distract himself and get on with the day.

'Hi Ruth, it's me again,' said Will twenty-two minutes and thirty seconds later. 'I just wanted you to know I was thinking of you. Although you know that already.'

Okay, thought Will. *Time to move on and get some stuff done. Time to sort the things that need sorting and to fill the forms that need filling and to write the letters that need writing and talk to people who need talking to.* Five minutes later...

'Ruth, I am sorry, I don't mean to plague you with messages. Just now I meant to leave you in peace but there always seems so much to say. This call isn't a call as such but is an apology for the call earlier. So, can you count this as one call from me and one mistake. Well, not a mistake, but an apology for the excessive call earlier. This isn't a call at all: this is an apology.'

Will made tea and opened rich tea biscuits – a combination guaranteed to mend a wounded soul. He dunked a biscuit in his tea and began to utter the words, 'she loves me, she loves me not' under his breath before removing it. Sadly half of it remained in the cup and bits of sodden crumb floated desperately in the meniscus of his tea. Meanwhile half a biscuit sat at the bottom of the cup waiting to spoil a random sip. Will figured this must be a metaphor for his life and then pinched himself and tried to pull himself together. He had to stop moping about and get on with the day. He needed to be strong, firm, more James Bond and less Mr Bean.

'Hi Ruth, I wondered if you were there and whether you fancied meeting up. I mean, I know you probably have better things to do that waste your time with me but if you did happen to be free it would be nice to spend some time with you, even though you might not enjoy it very much if you see what I mean...'

Will fished the remnants of biscuit from his cup and tipped them into the bin. He tried dunking another biscuit and this one remained perfectly formed with just the right amount of soggy texture and warmth. Surely a sign from above that all would be well. Who was he kidding?

'Hi Ruth, sorry about the last call. I didn't mean to say

that you would have a crap time with me as I hoped you would have a lovely time. I wouldn't set out to make you miserable, obviously – I would do nice things, not horrible ones. I can also guarantee no text messages as I have thrown my phone in the rubbish bin so that I can't look at it.'

Will washed his few bits of crockery in the bowl by squirting a short burst of Fairy liquid at them. The liquid had indeed lasted a mighty long time, just as the adverts claimed.

'Hi Ruth, obviously I hadn't thrown the phone away then as I was still using it to speak to you. Clearly, I need the phone otherwise I am truly fucked (apologies), as they say. What I mean is that as soon as you give me the all clear, I will dispose of the phone and replace it with tin cans and string. I will arrive at a place of your choosing with my tin cans tied to my legs and anyone who wants to talk to me will have to borrow a can. I know I won't technically need the string and the cans as, by definition, all someone would need to do is to shout loudly at me and I could hear them. Call me.'

Will browsed through his iTunes app and debated creating a break-up playlist. He began scanning his collection of 16,568 songs and many struck a chord. He didn't even have a copy of 'Y.M.C.A.' so he quickly remedied that with a couple of clicks on the browse button.

'Hi Ruth, it's me. I was wondering if you needed a footstool. You know that scene in *Alice In Wonderland* where the Queen of Hearts calls for pigs so that she can rest her feet on them? I wonder if you have any requirements for that sort of thing and what the hours might be.'

At this point Will shook himself. What was he thinking? He was being completely pathetic. Where on earth had his manly dignity gone? He was acting like a fop from a restoration comedy. All he needed was a wig and a velvet suit and he would complete the picture.

'Ruth. I don't want to be your footstool. What I want to do is to come over and put my tongue in your ear. Sorry, I don't mean that, I mean I would like to whisper sweet somethings … Fuck it, how do you re-record the messages on here? This is crap.'

'Hello. This is a message from O2. Will would like to apologise for the last message as that was not right at all. It failed to convey the true meaning of passion and commitment intended and ended up being a complete cock-up so please delete it from your phone. You have not been charged for this message.'

Will had now lost count of how many calls he had made and how many counted. He was getting more and more annoyed with himself and turned his attention once again to his playlist. He decided he would create it and send it to Ruth. Not an amazing gift but the traditional mixtape had always held a special place in his heart. He began dragging songs into a newly created playlist entitled 'Songs for Ruth' and then spent some time putting them in the right order. He wasn't sure whether it should be songs that she already liked or whether the songs should have some sort of connection to their relationship. Once complete he composed an email to explain them as some were a bit obscure. This is what he came up with:

- 'Scooby Snacks' by Fun Lovin' Criminals – This one starts with a robbery, just like us.
- 'A Case Of You' by Joni Mitchell – I sat in The 10 Cases wine bar and all I could think of was that I could drink a case of you and still be on my feet.
- 'Inside of Love' by Nada Surf – This was playing in the 10 Cases when we met on our first date. Bet you didn't notice.

- 'Streets of London' by Ralph McTell – To remind you of the happy times you spent looking at the world over the rim of the teacup.
- 'Art for Art's Sake' by 10cc – Crap song but necessary given our trip to the gallery.
- 'Hong Kong Garden' by Siouxsie and the Banshees – In recognition of a most excellent Chinese.
- 'Y.M.C.A.' by the Village People – To remind you of the kiss at the wedding which I can still feel when I close my eyes.
- 'Close To You' by the Carpenters – Don't ask why this is there but it is. Much to my embarrassment.

Will surveyed his list of songs and realised he actually didn't like many of them. But perhaps the thought would count. He emailed a link to the playlist and sent his email with a simple covering note:

Ruth, it's me. I have just sent a playlist with some crap songs but they remind me of you. I hope you like them xxxxx

Then three minutes later:

Hi. Don't get me wrong, the songs don't really remind me of you but of things that have happened and the situations we have been in. I don't want you thinking you are a drug dealer or a sad old homeless person because obviously you are not!

Will stared out of the kitchen window and debated his next move. He flicked through his phone contacts but doubted anyone would be free at this time of day. He sighed a deep sigh and pressed Redial.

'Hi this is Ruth, sorry I can't pick up but leave a message and I will ring you back,' said the voice for the umpteenth time that morning.

'Hi Ruth. Sorry I have been such an arse. Ring me and let's talk this through.'

A few minutes later the phone rang and Will was able to answer within two seconds. Mainly because he had spent the morning staring at it.

'Ruth, it's you!' he exclaimed with no attempt to disguise his enthusiasm.

'Yeah. I can see you have left a load of messages but I have been in the bath.'

'So did you listen to them?'

'No. I just rang you back to see what you wanted. I had so many missed calls I thought it must be an emergency.'

'Delete the rest, trust me. They all say the same thing.'

'Which is?'

'I miss you. Can we meet and sort this out?'

'Thanks for the curry last night, by the way. Sorry I had to rush off but I needed to get the hell out lest other arrangements arrived by carrier pigeon.'

'Ruth, I am so sorry.'

'Well, what explanation do you have this time? Let me guess. Colin is in fact a transvestite and has taken a shine to you. You have been secretly cross-dressing and have arranged to meet to try on shoes.'

'Ruth, I'm –'

'Or was it that Colin was meaning to write to his loving wife and sent her a text about her birthday lunch but accidentally sent the text to you instead of her? Which sadly means that Mrs Colin has no Birthday lunch this year and Mr Colin is being Billy No Mates in a restaurant as we speak. Or was it a note from the CIA explaining where you need to meet a contact this week, and "xxx" is actually code for Whitehall Post Box 20?'

'Jeez, Ruth, please.'

'Oh, I have lots of potential excuses for that text, Will. I have been playing a variety of scenarios in my head all night. A night in which I had very little sleep, no thanks to you.'

'That was probably the bhajis.'

'Will, don't be absurd. Now I guess you have had time to think about this, so let's see what you come up with this time. I will pause for breath and this is the part where you give me a reasonable explanation.'

Will took a deep breath. He had thought about this question and what he might say. He had played around with a variety of options and thought through what might create the best outcome. He didn't think that using Colin again would work. Ruth had seen through that last time. He could pretend that he had no idea who the text was from, but that seemed ridiculous and of course he knew who sent it. He debated in his head claiming it was a different work colleague, but he knew he would get quizzed about the kisses. And then there was the indisputable fact that the text seemed to come from someone in his phone book called Colin. None of it made for a comfortable explanation.

'It was a text from Jen,' he admitted. 'When I met her for lunch, we made a joke about same time next week and that was a text from her to see if we were meeting. I had no intention of saying yes. I am so sorry that you had to see that.'

'And Jen is called Colin, is she?'

'I stored her name as Colin in case she rang the number when I wasn't expecting it.'

'Wow, that really inspires me with confidence, Will. So when Steve rings, is it Steve or a girl called Hannah? Is your whole address book some sort of code to disguise the double life you lead?'

'Ruth, I am sorry. It's nothing like that.'

'Well,' said Ruth, 'the trouble is, how do I know?

Within a bloody short period of time, you have met a girl for an illicit lunch, lied to me about it, disguised her name in your phone and now apparently you had no intention of meeting her again. What the fuck is a girl supposed to believe here? Do I have "sucker" tattooed across my forehead? Do you sit around and think about how you can stitch me up and make me look like an idiot? What would you do if the roles were reversed? Supposing I secretly met some bloke for lunch and then started getting texts from a fake name. What would you do?'

'I like to think I would give you a chance,' mumbled Will.

'Oh, as if. That's so easy to say but you are proving to be untrustworthy and I am not putting up with it. Plain and simple.'

'Ruth, I met her and that was a mistake. But I haven't lied about her. Nothing happened between us. I didn't know she was going to text and this is the first conversation we have had about it. I resolved to be straight with you and I am. I feel terrible. What do you want to do?'

'What do I want to do?' said Ruth. 'Interesting that now you ask my opinion. The truth is that I don't know. I want to get off the phone. I want to dry my hair and I want some space from you. And you in the meantime need to think about your behaviour and what it is you actually want.'

'Would you like to meet up and talk this through face to face?'

'Frankly, no. You can't just brush this under the carpet, Will. This is happening too soon in our relationship and maybe we won't survive this. We are supposed to have many years of happiness before we have major disagreements. And here we are in the heat of battle so quickly. It doesn't bode well, does it?'

'I guess not.' Will sighed with a sound of deep resignation.

'I am getting off the phone,' said Ruth, 'and I am not spending my day going over the same old crap from you about this.'

'Ruth, I am sorry.'

'Yeah, so you keep saying. It doesn't carry much weight, to be honest.'

'I guess not. Well…' Will racked his brains for something meaningful to say, but fell short. 'Have a good day, whatever you are doing.'

'Sure. See you, Will.'

With that Ruth sat on the bed with tears flowing down her cheeks. She determined to be tough and resilient but as soon as the phone went dead she was overcome with a feeling of hurt and betrayal. She grabbed a wet wipe and did her best to remove the smears on her face. She scrolled through her phone. She didn't want to do anything or see anyone. She stumbled across an email from Will with a random list of songs which were old, terrible or both and only served to remind her of what she was missing. She'd put such faith in him. She'd been so fed up with being alone and for the first time in a long time she'd felt part of something. And yet she'd been messed around and lied to, and that was not the basis of a healthy long-term relationship. It was surely a recipe for disaster.

Ruth spent what was left of the day reading, dozing and pottering. She browsed the TV, read pages on the iPad and generally hid from the world outside. She checked Facebook a couple of times and could see that Will was online. She couldn't help but wonder who he was chatting to.

Eventually she turned off the TV, plugged the iPad into the charger and wandered into the hall. Her eyes were drawn to a white envelope on the floor. She bent down and picked it up and recognised Will's handwriting immediately. A shiver passed down her spine as she realised he must have come over to post this by hand. Inside was a red Lego brick and a handwritten letter.

Dear Ruth,

This is not how things were supposed to happen. I met you and I thought I had met my soulmate. I fell for you in a way that swept me off my feet and made me smile from the top of my head to the tips of my toes. The expression being head over heels in love made no sense until I met you but as soon as we met, I understood what it meant. I walk about thinking of you the whole time and I bump into things as I search for text messages from you. It seems that every nice thing that happens to me reminds me of you. And if the day goes badly for any reason I figure it will be okay because I get to see you and everything will be alright.

I have been a classic fool by responding to a girl from the past and spending ninety minutes in her company. Do I regret the time I spent with her? I guess not, really, as it is nice to catch up with old friends. Do I regret the way I handled it, the way I treated you? A thousand times, yes. Do I wish for the ability to turn back the clock and change my behaviour? I long for time travel and a machine to go with it. Sadly, I don't have that ability. I am stuck in the here and now and the overwhelming sadness that I feel and the sound of hurt and anger in your voice.

I love you, Ruth. I am sorry. I want to put things right. I am enclosing another red brick for our tower. I hope that this dark hour of our relationship makes us stronger. Perhaps some of the red bricks need to be moments of regret and sadness to bind the good times together? I promise to keep them to a minimum, though!

I am sending lots of love and lots of hugs to you tonight. And if you need them delivered in person, you only have to ask and I will come running.

All my love,

Will

Ruth held the letter tight in her grasp and sat on the stairs. She read it a second time with fresh tears welling up with every new paragraph.

She went to bed but found sleep hard to come by. She was tired from so little sleep the night before and tried reading and dozing in equal measure. The streetlight shone through the cracks in the curtain and a three-quarter moon rose over the tops of the houses. Sounds of laughter from drunken revellers on the street kept sleep even further away. She tossed and turned and checked her phone again. She managed to sleep for a short while but woke either because her restless dreams disturbed her or something in the street stirred. Her clock read 4:00 a.m. and she turned this way and that, attempting to mould her bed into a shape that would provide the comfort she needed for sleep, rest and respite. The bed refused to bend to her wishes and no position seemed right. In the end she got up, turned on her iPad and began to type.

Dear Will,

Thank you for your letter. It seemed odd that you came round to put it through my door without announcing yourself but I guess I can understand why. Thank you for the brick too. I will put it with the others. You have to understand, Will, that you have made me miserable recently and that's not supposed to happen. I had such high hopes for us and you dashed them on the rocks. Have you any idea how heart-breaking it is to be so near and yet so far from a proper romance? I thought you were the one. I thought we were made for each other. I guess you have to understand my past to understand how I am responding to the present. Let's just say that I have had more than my fair share of betrayal in my time and my tolerance is low. No relationship can exist if based on lies and deceit and you rocked the foundation of ours.

I love the fact that you send me red bricks and I miss the idea of you terribly. I am lying in bed at 4:00 a.m. completely exhausted and unable to sleep as so many things run through my mind. I need you to calm my demons, Will, and there are plenty right now. I have doubt, worry, concern, suspicion all sitting on my shoulder and forcing me to look at the world through dark glasses.

I will be honest and say I am not sure how we can recover from such a bad start. But equally, I would hate myself for not at least talking this through. I will try and get some sleep now but let's meet tomorrow at 13:00. Let's go to the South Bank and have lunch in one of those cafés outside the Royal Festival Hall and maybe a stroll along the Thames.

Until tomorrow,

x

The email was sent at 4:18 and although she couldn't see it, Will had read it by 4:40. It was the first thing that had made him smile since their fight and he allowed a hint of optimism to colour in some of the pessimism that had greyed his world since then.

An introduction to her book, The Things I Wish I Had Said by Dr Dorothy Docture, published by Oxford Developmental Press, 2014

When I was younger I developed a love of everything Joni Mitchell stood for. I knew all the words to all the songs. She was the rock that sustained me through years of study and her voice would be one of the few I would allow into the hallowed ground of my research. In particular, the song 'Big Yellow Taxi' resonated with me. The song laments the demise of tradition and the destruction of mother nature all in the name of progress. Paradise, it seems, is to be replaced with cheap hotels and parking lots whilst the trees are cut down and the fruits are poisoned by insecticide. Joni argues that these losses are only noticed once they disappear from view. Hindsight and reflection focus the mind on the departure of things once held so precious. As a student researching my subject, I didn't really understand the kind of loss Joni was referring to. I hadn't experienced loss of any significance at an early age. True love had yet to venture into my world and everything seemed so new, so exciting and none more fascinating than my studies. But I loved that tune and I would sing along as if I were Joni herself. In fact, I came to believe I was as good a singer as she, a fact debated and discussed at length by those in close proximity to my rooms of study.

It is funny how experience brings new and perhaps wiser perspectives. I remember the loss of my first pet, the loss of my favourite relative and even the closure of the one great coffee shop in the city. One day they were here and part of my life. The next day they were discussed in the past tense. They were history and only mentioned in stories.

This got me thinking about the small avenue of time that exists between being and not being. Between existing and not existing. I have summarised the process in this diagram:

I soon realised that Joni's song was all about the emotions present in Box 3. This box can often be full of affection, sadness, love, perhaps even regret. I became fascinated by these feelings and began to interview people to explore this in detail and perhaps offer insights into how we can live our life with less regret and perhaps more appreciation of Box 1. I also made the assumption that I could do nothing or very little about Box 2. But my research here also surprised me. Perhaps we can change even the most dramatic of events.

It all started with a big reflection around my coffee shop. I walked around the corner, expecting to take my usual seat in the usual place, and to my horror found a 'Closed' notice on the door. Not just any closed notice, but a 'We have closed for good, thanks to all our customers who have supported us over the last twelve years' notice. I was mortified. I loved the coffee, the cakes, the vibe and even the rather odd choice of music played over the stereo. It was where my friends would gather. It was our place. I now had to move on, to accept this and to take all the aromas and tastes into a small file in my head and hope to rekindle them somewhere else.

Normally the story would end there, but because of my research I began to consider the following questions that fit neatly into Box 1 and perhaps might influence Box 2.

1. What would I have said to the owner of that coffee shop had I known I had just taken my last

ever sip from one of his cups? Would I have said something more profound than, 'Thanks, have a good day'?

2. How much love and appreciation did I share during my time there? How well did I connect with the owner? I considered myself a regular, but he left without saying a word. Clearly, I was not even close to being someone he would confide in. I knew the man superficially for the best part of eight years but he closed his shop and left without mentioning it.

3. If the owner knew how much we loved his shop, would he have still closed it?

A few things collided to kick-start the research for this book. Joni, plus bad coffee shop experience, a whole pile of regrets, a lot of study and many questions. I will explore these things in detail but for now, leave you with a question and an assumption. Firstly, the assumption: I bet as you get older, your experience of Box 2 is increasing.

Now for the question. What if I told you, you have just one more interaction with all the things you hold dear? Only one more chance to say anything or express any emotion? Are there things you would like to say, if you knew that would be the last goodbye?

Chapter 10: Smile In My Eyes

Ruth had a bit of a slower start than she wanted. She'd forgotten to plug her phone in properly overnight and woke up to a low battery. So, she flicked on airplane mode and waited for some much-needed power. She reflected on how it is funny how tied to the phone people were these days. She had seen people miss trains because they couldn't bear to look up from the screen. Days are delayed while the power is boosted to an acceptable level. The whole nation has a national obsession with phone charging while the makers of phones seem determined to run enough software to guarantee you will run out by lunchtime.

Eventually she made it out of the house, still ridiculously early.

It was a beautiful, crisp morning. London looked stunning. Ruth breathed in the majesty of the walk across the Thames and paused to take in a view of which she'd never tire. She's always felt that London was the best city in the world and this view proved it. The newness of the glass towers rising out of the city skyline in stark contrast to the old and traditional. Where Renzo Piano meets Christopher Wren and – despite the huge difference in time, craft and materials – transform the landscape for the better.

Earth has not anything to show more fair:

Dull would he be of soul who could pass by

A sight so touching in its majesty:

This City now doth, like a garment, wear

The beauty of the morning; silent, bare,

Ships, towers, domes, theatres, and temples lie

Open unto the fields, and to the sky

Ruth had learnt that poem for her A-levels and it was one of the few pieces she had never forgotten. Crazy to think that it was written in the early 1800s and yet still seemed so relevant and real. She wondered whether Wordsworth would have still found these words today.

She wandered along in no particular hurry since she had a good forty-five minutes to spare. Mind you, having said that she second-guessed that Will may be early. It would be pretty bad form if he happened to be late for this one. She heard a noise behind her.

***

Will read Ruth's email over and over and dissected it as if studying for his A-levels. He read each line and extracted potential meaning from it. He found words that gave him confidence and optimism, and words that gave him cause for concern. There were mixed messages in there for sure but the main thrust of the note seemed to be saying, 'It's not over till the fat lady sings', or words to that effect. He couldn't wait to see her and found himself leaving the house extra early. Besides, a stroll or a coffee would be a welcome pick-me-up after such a restless night.

***

Ruth was suddenly aware of a pressure building behind her. In movies, they are able to slow down dramatic scenes but in real life things happen so fast that it is almost impossible to react. She heard sounds that seemed not to be right at all. Ruth spun on the spot.

***

Will sat under an outdoor umbrella in a waterfront café

and was enjoying a double shot latte and one of those little macaroon biscuits they provide for such occasions. He never could understand why the macaroon was such a popular choice and, if asked, he would have gladly swapped it for a McVitie's Chocolate Digestive. You know where you are with a chocolate digestive and Will had the capacity to eat many at a time.

***

In the next moment, Ruth's world stopped. What she needed was a pause button. She would have pressed it and instantly halted the white van that sped toward her. Instead she tried to flee on instinct by diving towards the wall of the bridge. Maths, velocity, momentum and speed of reaction were not on her side. The van kept going, crushing Ruth in its path. Around her people screamed and the van carried on. The world citizens on the bridge were reduced to mere tenpins as the driver swerved and accelerated and swerved and accelerated on and on through the crowd. Behind him was a scene of carnage rarely seen on a London street. Parents, children, commuters, tourists, cyclists, toys, pushchairs, wheelchairs and backpacks were thrown randomly into heaps on the ground. Screaming, bleeding, crying, cursing and worse still, complete silence came from those left like rag dolls on the black and rose-tinted surface.

***

Will could hear some commotion from above. He looked up and couldn't make out what was going on. To his horror, he thought he saw someone fall from the bridge and land in the Thames below. It was so quick, he couldn't be sure. Over the hum of the traffic he swore he could hear screaming and he strained his neck to get a better look. Quickly the sound of sirens filled the air. Amazing how fast the police are able to spring into life. Something was happening on the bridge. He could see flashing blue lights converging from all corners. A police helicopter came into view and began to hover over the South Bank. Will picked up his phone.

Hi Ruth, I'm here early but all hell is breaking loose out here. Police everywhere. No idea what's happened but I am near the Royal Festival Hall in one of those cafés. Give me a ring when you get here. We may need to meet somewhere else.

Will kept an eye open from his limited vantage point. Eventually he left the café and walked towards the bridge where the stairs up were blocked by a policeman with yellow tape tied from railing to railing. A crowd gathered and any attempt to climb the stairs was clearly going to fail.

'Tube is shut,' someone shouted. 'The bridge is closed. Police advise to get out of here and try somewhere else.'

Again, Will pulled his phone out of his pocket.

Tube station shut, apparently. I guess that may have a knock-on to Waterloo and everywhere round here. I am guessing you may be stuck underground. Ring when you surface and get this message.

The blue lights and sirens kept coming. Will accessed his BBC News app and watched the breaking news section. A white van had run amok on Waterloo Bridge. There wasn't much there but Twitter was always reliable. He smiled when he recalled that someone had posted a picture of an office fire poster that said something like 'In case of fire, please evacuate the building immediately rather than stand around filming it for Instagram'. How true that was these days. Seems that a natural reaction to extreme chaos is not to run away but to get the phone out. Ideally people want to take a selfie with burning building, hurricane or murderer in the background. Posting something like this online attracts many 'likes' and builds instant popularity.

Twitter was full of postings that seemed confused, unnerving and extensive. Reports of carnage, death, terrorism, white vans, police, knives, shootings, closures, ambulances, helicopters, wounded, stretchers, doctors, screaming, roadblocks, Tube closures, heroism, fear, loved ones, all linked with hashtags and Waterloo Bridge.

Will scrolled through pages of random tweets. Some clear and some contradictory. It was amazing to see so much content but not to fully understand what had happened. As the word 'terrorists' appeared more and more frequently, he began to feel sick. All reports suggested men armed with knives and a foot flat on the accelerator. How dare they abuse his city, his town? It became devastatingly clear that many were suffering up there. The first report said one person had died and many were injured but Will knew enough from the images to know the numbers would rise.

In times of crisis, a strange thing happens to British people. They talk to complete strangers. You will notice that a whole carriage of passengers on a train will sit in silence until told that they have to all get off at the next stop. At this point everyone will start chatting like old friends. The crisis gives them a reason to open up and, since everyone is experiencing it, there is something common to talk about.

And so it was that Will found himself passing the time of day with complete strangers.

'I am supposed to be meeting a friend here but she will struggle to get out of the Tube, I expect. You know what it's like when they start closing the network,' said Will.

'Blimey yeah, I remember when there was an electrical fire at South Kensington a few years back. Stuck in the drains for two hours, we were. Bloody unbearable. Shop was packed with people going to Harrods and Harvey Nicks and no one could move.'

'You might be here a long time, mate.'

'Yeah, I guess so,' said Will. 'Mind you, I can't imagine the whole network is shut.'

'Depends on the reports. Has been known to close things as a precaution. I have to get home to Brixton so fuck knows how long that will take.'

Will didn't know what to do. His phone battery was rapidly running dry from constantly checking his phone for messages. The news from the bridge was getting worse and worse. Stories of multiple casualties and a rapid police response. It seemed madness that the carnage described was less than half a mile away and yet here he was with a seat, another coffee and a stunning view of the water. He was looking at headlines of *London Carnage*, *London at a Standstill* and *City Under Siege* as he licked the froth from his spoon and nibbled on his second macaroon of the morning. He imagined a foreign reporter stumbling upon this part of the South Bank looking for a story and interviewing Will.

'So, what can you tell us?'

'Well, it has been a chaotic morning as you can tell. A lot of noise and much confusion – see that guy over there? He spilt a lot of coffee earlier which needed some pretty rapid cleaning. There was also a drunk guy who staggered by earlier asking for 50p for a can of Strongbow. So I gave him £1 and asked him to get me one. Other than that, I am waiting here for someone who is clearly having trouble getting here.'

Will reflected on how the news was able to magnify an

incident and make it seem so much bigger that it was in reality. For sure, what had happened was tragic, unimaginable and unforgivable, but the camera lens trained on a few square feet of the capital would give such a wrong impression. Here he was in relative calm. People had stopped staring and the crowd had dispersed. Only the steps to the bridge remained closed and he assumed there was still some disruption to transport. At the end of the day, life goes on.

After over an hour, Will wondered what would be the best thing to do. He had heard that the Tube station would be shut for a good few hours and the closure of the bridge had meant he was standing in an inaccessible area. Buses, cabs, cars and even bikes were struggling to get near to the bridge and the local stations. Will flicked his phone into life and began to type.

Hi Ruth. Still traffic chaos here. I am going to grab the Tate to Tate Boat and hang around near the Tate Modern. Will be easier to meet there. London Bridge Tube is fine, apparently. See you soon x

Will walked along the Thames towards the London Eye and found a small pier that served the Thames transport system. He loved these boats. Whenever he went to the O2 arena to watch a band he preferred to travel by river. So much nicer than the jubilee line. Mind you, not that you see a band at the O2. What you see is a large TV screen with average sound while experiencing a severe attack of vertigo. Unless, of course, you are prepared to pay prices that make the Last Night of The Proms seem like a bargain night out.

Will kept one eye on his phone in short bursts, hoping this would preserve his battery. Still no sign. He leant on the railing and absorbed the view from the water. *Ruth would love this*, he thought and smiled when he remembered his failed attempt at taking her to an art gallery. Then another thought struck him. What if she had changed her mind about coming to see him? He wanted to re-read the email but didn't want to lose the power completely. What was it that she had said about worry and concern and starting to see the world through dark glasses? Maybe she had a change of heart overnight. Maybe she wasn't coming after all. Or worse still, perhaps this was some kind of punishment. He had read an article recently about women who make men suffer in order to gain attention. Maybe she was never intending to meet him and was right now having a good laugh at his expense. Was she perhaps in a coffee shop with her mates, laughing over the texts and voice messages?

On reflection, Will didn't think this sounded like her. He hopped off at the Tate Modern and found a bench to perch on. He could watch the stream of tourists strolling by, many clutching bags branded by the gallery as they took home souvenirs of mostly long-dead artists with a flair for colour and the ability to shock and surprise the viewer. Will liked modern art. Not all of it, no one could like all of it. Today's exhibition was called *Roy Lichtenstein In Focus* and Will recognised some of the paintings on the poster. He wandered into the gallery for a few minutes to use the gents and found his phone signal reaching the depths of his phone battery. Funny how phones now use so much power that they often need charging by lunchtime. He wondered when Apple would create a solar-powered iPhone or one that charged like watches seem to by movement alone. *That would be quite a good fitness app*, he figured. *Your phone would only work if you did enough exercise. You would have to jog along the Thames for five minutes to make a call, for example.* Will made a mental note to write to Apple when he had a spare moment. Perhaps they would give him royalties for his idea.

By 15:30 Will was bored, hungry and worried. Still no news from Ruth which either meant she was not bothering to call or she couldn't for some reason. Will's phone was now on 8% which meant that any second his battery would fail. The phone didn't like operating at lower than 10% and tended to randomly give up at any moment. Quickly he opened the text app.

Phone battery dead here. Hardly any life left in it. I am at the Tate Modern outside the main door but will head home in 30 mins. Don't know what else to do. Hope you are okay and haven't given up on me xx

He pressed Send and heard a faint swoosh as the message left his handset, flew into the air and made its way to the phone located in Ruth's handbag, which was left on Waterloo Bridge surrounded by forensic experts, tape, debris, and a line of abandoned possessions. Her phone beeped but there was no one there to receive the call. Has a message really been sent if there is no one there to read it?

***

Silence and dark. Quiet. Movement but no sense of touch. Sound but nothing audible. No pain, no feeling, no senses. A dark room with barely any light. In the corner, a number counting down. Starting at 96% and dropping quickly to 30%, then 20. Now the meter hovers at 8%. With 8% comes resignation that it is okay if the number drops to zero. There is silence, peace, tranquillity. The void becomes real. The void begins to envelop and becomes one with everything it touches. Only a few thoughts flicker. I think therefore I am? Really, is this all I am? Is this being? 7%, I welcome you. Cold. Cold. Cold. Temperature dropping until the cold stops. There is no such thing as cold. This is not cold but an absence of heat. Memories, faces, a family scrapbook. Is this my life flashing before my eyes? Where is Mum? I can't see her. Nothingness. No colour, sound, smell, feel or taste. Senses are shutting down. Senses have shut down. 6% and relax. Embrace the silence. Welcome the absence of reality. Reality has gone. Instead, only dreams. But even dreams have abandoned this frame. Imagination has left the building. Creativity, passion, energy, drive, commitment have all evaporated. What is left? What remains? A few signals of thought. A body that no longer responds. Ears that cannot hear. A voice that cannot speak. An inner voice that is running out of things to say. Memories escaping fast and hoping to find a receptacle.

Breath, heartbeat, pulse, signs of activity. Signs of life. Slow them, slow them. 5%. Be at peace, my love. There is no fight, no resistance, no spark and no flame. Remove the colour and welcome shades of grey where motion once made an attempt to escape. Let it lie down and rest. Rest. The battery has run down. There is no charger. Power down. Power down. Power. Down.

***

Will sat on the Tube home without a working phone so was forced to look at people. He couldn't help but check the floor for suspect packages. He heard the recorded messages all the time about these things but a major incident in the capital always heightened awareness for a few days. Over time people would go back to being immersed in the *Metro* or playing games on the phone or even books made of paper.

He trudged back to his apartment and immediately plugged in the phone then went to the loo in that order. As usual, the need for signal was more important than any bodily functions including eating, sleeping and pissing. In fact, Will was sure that many people would forget to eat but would walk miles for a phone charger.

Coffee and toast made, he flicked on his laptop and opened up Facebook. A memory from nine years ago showed him in a pub in Hackney with Steve and a couple of others. No point in sharing that. He had a quick look at a post featuring a train going through a waterlogged station and soaking the passengers, which apparently was hilarious, 'lol'. He noticed a '1' in the message box, which he opened. And then he ran.

***

He met Ange in a corridor outside the ward and they hugged the way two people might who have been brought together in such bleak circumstances.

'Ange! I saw your message about Ruth being in hospital and got here as fast as I could. Where's Ruth?'

'Thank God you were on Ruth's Facebook. It's the only way I could get hold of you.'

'We were supposed to meet today, but she didn't show up. What happened?'

'She … she was on Waterloo Bridge, Will. One of the casualties they mention in the papers who you don't really think about. I guess until now.'

The hospital lights became distinctly brighter, there was an odd ringing in his ears and Will had a sickening feeling his world was collapsing in on itself. 'Oh my God. Is she okay? Can I see her? Ange, is she … dead?'

'No, Will. Not right now. The place is chaotic, as you can imagine. The trauma unit is stretched to breaking point and they seem to be dealing with the life-threatening cases first. She was in surgery when I got here and that's all I know.' Ange paused to wipe a stray tear from her cheek.

'Jeez, I can't believe it. I was waiting for her not a stone's throw from the bridge. I assumed she would be coming out at Waterloo and would be nowhere near the carnage that unfolded. I thought she was just stuck on the Tube or something.' Will's words were tumbling over themselves as he struggled to make sense of what happened.

'They picked her up on the bridge and brought her here.' Ange lowered her voice. 'They only got hold of me 'cause I happened to give her a new business card the other day and wrote "New card, what do you think?" on it.'

'I've been calling and texting all day –'

'Well she's hardly in a state to answer the phone, is she?' Ange snapped. She took a breath. 'I'm sorry, I didn't mean to bite your head off. It's been hard here, on my own, not knowing. We just have to wait, Will. When I got here, the doctor told me that I shouldn't expect any more news for at least a couple of hours.'

Will and Ange trudged to the hospital canteen where visitors could seek refuge from the constant sound and smells of the ward. No one likes hospitals. They have a smell of their own and apart from the birth of children maybe, they represent somewhere you don't want to spend much time. They ordered a small pack of biscuits and two cups of tea, which were served in stainless steel teapots with small cartons of something that claimed to taste like real milk without actually being real milk. Will wondered what it was. Perhaps some Tipp-Ex mixed with water.

Will's complexion was grey as the seriousness of the situation began to sink in. Earlier in the day he had found himself thinking that the Waterloo Bridge incident hadn't made a dent on a city which was open for business as usual. He remembered watching a war film once when a nameless soldier gets shot in a battle. Normally the camera leaves people on the floor and moves on. But for this one example, the camera panned back and focussed on a senior officer writing a note. And then the camera followed the note to somewhere back home to be opened by a mother, lover or some other close loved one. It was a reminder that even the faceless and unknown soldiers in the movie have stories and connections. And here he was, feeling the full impact of the reality of an attack on the city.

He was struck by the randomness of the whole thing. If only they had agreed to meet at 12:30 instead of 13:00. If only Ruth hadn't walked over the bridge. If only he hadn't gone over to her place with the pleading love letter. If only she hadn't read it straight away. There were so many alternative endings and timings possible here, but something conspired to put her on the bridge at exactly the wrong time.

'How are you doing?' asked Ange.

'Not great, to be honest. I feel so bloody guilty. She was supposed to meeting me. If I hadn't been such an arse, we would have been nowhere near the place.'

'You can't blame yourself.'

'Well frankly I am the best bet when it comes to dishing out blame. Have you seen the Twitter feed? Christ, we get more information from there. Apparently six people dead, fifteen in hospital, with four in a critical condition, whatever that means. We don't even know what state Ruth is in. Oh and the police think they have killed anyone in the car, which crashed a few yards up the road. So here we are. And what on earth has Ruth ever done to hurt anybody? My God. She doesn't deserve this.'

'No, she doesn't. I got hold of her parents, by the way.'

'Oh, of course,' said Will feeling immediately ashamed that he hadn't considered the other people who might need to know. 'What did they say?'

'They're devastated. They're touring New Zealand, on holiday. They are desperate to get back and I left them looking for the earliest flights out of there. I gave them as much information as I could but it will be a good day or so before they get here. They will ring for updates so I will give them your number as well.'

'Is there anyone else we need to tell?'

'I've been in touch with people through Facebook Messenger and WhatsApp. Mostly friends. I haven't contacted her work yet – we need to do that. I have told people to stay put. There is nothing they can do here. Last time I saw you was on an early date and I was the unwelcome gatecrasher.'

'Yeah, that was funny,' said Will. 'I was more than a little surprised to see you there. At first I thought I had misread the signs and had mistaken date night for a social gathering.'

'Well, I hope you two get to laugh about that together for a long time to come.'

'So do I, Ange. So do I.'

***

18:47 – Waiting for important news is always a strange experience. It is amazing how easy it is to fritter away a day hardly being aware of the time and to use expressions like 'I just don't know where the day has gone'. But add an important event into the mix and things change. It's not that clocks move more slowly, because obviously they don't. But by focussing on minutes, seconds, and hours, the awareness of time can stretch it. Will wondered if it was possible that bored people believe they live longer. Not because they live longer in reality but because their perception of reality means that the days and evenings drag, and weekends are empty extensions of nothing in particular. Thus the week seems longer than anyone else's. Will wasn't in the mood to test the theory.

19:12 – Maybe time for some more coffee. At least that would be something to do.

19:14 – Drinking coffee that is called a latte from a machine. Anyone from Italy would demolish it in an instant. Nescafé plus froth doth not a latte make.

19:22 – Meet someone else who is waiting for news and enter a competition for the most distressed visitor. If you have been waiting to hear something for five hours, they will have been here for six. If you are worried about your patient, they will be worried sick about theirs. Any emotion you have, they can better it. Will wondered why people do this.

19:30 – Find some magazines in the waiting room. Will browsed through the 2015 edition of Sewing News Monthly and a well-thumbed, three-month-old copy of Hello! magazine full of people he had never heard of. He didn't think he would be making the cushions and someone had already stolen the pattern for the stuffed alligator.

19:40 – Take a stroll to the hospital shop and look at flowers, grapes, books and knitting patterns. Buy a Boost bar and return to the waiting room.

19:43 – Visit to the lavatory to sponge bits of chocolate from clothing. Inspect features in the mirror and declare that hospital mirrors have a slight curvature and light filter to make you look ill. Then when you go home and see yourself in the regular bathroom mirror, you believe your treatment has worked. Will wondered whether they have fat mirrors and thin mirrors at Weight Watchers. They could use the fat ones at the start and the thin ones as you progress. Who knows?

19:47 – Browse Facebook but dare not post anything. The truth is too painful and no words can do justice to the emotions in a hospital waiting room. If people feel the need to be sympathetic, they should turn up ready to hug people. They should not be allowed to click 'Like' or whatever to a post about illness.

**

At 19:52, a doctor came out to talk to Ange. 'Hi, I am Dr Burrows, one of the team working with Ruth,' he began.

Will rushed over and introduced himself as Ruth's boyfriend. A label he disliked but would serve well for now. 'Can we see her? How is she?'

'Let me explain what's going on. She was admitted with lacerations down both legs, severe bruising on her back and signs of bruising across her body. She was unconscious and bleeding badly from these wounds. She was taken to theatre where we discovered five fractured ribs and a punctured lung. Her right leg is fractured at the ankle, which has now been set. More worrying was the swelling on her brain revealed by her scan results. Due to concern about potential lasting damage, we have administered drugs to bring about a comatose state. Put simply, we have given her anaesthetic to reduce the activity in her body to give time for that swelling to go down. When you see her, you will find she has tubes down her throat and she is connected to machinery, which I appreciate can appear quite distressing. The machinery is taking over the working of her heart and lungs and we are monitoring her closely. Right now, she is off the immediate critical list. She is stable but unresponsive. If the swelling doesn't go down, we may need to consider burr holes to reduce the pressure in her brain. These are quite common in this kind of injury.'

'And how long will she be like this?' asked Will.

'It's hard to say. If it looks like the swelling is going down, we can reduce the anaesthetic and remove the tubing to make sure she can breathe unaided, and then see if she can wake up from it.'

'But she will be okay?'

'I can't make any promises, Mr Graden. To be frank, I have seen patients make a full recovery and I have seen others never recover. Some patients wake but experience the loss of critical functions such as movement or speech. But she is strong and seems healthy enough. We are moving her to the ward. She will be in a private room shortly and yes, you can see her there. But don't expect too much. She won't be waking for a while, I can promise you.'

'Will she be aware of us?' said Ange.

'We don't really know. There is some evidence to suggest that hearing and brain function remain active but I am also certain that some patients shut down completely. My advice is to keep an eye on her. Manage the visitors if they come to make sure she is comfy. Chat to her if you like. It is more important that you are around if and when we reduce the levels of anaesthesia.'

'What do you mean if?' Will and Ange exchanged concerned looks.

'Well, we have to accept that internal trauma can be unpredictable. Some people don't recover and some have lasting damage and need extensive care. Others go on to lead normal lives. It just depends.'

'Depends on what?'

'Many things. Now if you will forgive me, I have more work to do. As you can imagine, today has been testing for us all.'

With that the doctor turned and strode back through the swing doors behind him. Will and Ange stood somewhat stunned by the news. They hadn't been sure what to expect but now the doctor's words hung in the air and pressed down on their shoulders. They both shrunk a little in that moment. Will immediately focused on the negatives, of which there were plenty. Ange tried to be the optimistic one but they both knew her words were contrived to create hope. Right now, neither of them had much of that.

Truthfully, Will had been hoping to be called in to see Ruth sitting up in bed with a smile and maybe a bandage and a tube in her arm. They always seem to have those in hospitals. He could sit by her bed and discuss the perils of hospital lunches and the lack of Wi-Fi. Instead, he was to be confronted with complete silence and nothing to hang on to but hope.

Ange excused herself to make a call. She had promised to update Ruth's parents as soon as they heard some news. Will could hear the inflection in her voice that was trying to inject some false optimism into the conversation so that they wouldn't worry too much. Who was she kidding? This was Ruth's mum and dad she was talking to. People who could go into a state of panic over a splinter or a graze.

Afterwards, Ange and Will found the ward and located Ruth's room. A kindly nurse showed them in. Ruth was lying flat on a standard issue hospital bed, surrounded by the inevitable wires and tubes.

'They even have a machine that goes ping,' said Will as tears welled in his tired eyes.

Ruth looked terrible. Neither Will nor Ange was prepared for the bruise across her head that changed her complexion from porcelain white to purple and grey. Both of her arms were strapped up. Her right leg was showing and she had strapping all down the side that was clearly keeping it straight. Her skin was covered in bandages.

Plastic tubing reached into her throat and connected her to pale blue machinery. She was wearing a hospital gown and they could see the trace of yet more bandages across her neck, back and chest.

'Oh Jesus, Ruth. What have they done to you?' said Will.

Ange walked around the bed and stroked a small patch of exposed skin. 'Hi Ruth, it's Ange. I must admit you have looked better. Blimey, what have you been up to? Don't you worry, we are here. Will is here. I am here. Your mum is on the way and the doctors are looking after you. Everything's going to be fine, you'll see.'

They stood in silence for a few minutes, watching for signs of Ruth breathing. Only the sound of machinery and the distance hum of the ward made an imprint on their ears.

Ange agreed to sit with her while Will ran home to grab a few things. He was staying with Ruth and nothing would convince him to do otherwise. He packed a toothbrush, a couple of items of clothing, a phone charger, an iPad and a few snacks and ran back to the hospital as if Ruth's life depended on it. Of course, nothing had changed when he returned and Will was glad. In his darkest fears, the machine would make that flatline noise and she would be gone forever. To his relief, the same sounds and same sights greeted him. He convinced Ange to go home at last and thanked her with every positive adjective he could muster.

Will sat on a chair by the bed, stroking Ruth's hand. It was one of the few areas of untouched skin although the back of it seemed rough as if rubbed the wrong way by coarse sandpaper.

***

Silence. Currently 6%. No pain. Cold. No sound. No voices. Just quiet.

***

Will sat back and felt sick and scared and worried and panicked and empty and terrified all at the same time. The trouble was, he felt incredible pressure to put on a brave face and to utter words of reassurance even though, judging by Ruth's state, he didn't believe them himself.

If the day had seemed long, the night seemed longer. Will dozed in his chair and checked and stroked. In his dreams, Ruth would wake and would be fine. But when he opened his eyes, she was in the same position and with no sign of movement. Occasionally the sounds of the ward would waken him. Hospitals are never quiet. The sounds of the sick, and the dying seem to permeate the corridors trying to suck the life from those who seem to be on the mend.

'I'm here, Ruth. Right here. Don't you worry, I am not going anywhere. You let me know if you need anything.'

Will hoped his words might permeate Ruth's coma but even if they didn't, they might make him feel better.

And so he stayed. Will camped out in the hospital for three nights in a row. He made a call to his new boss to explain what was going on. Technically there were no provisions in his conditions of service for taking time off for compassionate leave, since he was still working his probation. But his description of what happened to Ruth and the story behind it prompted a most caring response. His company suggested he take a week to look after her and to keep them posted. Will was beyond grateful for their kindness and consideration and vowed to work for them forever. Meanwhile, Ange rang Ruth's office to make sure they knew what was happening. Ruth's colleagues clubbed together to send flowers and a big card full of well-meaning hopes and prayers. No doubt there was much personal and collective debate about what to say in a card when someone is not awake to read it.

Visitors came to see Ruth and paid scant attention to Will's dishevelled look. His clothes were as creased as the lines on his face. His hands smelt of antiseptic handwash and his breath smelt of Nescafé and chocolate. His socks needed changing and his skin adopted a grey pallor, as if he had been locked in a darkened room for days. Which, to a certain extent, he had been. He hated leaving Ruth even for a few minutes. He feared that the best or the worst might happen if he was not there and he wanted to be there, whatever the outcome.

Doctors would come and shine lights and check pulses and reflexes. The drips would be changed and the tubes removed and then reinserted. The machinery would be reset and would carry on making the same monotonous sounds. Occasionally it would do something odd or an alarm would sound, prompting a nurse to hurry round, take a quick look, press a button and then leave.

'We are reducing the anaesthetic,' said Dr Burrows on the fourth day. 'Not by much but a little. We will check for a response and see if any damage has been done. We have also removed the breathing tubes and she is now breathing by herself. Try talking to her. Sometimes sounds or smells of home can get things going inside. You never know.'

Will nodded, resenting the doctor's cold bedside manner. At least this was some sort of progress.

***

Quiet. Perhaps a flicker of something. Numb. Empty. Silent as the grave. Quiet as a mouse. What is that? Spots before the eyes but the eyes have gone.

Wait. What is that? Something. Somewhere. Sensation. A dream. What is a dream? Where am I? What am I? Who am I? Connections. Sparks. Black as the night. Empty as my soul.

Hold on to something. Time? What is the time? Does time wait? Does time exist? Memories. Is that a memory in the corner? Memories waiting for me to find them? My God, what is this? God, do I believe in You? Do You believe in me? Are You even there? Did You make this happen?

What is that? Scent. Familiar and yet not wanted. I don't like this. I don't like this at all. Take it out. Take it away. White noise but what colour is white? Any colour you like, as long it is white in all this blackness.

Ouch. What was that? I felt that. I don't want that happening again. What was that? 11%, whatever that means. What disguise is this? Am I visible? Invisible? Is this death? Is this what I have become? No one tells you it will be like this. Where are the angels? I want angels, damn it.

Ouch. That hurt. What is that? Who is that? Why are you doing that to me? Are you getting this? Are you taking this down? What is that picture? The one over there. Faded corners, I see. Must be an old one. Old photos are the best. I have plenty. Want to see? I just need to see where I have put them.

Ouch. How dare you! What is that? Don't do that. Why would anyone do such a thing? I hate that. Colour. I see white. Is that colour? Is white a colour? Have I asked that already? Now, where did I put that photo? See. Here it is. Who is this, does anyone know? Can someone look this up? Anyone? Is anyone actually listening to me?

Ouch. Stop doing that. Give me something for that, will you? Mum, is that you? Can you get me something for this? I don't know, someone keeps doing something. Where is everybody? Where is anyone? Can you hear me? Am I even here? And where is here?

Ouch. What is that? What is that sound? I know that. Does anyone know what this is? Where is a mechanic when you need one? Join the dots, will you? These things need connecting. You need to put that in there and then join that to this one and then who knows, maybe this thing will work. Doesn't anyone do any work around here?

What is that? I know what that is. Give me a minute. However long that is. Is my time up? I have no idea what that is. I know that. I know what that is.

Ouch. Stop hurting me. That is not nice. I have told you before. This has got to stop.

Ouch. I have had quite enough of this. And what is that over there? Something is happening over there on the other side. Do I have sides? I guess I have sides. On the side that is not this one, something strange is happening. I feel it. Is that truth? Is feeling a thing? Did I just learn to do that or did I always know how to do that? Well, that's better than the other thing that keeps happening over there. I wouldn't mind some more of that, thank you very much.

Ouch. That hurts. That is pain, that is. I am glad I can see it for what it is. I never did like pain. See, I can remember that. Where are those photos? Has anyone found them? Join the dots and choices. It's all about choices at the end of the day. You can get busy living or get busy dying. Who said that? Did I say that? Can I speak? What is speech anyway but the expression of thoughts? I have thoughts. I can prove it. Here I am thinking, see. That must be a good thing. Has anyone found my photos? Show me just the one.

Oh, there you are. I can see that, whatever your name is. Is that you I can hear? Sound. Oh yes, that is sound. What is sound but the absence of silence? Are we able to measure silence or is it only noise we can measure? Are noise and silence opposite ends of the spectrum or is silence just the word we give to very quiet sounds? I know that sound. What is that?

Ouch. We need something for that. That needs sorting. If you need a job doing, you better do it yourself. Now what were you saying? Well, that makes no sense at all. I am not doing anything at the weekend. I have no plans. I need to join that up and connect those things. I need more lines on my signal. You know, those lines on the phone that tell you about signal strength. I need some of those. Right now, the signal is crap. Can somebody sort this? How long does it take to get anything done around here?

Ouch. That doesn't get any better. Wait. I remember you. I have a picture somewhere and a word that goes with it.

Ouch. This is pretty fucking unbearable! I am not putting up with that much longer. Someone better do something.

Slowly.

One thing at a time.

Prioritise and think it through.

Let's be calm, everybody.

Now I want someone to connect that noise to the picture in that memory box with that word on the side. Is that too much to ask? We haven't got all day, Will, and I can't make this weekend. I am stuck here for some reason.

Will.

I remember.

Well done, everybody! Will. Yep, now that is a start. Do we have any other pictures back there? Any will do but hurry up. Time is money, everyone. Oh, that's a nice one. That one sure is a bolt out of the blue. I had forgotten that. Nice smile, don't you think? Any more for any more? Now you don't need to show me those. Those are the private ones and not for public consumption. I took these when no one was looking and filed them somewhere for safe keeping. I had forgotten where I put them.

Yes, the flowers are lovely, Will, and get some water if you need to. Have you seen this picture of you? Not your most flattering pose I agree, but those shoes had to come off somehow! Put that memory back in those little clouds over there. Somewhere I can reach if I need to.

Now, Will, what are you doing?

You can keep doing that. That's nice. Now what am I doing here again? I honestly have no idea. Can I get up now? Or is this it? I am not making a lot of sense to everyone else round here. Hey guys. What about a little help? Can we move something maybe? Anything? No? Okay, well, one thing at a time, I guess. Maybe I can force a smile. Not that I have much to smile about. Apart from you. Can you hear me? I can hear you.

Ouch. Someone needs to do something about that. I am not putting up with much more of that.

States of Consciousness: Research into Coma and Vegetative States

Case evidence summarised by Hector Winslow, July 1983

Case one

Miriam Enderflower was in a coma for four months. She was unresponsive to any external stimuli. When she woke, she was able to replay complete conversations that had taken place within earshot. She divorced her husband immediately because she overheard calls he made to his lover. The husband denied this but further investigation revealed that he was engaged in a clandestine affair. The divorce was granted.

Case two

Steve Atkins was unconscious for eight days following a car accident. During this time, he was linked up to an MRI scanner and his brain activity was recorded. Scientists noticed a rise in brain activity when he was played recordings of familiar voices. Recordings of his wife speaking resulted in a significant spike in activity, for example. During the experiment, a radio was placed in his room and at one point played football commentary of Liverpool vs Chelsea. As a life-long Liverpool fan there was an expectation that this would generate a rise in activity. None registered, however. On waking, Mr Atkins suggested that he'd recorded the football and didn't want to know the result until he could view the matches himself. Instead, he claimed to have spent the whole time the radio was on distracting himself with mental maths and problems.

Case three

Gemma Walker was in a coma for six weeks. When she

woke, she sued the hospital for malpractice as she believed one of the orderlies had abused her on her bed. The court rejected her evidence as inadmissible. Six months later the same orderly was dismissed when CCTV footage caught him behaving inappropriately in the morgue.

Case four

Maria Galbreni's husband was a master chef and sat by her bedside talking about food and recipes as he created new ideas for his kitchen. After nine weeks in an apparently vegetative state, Maria awoke and was able to recall the recipes and critique them. Her opening words when she regained consciousness were, 'You have too much salt and not enough basil with the asparagus.'

Chapter 11: The Glory Of Love

Well, it sure is quiet around here. Should I eat anything? I'm not sure I can do that right now. What about water or a nice cup of tea? If I am not eating or drinking, how am I keeping fit and healthy? Or maybe I am not keeping fit and healthy. In the absence of a mirror, maybe a memory will do. Do we have one of those? Oh yes, that looks like me. I don't like the shoes, though, we need to go shopping. When can we do that?

***

'She seems stable today, did she have a good night?' asked Ange.

'Yeah, pretty much the same. I hoped for some sort of sign but she didn't move,' said Will.

'You look tired yourself.'

'Yeah, I am. I am going to go home for a bit today to freshen up. I will come back later. Her parents came in yesterday and they are back this afternoon so I can give them some time alone and then come back when they have gone. Thanks so much for all your help, Ange. It has been brilliant having you here.'

'God, don't mention it. I wouldn't be anywhere else. Let's hope this doesn't go on for much longer and we see some signs of improvement.'

'I hope so too. Apparently, the meds are reduced now but it doesn't seem to be making a damn bit of difference.'

'Hmm. Oh, you may get a visit from Megan and Helen later. They were going to try and come after work. I sent a message to put them off but they are close friends and I couldn't think of a good excuse, so you will have to entertain them.'

'Well, as long as they are on the close friend list. I am

not having any distant friends cluttering up the place.'

'How will you know?'

'I am developing a "How well do you know Ruth test" and they have to pass or else they are sitting in the waiting room and just being shown charts.'

'Fair enough,' said Ange. 'We don't want the undeserving getting through. Mind you, I'm not sure I would pass myself. What sort of questions are there?'

'What is her favourite colour?'

Red

'What perfume does she wear when she goes out?'

Jo Loves Pomelo

'What does she wear in bed?'

'Hey, that one's a bit unfair, Will!'

'Yeah, maybe you're right about that.'

Silk pyjamas with flowers woven into each sleeve

'Where did she work before her current job?'

MDA Marketing

'What was the last movie she enjoyed at the cinema?'

Oh, this is a hard one. I saw La La Land *but wasn't sure I liked it. Does that count?*

'Blimey, I think I am going to fail the bloody test,' said Ange. 'You'll have me stuck in the waiting room looking at charts next. Go home, Will. Freshen up. Have something to eat and come back when you are ready. In the meantime, I will stand guard here. If her mum and dad arrive, I will talk to them then clear off for a bit, but I will be here until you get back.'

'Are you sure?'

'Of course.'

'Thanks Ange, you are an angel.'

***

Oh, that's where they are. I wanted to know where the angels were hiding and it turns out they are all around when you need them. I was expecting wings and halos and for them to be called things like Gabriel and not Ange, but there you are. How wrong can you be? Those Christmas cards have had it wrong all this time, not to mention a myriad of stained glass windows. Oh, and that chapel in Rome with the big ceiling? Bloody picture of angels and cherubs everywhere and they are all painted wrong. Makes sense when you think about it. Angels are people, you see. They are the ones that come down to help when you need it. Just normal people who are kind. Mind you, I expect the chapel roof would look a bit odd with a picture of Christ and a girl called Ange next to him. Especially if she was doing her nails or something.

Anyway, what was that game? Things we know about Ruth (me). I think therefore I am. I am stuck on the movie question. I want to say La La Land *but I think it must have been that film with that bloke from that series. You know the one. He does that advert sometimes that you can see on Saturday night during the breaks on the Ant and Dec show. You know him.*

I can't remember. The box of memories is sometimes locked. If I remember one thing, it can have a domino effect and open some others. One thing remembered and many things remembered.

Where has everyone gone? Funny, they say hello when they arrive but mostly just disappear without a by your leave. Most rude. How am I supposed to know when they have gone? Sometimes I think they have gone and then they do something to prove they are still here.

I want to use the word 'yesterday' but I am not sure the timing is right. What I am thinking of was before now but I am not sure how long before now it was. It could have been minutes, hours or days. I don't think days because that doesn't seem right. There was a measure of time when something happened and that's what I am thinking about. I am sure I saw colour. Well, maybe something white. See the thing is, it is dark here. I can hear things and I get sensations from different places, which I think are connected. But the dark is overwhelming. Yesterday (if that's when it was), the spots that sometimes blur across my vision changed and I had a sense of brightness. I don't know what it was, but it was different. Hello, does anyone know what that was? You could go quite mad in here, you know. Hardly anyone answers. I might rest and give that some thought.

***

'Hi Ange,' said Will. 'I'm back. How's it been?'

Ange was slumped in a chair, half browsing an iPad and half checking on Ruth. 'Doctors came in and did some checks. Shone the torch into various places, prodded and manoeuvred various limbs. Changed the bag of fluid and made some notes on a chart. Then we had some nurses pop in to check on us both, which was nice. Made sure I had a cup of tea and some cake, but no news really. Her parents came and fussed for a couple of hours. They are lovely and her mum chatted away without pausing for breath. I think she is probably the same with everyone.'

'I bet Ruth is in the perfect state for her to chat away to.'

'You are not wrong. Her dad hardly said a word, bless him. He just sat staring at her and holding her hand. They kept asking questions about progress, when she would be home. Was she eating enough (don't ask). In the end, they left. They wanted to stay longer but I said you were coming and I was here. They will be back tomorrow afternoon to see how she is. They looked so devastated, Will. Understandable, I guess, when you see your little girl like this. It's not what is supposed to happen, is it?'

'Yeah, must be tough on them.' Will sighed. 'A lot of parents are having a hard time this week. Some worse than us, of course. Some poor bastard has had to bury his children. Did you see the faces in the paper? Jesus, some were so young. It makes me sick.'

'Yes, me too … Anyway, I'm going to shoot off now that you're here. You will have Megan and Helen arriving at some point. Are you staying the night again?'

'Yep. Couldn't sleep at home so I'm staying here just in case she needs anything.'

'She is lucky to have you. She may not know it. Mind you, when she wakes up I'll tell her you couldn't be arsed and only popped in once, smelling of drink and stale perfume!'

'Ha. Thanks, Ange. That's perfect.'

'You are most welcome, Will.'

Will and Ange hugged and Ange disappeared down the corridor. They were becoming close friends through this ordeal. Ruth would be most surprised to find out how much of a bond was forming amongst the regular bedside visitors.

***

Now why exactly would someone be burying children? What's that all about? I am glad Ange was here, although the truth is I didn't know she was here until she said she was leaving. And Will. You smell nice. I can smell something of your aftershave and that lemon burst shower gel you use. Sort of spiced lemon flavour. Thank you for coming. I am sorry I am here and I don't understand much. Maybe things will become clear.

***

'Hi, Will?'

'Megan, Helen. So nice to see you. Sorry it always seems to be traumatic occasions when we meet.'

'Hi Will. Is it okay to be here? We weren't sure about visiting to be honest,' said Helen.

'Oh, it's fine. Of course. Can I take those?'

Megan had brought flowers that were conveniently already held tight in a plastic container and a small furry bear. Helen clutched a large box of Cadbury Milk Tray and some grapes. 'I brought hospital food for her,' she said, not fully grasping what she was dealing with. 'Has she woken up at all?'

'No,' Will said gently. 'I'm afraid she has been in a coma since the incident on the bridge. The doctors have begun to reduce the levels of anaesthetic but there's no sign of progress so far.'

Megan and Helen exchanged glances. 'Can she hear us?'

'Maybe. We are not sure but I like to think so. I like to think she knows we are here and she is loved.'

'I couldn't believe it when I heard,' Megan said. 'You read about these things and it's always someone else, isn't it? You see pictures in the paper but they are not *real* people. Not to me, anyway.' Her voice began to falter. 'Why would anyone do this?'

'We will never know,' said Helen, reaching over to squeeze her friend's shoulder. 'The police shot the blokes in the van and have arrested and released other people. All anyone else says is that they know nothing and can't believe they would do this. They interviewed a brother or some other relative the other day, and one of them was described as a loving father and committed to his family. And now he's dead and Ruth is like this. Some loving father he was. Shame he is dead in a way. I would love to ask him why. Why these people? Why Ruth? It's so tragic and bloody random. I often walk over that bridge. It could easily have been me.'

'The government needs to do something to stop these people coming into the country,' Megan muttered and the room descended into an awkward silence.

Will wondered if Helen and Megan were nervous and

not sure what to say or what to do. Finally, they pulled themselves together and did what they came to do. They focused on their friend and spoke words of quiet comfort while stroking her hair and her hand.

'What's going to happen to her, Will? I don't know what I expected when I got here but this sure brings it home, doesn't it?' Megan wiped a tear from the corner of her eye with a fresh tissue. Meanwhile Helen linked arms with her in a show of bedside solidarity. 'It seems that life has left her for a while and this is Ruth's housing but no one is home. And all these machines! I was hoping to ring people with good news but right now, I don't know what to say.'

Will sighed. 'I have been here since they brought her in on and off. Sometimes I feel positive and think things are going to be alright. But then I have real dark moments. I think I detect movement but then I think I have been kidding myself. It's just tricks of the light in here. At the end of the day, you need faith in the medicine, faith in the doctors, faith in the family and friends and, of course, faith in Ruth and her ability to beat this.

***

Faith? Well faith may move mountains but it won't shift my little finger. Nice words, lovely sentiments. Thanks for coming. I am not sure who you are, though. I have been looking but the box with the pictures in isn't opening. I mean, I know that I know you. Your pictures are filed under 'known people' but the labels have fallen off. It makes it difficult to work things out. Will, I know. I remember parts of him. Or at least parts of his story.

***

Will recalled going to hospital to see his great Aunt Daphne. Now there's a name you don't hear often. He would arrive with a packet of her favourite After Eight mints, to find her in a comatose level of sleep. The levels of methadone being administered kept uncomfortable waking hours to a minimum. So, he would announce his arrival in a slightly raised voice. State clearly that he had chocolates and that other people sent their love. And he would take a seat. He would look at his watch and scan the ward for signs of life. He would sit there for fifteen minutes and wonder if that was long enough to count as a visit. The trouble was, he reflected, he had no idea whether his aunt knew he was there. So he began a debate in head as to whether he was now wasting his time sitting on a grey hospital chair. He concluded after three visits that an average of twenty-two minutes was sufficient. It was long enough to show willing. Long enough to prove to the other patients that Daphne had a loving family who cared for her and long enough to signal to the hospital staff that she was not alone. So that's what he did. Once a week for twenty-two minutes for three weeks, with two boxes of After Eight mints and some grapes. And then she died in her sleep. Will remembered people at the funeral being pleased that he had visited her and how smug he felt compared to those who wished they had found the time and who were planning to go the following week. As he listened to Helen and Megan and their bedside mutterings, he hoped they would leave quickly. As twenty-five minutes passed he found himself thinking, *Hey, that's more than enough time now. You have turned up and showed willing, made all the right noises and expressed concerns, and now you can go. Go back to your lives where you go to the pub and meet after work and spend your days in the dullest of meetings.* Clearly Helen and Megan hadn't worked out the acceptable hospital timescales for visiting those who are not responding.

Eventually they left after forty-seven minutes. Although twelve minutes of that time didn't count as they wandered off in search of a coffee machine and Megan needed a cigarette. Will had visions of her joining the cancer patients by the ashtrays near the carpark, some dragging oxygen or drips behind them. A strange concept: illness and smoking. You don't need a picture on a packet to warn you of the dangers of smoking when you start dragging an oxygen cylinder behind you. But it didn't seem to deter people. It seems not only will some smokers put up with a little rain and the cold for the drag on a cigarette – some don't mind operations, emphysema and hospitalisation for a final fag.

And so Will found himself alone with Ruth once again. He was glad the visitors had gone and no more were due to arrive. He scanned the range of cards and flowers that now acted as a temporary stage set to Ruth's hospital bed. The well meaning and disconnected had sent notes saying they were thinking of her. And they were sure she would be back on her feet soon. Some had added a few notes of news which suggested they hadn't spoken since Christmas or even before that. Will picked up a large card that was clearly from people at work. He counted twenty-seven signatures in a variety of pens. Some with short messages of encouragement and some simply signed 'Best Wishes' with a name next to it. Will could see the dilemma landing on each desk. How to write something profound for someone caught up so randomly in an act of terror. In the end, the best wishes would do. Ruth's bedside drawer was full of chocolates and sweets. *It's like flowers at funerals*, Will reflected. *The deceased never see them but those attending or even those not present can show that they have been or were there in spirit.* He noted a great deal of the rituals around hospitals were for the benefit of the visitors rather than the patients.

Will popped a Werther's Original into his mouth. A packet brought in by Ruth's dad just in case she needed something soothing and sweet to suck, he'd said. He tidied a few of the cards to make sure they were well balanced and made room for the newly acquired bear.

'Hi Ruth, it's just me here now. I am not leaving. Just popping to grab a class of water and to stop by the loo. I will be back in a couple of minutes. Let me know if you need anything.'

***

Actually, I do need something. I haven't quite worked out what is going on. What is happening and what is not happening. Those girls seemed fun earlier and then sad. Did I detect crying? I could do with talking to someone about this if there is anyone. The sign says 24% and that's better than it was but still pretty useless. Is there a button perhaps? Jump leads? Defibrillators maybe. I have seen them work in movies. I also remember some movie about a man who is poisoned and he goes to his car and has to inject himself and use a defibrillator to restart his heart. Is there anything like that, maybe? I am also noticing things. I am not thirsty or hungry but I am also not noticing eating or drinking. So, I would like to be thirsty. That would be a good sign. Not being thirsty seems odd, especially when I have been here for however long this is. Water. Yes, I would like to need some of that. But I don't.

***

'Hi, I'm back,' said Will. 'A surprisingly satisfying pee, to be honest. Sometimes you think you need to go and there is so much more to give than you expected. It was actually quiet embarrassing. As I was mid-flow, a man wandered in and used the cubicle near me. He had finished and was washing his hands while I was still going. He must have wondered what I had been drinking, that's for sure. Men never say anything, of course. There is an unwritten law about these things. I am amused by toilet doors, though. They have all these signs about washing your hands. Now I always do. But some blokes don't. Disgusting, I know. But then we both have to open the door to get out. So, I get all the germs left over by Unclean Boy over there and start spreading them about. We need soap dispensers, air driers and automatic doors that don't have handles or things to press. No wonder germs spread so damn easily. Anyway, I am sure you don't want to hear about that. So what else can I tell you?

'You need to wake up to try some hospital food. I had a Cornish pasty in the canteen yesterday and I think the contents need examining. There were definitely diced carrots in there, but the meat? Well, I couldn't be sure what that was. It was served with chips and brown gravy with a skin on it which was only broken by a forcible blow from a metal ladle. You need to wake up and see what a taste sensation you are missing, Ruth.

'Ange has been fantastic. She has literally dropped everything to come and see how you are. Funny, I hardly knew her before but she is becoming a good friend. You and I need to take her out for dinner sometime. Somewhere nice.'

***

I am interested by the word 'before' that people drop into conversation. The concept of before and after makes perfect sense until you realise they are talking about you. You before and you after. Which means something is not the same. I guess people change all the time, though. Hair, make-up, clothes, shoes. That reminds me, where are my shoes? I don't think I need them but

I'd like to know where they are. I must find the photo of the new pair. I have forgotten what they look like. 29%.

***

Will stopped babbling and filling the space. Sometimes it gave him comfort to chat away. He had no idea whether any of his words were landing but he felt so alone in there. So incredibly sad and lonely. He didn't believe it was possible to share such a small space with someone and yet to feel abandoned on every level. One-way conversation seemed better than none.

Will allowed the quiet of the room to creep over him. Closing his eyes, he sat holding Ruth's hand and dozed off. For a while they were both just two people sleeping. Sharing a bed, touching and being together. Will's metabolism slowed into light sleep and his head came alive with dreams.

A sudden noise from outside woke Will from his state of slumber and he sat up and looked at his watch. Then checked his phone. Old habits die hard, it seems. He stretched and looked around the small room.

'You okay in there, Ruth?' he whispered. 'We need to get you out of here. I have to tell you; this room is depressing. It need a good paint job, we need to get rid of these machines and put a TV in here. Do you want a cup of tea or something? No? No worries.

'The trouble is, Ruth, before I met you, I was miserable. I didn't know it because the monotony of life took over. I would fill my days with trivia like Facebook and Twitter and video games. Have you any idea how many hours I have spent looking at the lives of others? I have peered in on their day-to-day trials and tribulations and found myself watching endless pictures of babies, puppies, cats and dinners. I have played countless hours of FIFA and progressed through tournaments. I have scored great goals, won penalty shootouts and been awarded cups and medals. All from the comfort of my armchair and connected to people I barely know through a headset. I have sat in meetings that drone on and on and have convinced myself that sitting through such torturous events is what I am paid for. I have eaten the dullest of sandwiches wrapped in plastic, accompanied by a variety of crisps and snacks. All designed to be eaten on-the-go to provide minimum disruption to the day. I have gone for drinks with people who don't matter and convinced myself that this is a social life. I have handed out business cards with a smile and not meant it. I have clicked 'Like' on thousands of things I don't care about. I have many 'friends' but no real friends.

'Oh, don't get me wrong, not every second was awful. I do have a couple of good mates and we still create a few stories and share a pint and put the world to rights. But most of it? Well, most of it is just bollocks. Facebook is just a sham. The friendships are not real and I am bored with the competition. I found myself playing a lonely game of FIFA the other night and became aware of how absurd it was. Any sense of achievement is created by a few programmers who insert cheers and challenges into the game. I am no soccer star. Just a sad bastard with a well-developed thumb.

'And then I met you. And do you know what? The days at work were still crap but now I was excited to be in them. I remember the first day we were due to meet. Time couldn't go fast enough. Adrenaline rushed through my veins and I was like a new puppy with my tail wagging and a lust for life. You would laugh: I had a good look at my wardrobe and decided nothing was good enough. I threw away all my socks in the sock drawer and bought new ones. I threw away all my pants and bought new ones of them as well. The jeans I was wearing when we met were fresh from the shop and my shoes didn't need a polish, as they came out of the box like that.

'I remember our first date and how lovely you looked. I didn't know what to order in there. The bloody wine list was overwhelming. All I wanted to say was, "I'll have what she's having".'

Will chuckled. 'Do you remember the date after that when I tried to impress you? Damn the perils of *TripAdvisor* and the internet. I planned what I thought was the perfect date. Have you ever seen that movie called *Hitch* starring Will Smith? He's the guy who sets people up and plans the most romantic of things. In the end, nothing was as I planned. Apart from you. Apart from you. As the day collapsed around me, your smile was the one constant.'

Will paused for a moment and brushed his hand over the growth of stubble on his chin. There was something he needed to say, but he didn't know if he should. But if he didn't say it now, would he ever? Would Ruth even hear it? He decided to bite the bullet just in case he never got another chance. 'There is something we need to talk about though, isn't there? Lunch with Jen and the text message. In the midst of all this chaos, I had allowed that to go to the back of my mind. I know we were due to talk about it on the South Bank. Jeez, if it hadn't been for all that going on between us, we wouldn't be here now. We would have woken late, stayed in bed a while. Not been heading to the South Bank for self-directed relationship counselling.

'Anyway, here is the deal. Jen and I were more than friends at Uni. We were never quite an item but we stuck together like glue. We were inseparable and other people joined our names together when we were discussed. People would say things like, "Are Will and Jen coming over?" We lost our individual identity because we spent so much time together. We used to tell people we were more brother and sister than lovers but the truth is…' Will stopped, sighed and rubbed his eyes. 'The truth is I obsessed over her. I was such a coward, though, and I never really told her how I felt. We had a few moments of intimacy usually when drunk, but always laughed it off. Then, two years later, Jen had a work placement that took her to Cardiff. We chatted, of course, but ultimately drifted apart. Whatever we shared at university dissipated as the real world came crashing in. She met someone. I pretended to meet someone too, to make her jealous. In the end she dropped out of her final year and we went our separate ways. I got a new girlfriend a while later and tried meeting up with Jen but the new girl was super jealous of someone she perceived as an ex-girlfriend. I don't think Jen's boyfriend liked the idea of me either. So in the end, I stopped writing. For years I thought about Jen every day. I wondered how she was, what she was doing, who she was with. It felt like unfinished business. We were so damn close and then … nothing. I couldn't work out how it happens in life that you replace your soulmate and best friend with a complete void. In truth, I couldn't accept that she had abandoned me like that and never saw my complete and utter adoration of her.

'After that I heard stories and reports about her in various jobs and with different people. Over time I lost track of her. You know what it's like. I found her on Facebook but didn't learn much. And then she turned up at the wedding. Talk about bad timing.

'I am so sorry I treated you badly that night. It started so well but when Jen arrived it was like a sledgehammer smack in the head. I couldn't believe she was there. In one of the quieter moments she handed me a card with her mobile number, saying we should catch up. I'll be honest, Ruth. It was a conversation I had waited a long time to have. So, a couple of days later I sent a quick text and we agreed to meet.

'The thing is, I have learnt over time that ex-girlfriends and new partners don't mix. No matter how you try and present it, the reality is that you are spending time with someone with whom you share a history. You have secrets, habits and code words that bind you together and that seem threatening to any outsider. That's why I put her number in my contacts under the name Colin. I didn't want you to be threatened, because I didn't know where this was going, if anywhere. So, I arranged a clandestine lunch at the Cork & Bottle. I have to be honest, I was nervous and excited about meeting her. It had been so many years and I had stored up questions that I needed answers to. So we met and fussed over the wine list and sat down to talk. Do you know, the strangest thing happened? I discovered something I didn't know. She was mad about me and the fact that we never properly got together. She wanted rescuing from Cardiff and I never came and she felt abandoned. You could have knocked me down with a feather. All the time I thought I had been dumped and instead I uncovered her jealousy and resentment. Again, I have to be honest: that made me feel a whole lot better. For years I thought I wasn't good enough. I thought I was the guy you got to know a bit and then moved on to something better. Those voices in my head sat with me for years. Suddenly, I find myself sitting in the Cork & Bottle thinking, *Hey, Will. You are an okay guy. You could have made this work if you'd wanted to.*

'Anyway, we sat there for a while and I discovered another strange emotion. I glanced at the clock on the wall and began to feel slightly bored. I started wondering when I might leave. You must have had that feeling sometimes, when you are out with someone and decide you've had enough. Jen was full of stories. She loves to present herself as a free spirit. She said her favourite song was 'Beeswing' by Christy Moore, about a girl impossible to pin down. (I did correct her that it was a Richard Thompson song, don't worry.) As I sat there listening to story after story, I began to realise that she was trying to convince me that she was a wild and fun person. She would explain this happening and that happening and she got so drunk and it was all hilarious. But I have come to the conclusion that really fun people are authentically fun to be around. They make you laugh. Jen was presenting an image, an ideal if you like. She hoped the stories would craft the image, but I found myself sitting there and nodding and smiling in all the right places. Eventually I told her some lies.

'The first lie was that I had to go as I had a meeting to get to. I didn't.

'The second lie was to agree that yes, it would be great to see her again. I didn't know what to say after that. When people say that there is normally an implied "sometime" at the end of the sentence. As in, "It would be great to see you again sometime." This at some random point in the future not, as it appears the week after.

'I had a text from her asking about meeting again soon after. The trouble is that once you have told someone it would be great to see them, it is hard then to say no. So I was vague. She mentioned a time and place and I texted back to say that it was possible.

'Trust me, I had no intention of seeing her again. This is how blokes let girls down gently. Most of us are too cowardly to say no, so we say things like, "Sure, that would be great." And then, "I need to check my diary", followed by, "I think I have something on that day" and finally, "I'll call you", followed by silence. That was the path I was on when her message hit my phone.

'You know the rest.'

Will paused. He had no idea whether Ruth could hear

him but it was cathartic to say the words out loud in her presence. He sat back in his chair and stretched to ease his back. His hand fell on Ruth's hair and he lent forward and kissed her forehead and lightly brushed her lips with his own.

'If Walt Disney was in charge of this hospital, that would have worked, Ruth. I have seen that movie where the princess is woken by true love's kiss. Where is Walt when you need him? Or God, even? How come those with the power to impress don't show up at times like this? Walt would never have missed the opportunity for cinematic romance. If God exists, now would be a pretty good fucking time to show up.

'I miss you, Ruth. I am here. I am not leaving, I promise.' The volume of his voice quietened to just above a whisper. 'You are the only one I care about, Ruth.'

Will squeezed Ruth's hand and grabbed a tissue. His emotions had left light tear stains on his cheeks and his eyes felt swollen and sore.

Will blew his nose in the tissue and wandered out of the room. *Time for some more Nescafé and froth*, he thought.

***

That was nice. I felt that. I could feel my hair then and I could feel something warm on my head and my lips tingled. I am sure that is Will chatting away. I can't quite get what he is on about but it sounded lovely. There were some loud parts and quiet parts and I know it was him. 32%. Not bad.

***

Will spent the night on a fold-out bed on the floor. He slept as best he could, waking to check on Ruth and waking because the sounds and smells of the place are designed to keep even the soundest sleeper from slumber. At 6:00 he woke and headed off for an early morning coffee and pastry. He spent a while sitting in the canteen, sending texts to those wondering how Ruth was doing and of course wondering how he was doing. Plenty of sympathy for those looking after the ones who are truly suffering.

Will was worried about the power in his phone. He reached into his pocket and pulled out a charger with an extra-long lead. Plugged it into the wall and was pleased to see the lightning bolt flicker over the battery indicator. 19%.

He paged through his text messages and stumbled upon one from Ruth. A message that had arrived a few days ago. *What ya doing?* was all it said. He hadn't replied as he had picked up the phone to that one. He thought now was as good a time as any to reply.

Hi Ruth. Just sitting here with a cup of coffee and hoping to see you later xxxx

He pressed Send. 22%.
And then a few minutes later,

Wondered if you fancied a gallery or a theatre or something. I promise not to have blood splatters and screaming this time. How are you doing? xxx

26%.

You know I am a bit bored of this place. Want to get out of here? xxx

33%.

I love you, do you know that? xxx

37%.

And so the messages left the phone and the battery powered up. They flew into the air to be picked up by satellites and were bounced from one to another. They flicked off the rooftops, streaked along the streets and searched for the coded destination. One by one they found their target and let out a small sound as they landed.

Will sent one more.

I tell you what, I am not taking you on a date in this restaurant. Too many weird people in here and the coffee is shit. See you in a minute xxx

51%.

Meanwhile, a duty nurse popped in for a regular check-up. She scanned the charts at the foot of the bed and padded over to Ruth. Her training meant she focused on stability or change and she was trained to detect anything that was concerning or indeed, encouraging. To her, Ruth was a patient in waiting. She was neither unwell, nor unsafe. She was simply there. If Ruth had been awake, she could have discussed how she felt, pain relief, hydration, temperature, blood pressure and emotional wellbeing. Instead, there was nothing to discuss. All she could do was monitor. It seemed that Ruth's life had been put on hold and her wellbeing detected by machines, devices and the light touch from trained professionals. There had been discussions in the hospital about the state of coma patients. It was clear that some were making the transition to a permanent vegetative state or perhaps even death. It was quite possible for some patients to simply slip away without anybody noticing. No fanfare, no tolling of bells, no grim reaper but someone could simply stop being. A final breath would signal the end of days and often no one was there to hear it. Those present at a final moment would report nothing more than a deep sigh and a sudden calm and stillness in the room. A moment that defined the end of something significant but somehow underplayed in the moment. When people pass away in the movies, their last moments are accompanied by a majestic soundtrack and rising strings. In a hospital there is no such sound, no such momentum. Just the movement from one type of quiet to another.

On the other hand, there was hope for some patients. Perhaps the good wishes and prayers from loved ones and the carers transmitted to those in need and made a difference. Perhaps recovery was nothing to do with external factors but an internal resilience that was possessed by some and coveted by others. Others believed in divine light and intervention from some higher power. People used words like 'it isn't his time' as if to suggest there is a chart already drawn up with a date, a how and a when. Some medical practitioners took a scientific view and attributed progress to the power of effective medicine and surgery and decline as a failure in the patient.

And so the nurse spent time with Ruth to check that she was alive, at least. She spoke aloud as she went about her work just so that Ruth knew what she was doing. Just in case.

***

Oh hello. Yes, you can lift that up and have a look. Yes, I can feel that. Yep, that feels fine. My, that is bright. Is that what you did the other day? That is so bright I can hardly look at it. 37%.

So my notes don't report much change. Temperature stable. Blood pressure stable. I don't know how long I have been here but it feels like a long time. I struggle to differentiate myself from the room, the bed, as I am sure there is one, and the environment. 'Let me know if there is anything I can help you with and whether there is anything else you want to know?' What was that you said? Let you know if I need anything. Well, I would like to know what happens next. 41%. I am getting fed up in here. And where is Will? I am sure he is here. If not, he is bound to send a message. 43%. Oh Will, what have I done? It seems I am stuck here and my memories of you are fading somewhat. Or are they coming back? To be honest, it is hard to work that one out. It feels like you are close and then I have memories and they seem quite distant. I am guessing reality lies somewhere in the middle. I can remember sweet kisses and text messages. I can remember red bricks and flowers. I can remember pain. Pain in the form of pain that needs bandages and pain that needs cuddling. I can't remember what anyone looks like but I am sure I recall their spirit.

That feels cold, what was that? 44%. While you are here, can you brush my hair? I am not sure but I don't think that has happened for a while.

How come it is so loud, all of a sudden? Have I slept through that? Will, can you shut the curtains, I can't sleep with all this noise. Also, can you stop these people prodding me with cold things? I am fed up with being prodded. 47%. How odd, I am actually feeling irritated. I haven't noticed an emotion like that since a meeting at work went on and on and on and I had promised to meet Will for lunch. Hey, that reminds me. That sensation of cold earlier. I had forgotten what that felt like. I think I have felt cold all the time. Like someone kept in a fridge. But whatever that was felt colder still. How did that happen? That must have been colder than me, I guess. 49%.

I just had an idea. I wonder if Will fancies popping out to town later. We could have lunch and grab a glass or two in Covent Garden. I love it there. We could wander round the shops and go to the Apple Store. I could do with a new charger and someone to fix my phone. Come to think of it, where is my phone? I haven't checked and maybe Will has tried to get in touch. 50%.

Will, what do you think? Shall we get out of here? Maybe it's time to get away from all this? Will? 50% is not bad. A half and with a half there is always the chance to argue that the glass is half full or indeed, half empty. Which way shall we go, Will? Up? Down? Stay the same? Choices, choices. What would you *like to do? Am I worth it? Are we worth it? Dammit, Will, we are so damn worth it. Ten, nine, eight, seven, six, five, four, three, two, one. Coming, ready or not.*

51%.

***

Ruth's eyes opened.

The nurse was about to leave the room when she glanced over. 'Oh, hello sweetie. So, you are awake. Now let me sit with you a minute. It might be a bit strange for a while.'

Ruth's eyes began to adapt to the shape, colour and brightness of her surroundings. At first, she couldn't make out anything at all. Then her eyes began to focus and the world came into view. She made out the shape of someone on her bed. Someone in uniform. She became aware of tension in her arms, her legs and on her face. She struggled to lift her arm.

'Take it slowly, you are connected to several things here. You have been sleeping for a while so things are going to be confusing at first. Shhhh.'

Will ambled back from his breakfast break. He knew Ange would call in and later, Ruth's mum. That would give him the chance to escape the confines of the hospital.

Approaching Ruth's room, he stopped in his tracks. Two nurses and a doctor could be seen through the screen. He always feared the worst in this place. He opened the door carefully.

'Oh, you're here,' said the nurse. 'Someone is awake!'

Will looked at the bed to see Ruth's eyes open and her head turned towards him.

'Oh my God! Ruth! You are back.' Will pushed forward and grabbed her hand.

Ruth made a slow motion to look his way and her dry

lips made a sound that no one could interpret.

'How is she?' asked Will of the doctor. Funny how he had learnt the rule of talking about people as if they were not there. Even though they now were.

'The signs are good. We need to run some tests and start to reintroduce fluid and nutrition. She will be groggy for a while. Certainly no long walks or dancing today, okay?' The doctor nodded in Ruth's direction and she nodded back and allowed a small hint of a smile to creep across her face.

Will bent down beside her bed and held her hand tight. For the first time, she squeezed back. 'You can't believe how good it feels to see you.'

Analysis of the poem, 'Breathe My Love – For I am With You' by Angela Lovejoy

Excerpt from an essay by William Hornby, published by Random Imagery 2018

Breathe my love
Not shallow gasps or rasping breaths
Breathe my love
Inhale the choice of life not death

Breathe deep my love
Find the root of resurrection
Breathe deep my love
Hold desire and resolution

Your body may be weak, my love
No shallow grave and early mourning
Breathe my love
Don't give in or heed the warning

Feel my love
Weaving patterns through the skin
Love runs deep, my love
Finding, healing from within

I am with my love
I am prophet, God and host
Awake my love
I am life's spirit to your ghost

In her poem, 'Breathe My Love', Lovejoy presents life in the balance. We know nothing about the characters in the poem but can surmise the suffering of one and the purest of faith and belief from the other. We are introduced to the severity of the illness through reference to final breaths and potential mourners at a funeral. The poem reads as a heartfelt plea from one to another. It is impossible to imagine these words could be spoken by a casual acquaintance or friend, and we immediately connect with the sentiment and the circumstance. The poem appeals to the emotions, hopes and fears we may feel should we witness the terminal suffering of someone close to us.

The final section is particularly controversial with the claim 'I am prophet, God and host'. There has been some notable backlash to this from certain religious sects, who deem it blasphemy to claim to be the voice of God.

I like to think Lovejoy gets to the truth of much religion. What is God but faith? In Descartes' Ontological Argument, we are presented with the notion or indeed the proof that God exists simply because the supreme being is present of the mind of others. In 'Breathe My Love', Lovejoy presents us with a theory that the concept of God resides in the body, spirit and faith of those who love us, perhaps even suggesting God is the concept of the love from one person to another – quantified as the sum total of love between people and magnified many times. As Paul McCartney says, 'When I find myself in times of trouble, Mother Mary comes to me.' According to Lovejoy, the nearest and dearest are our Magdalene, our Jehovah.

We are unclear whether the outcome of this outpouring of love and faith will be positive. Will the subject of the poem recover? Are words capable of repairing the wounds from within? Does faith trump medicine when it comes to healing? For all those caring for loved ones and spending hours on bedside vigils, let's hope so. I quite like the idea that the collective power of love is the incarnate deity we have sung about so often.

Chapter 12: Waterloo Bridge Revisited

Ruth was in hospital for another four days. Once she was fully awake, her body began to respond. Will was a constant bedside companion, helping with sips of water and then sips of tea. Her diet consisted of small pieces of bread and butter that Ruth could suck until dissolved. And bits of digestive biscuit that Will dunked before offering to her open mouth. Her voice began to come back. Not her thoughts, of course, they'd always been there, but the ability to frame them. Visitors came to see her. Only the close family and friends so Will didn't need to use his questionnaire, and everyone was overjoyed to see progress at last. Ruth's mum went straight into feeder mode and was prepared to shovel scrambled egg and home-made chicken soup into any orifice that would take it.

'What do you remember?' asked Will when she was ready.

'Honestly not much. I remember the view from the bridge and I remember hearing something that panicked me. That's about it. Apparently, I was lucky that the ambulance crew who tended me at the scene were equipped and trained to deal with trauma. They pumped me full of ketamine, which is a strong anaesthetic and effectively shut me down before I reached the hospital.'

'Did you feel any pain?'

'Not really. The only thing that hurt was waking up and then the bruises and the abrasions hurt. The bandages itched – still do, by the way. They're driving me mad. And I need a proper shower.'

'And what about while you were lying in bed? Were you aware of what was going on?'

'That was strange and I am not sure of the timing, so forgive me. At first, nothing made sense at all. I wasn't awake but I was so confused and everything was jumbled.

It felt like I was locked in a box with so many memories and thoughts but most I couldn't access. Then bit by bit, things started to make sense. I began to feel things without understanding what was going on. I have memories of hearing voices but I'm not sure if they were real or I dreamed them. A few people in my life drifted in to check on me and drifted away again. I seem to remember trying to recall a movie title for some reason. I also drifted in and out of a deep sleep state. I don't know what made me wake up. It was almost as if a little burst of energy came along and forced my eyes open. Was that you sending me vibes, Will, or the nurse's torch?'

'Give me some credit for sitting in this bloody chair for days. And while we are on the subject, how come you woke up when I wasn't there? I sit here for days, stroking your hand and I leave the room for a cup of coffee, and as soon as I have gone you wake up. Did you do that on purpose?'

'Will, you never left me. You were always there. I never thought you had gone in any sense.'

'Well, if you and I ever get married and the vicar says that stuff about in sickness and in health, do you mind if I mention I have done my fair share of in sickness for a while?'

Ruth grinned. 'I guess so. Thinking of which, at some point you and I have an outstanding conversation to have.'

'Don't you remember? We had a long, long conversation about that a few days ago. I gave you a full explanation of everything and you were perfectly happy with that. You forgave me completely for being a complete arse and we agreed to put it all behind us and start again.'

'Well, that's lovely. But only a bloke would say that. This is me you are talking to and whilst I had a nasty bang on the head, you are not brushing that under the carpet,' said Ruth. The forgiving smile on her face suggested otherwise.

'Damn, I hoped that was the end of it.'

'Well, you might like to think so but one day soon you can give me the full story. For now, you can help me to the loo.'

Will propped Ruth up as she shuffled along the corridor towards the toilets. The nurses were delighted with her progress as every day she grew stronger and her confidence returned. It was probably a good thing that she had so little memory of what happened on the bridge. Andy Warhol said that everyone would have fifteen minutes of fame. Ruth had hers. She was featured in a number of YouTube videos which scanned the debris and carnage left by the van. She appeared in photos in the newspaper and was quoted as one the casualties left critical by a few seconds of madness. An off-duty doctor on the bridge made sure her airways were clear and waited with her until the ambulance arrived. She probably saved Ruth's life and Ruth resolved to find her and thank her. On arrival at the hospital, the great NHS had performed the real miracles. People working long hours with stretched resources came together and built a comfortable place for Ruth to recover. She could never thank them enough.

The newspapers carried the story for several days and dignitaries from across the world expressed varying levels of outrage and sympathy. The police arrested people who knew people and who might have helped people. A couple of days after the incident the news was full of police raids in East London houses and suspects being pinned to the ground. Londoners and visitors to the City spent a couple of days looking over their shoulders and with an internal radar tuned into the sound of a van making a move. The councillors debated the best response and barriers began to appear in all the key tourist spots. Now anyone walking near the Mall was safe from a random and aggressive driver. But most of the City remained exposed and vulnerable. It was a time when gestures and signals were important.

A week later and the story had left the pages. It had become a memory, a statistic that would forever come to the surface when terror struck again, as it surely would.

Meanwhile, Ruth walked past doors to rooms containing people with shattered lives and distraught families. She glimpsed the sight of a young girl strapped up to machines and a young man in a seat next to her, struggling to make sense it all. She hoped the angels would visit the girl and make things right.

After four days of prodding, checking and poking, Ruth was allowed home. She was glad to escape the ward at last. There is something psychological about leaving hospital. It feels like there is a huge sign at the exit when you have been discharged that says, *You Are On The Mend*. Ruth's body was slow to respond and she tired easily but she was signed off work for a month and could take things at her own pace. The doctors were worried about her mental health as well as her physical wellbeing and gave her the details of a counsellor who could help her process the trauma of what had happened. Ruth had mixed feelings about this. She liked to appear strong willed, in command and confident, but the doctors were right. Now that she had time to process the attack, she had moments where paranoia held her in a vice-like grip. Her sleep was interrupted by dreams with catastrophic endings and in her waking hours, she found herself freaked by traffic and rucksacks.

Will was with her and helped her across the threshold when she returned home. She opened the door and was delighted to be greeted by lots of signs of people but not actual people. Her living room was alive with the colour of flowers and cards with warm and affectionate messages. She was able to slump into a chair and inhale the fragrance of her own space. She could shut the door without worrying that someone would rush in to check her blood pressure.

Will had been shopping and had done his best to buy 'girl food', as he put it.

'What's "girl food"?'

'Well, bloke food is easy. When blokes go shopping we buy the following: sausages, bacon, pizza, bread, butter, eggs, frozen chips, beans, cheddar cheese, pork pies, chopped up chicken in a packet, instant porridge, crisps, PG Tips, chocolate digestives, tins of beer. Bloke food assumes we need to spend the minimum time cooking for the maximum gratification. Nothing wild or fancy.'

'So, what did you get me exactly?' asked Ruth.

'Well, I bought some avocados, salad in a bag, smoked salmon, ciabatta bread, olives, cherry tomatoes, kiwi fruit, cous cous, pomegranate juice, wholemeal flour, pesto, fresh pasta, olive oil, balsamic vinegar, coleslaw, wraps, cheese with dried fruit in it (cranberry, I think), fizzy water, a bottle of white wine that won three medals, sultanas and nuts. I also bought two tea towels and some wrapping paper as they were on special offer.'

'Wow, okay. Thank you.'

'The only problem is that it all needs to be eaten by tomorrow evening. Best before dates and all that. So, you need to cram all the food in by midnight or we'll have to throw it away.'

'Oh, those dates are more flexible than that, Will.'

'Best before, worst afterwards,' he said. 'There is always some food that you should throw away rather than risk it, I think.'

'Really?'

'Yeah. Like coleslaw. You put some in the fridge and then a while later, you have a quick look and realise it is a week out of date. Frankly, I would be better off not bringing it home at all. I could save myself the journey and just dump it on the way out of the shop.'

'Sorry, Will, and you buy coleslaw because…'

'It goes well with salad.'

'It doesn't sound like you buy any salad.'

'Yes and therein lies the problem. I buy things that go with certain other things but don't buy the things they go with and so they go to waste,' Will admitted.

'Okay, well, with all that in mind, what shall we eat tonight, assuming you are staying, that is?'

'Thought I would grab a takeaway.' Will grinned. 'Indian, Thai or Chinese?'

Ruth threw a cushion at him. 'By the way, what's the wholemeal flour for?'

'I thought you might get the urge to bake something, you never know.'

'Uh huh. And the wrapping paper and tea towels?'

'Well, that's what supermarkets do. They always shove the things you need like milk at the back of the shop. And then you wander past displays of things that strike you as coming in useful one day and they are on offer. So you grab a couple of items and throw then in the trolley. Get home to find you have the ingredients for Sunday lunch and some shelving and vast quantities of cleaning products.'

And so they sat down to a unique mixture of curry and an odd assortment of salad. According to Will, once you started discussing the idea of a curry, you needed to have one. No other food would do. Ruth was happy to break bits of naan bread to eat with her smoked salmon.

'Ruth, can I ask you something?'

'Sure.'

'When you think about what happened to you, does it make you re-evaluate things? Do you have any regrets, for example?'

'Yeah, of course it does. Some people didn't make it, so I am one of the lucky ones. It puts all the boring meetings and time spent watching crap TV into perspective. I haven't spent enough time breathing in what life has to offer. You know that day you organised for our first date? More days should be like that. A bit chaotic but full of new flavours, sights and sounds. I've also thought about friends and family. You know those Christmas cards you get when you write "really must see you soon" in them?'

Will nodded.

'Well, the reality is that there is always plenty of time to see people but we allow everything to get in the way. I haven't seen some old friends for ages and I used to love hanging out with them. There are a couple of cards from them over there, saying the same things we always say. I need to break that cycle, Will, and see people and share good times with them. It's funny, when people ask me what I would do if I won the lottery, I always come up with holidays, houses and cars. But give me a near-death experience and all I can come up with is connections, love and family. I've also thought a lot about us.'

'That's nice to know,' said Will. 'I've thought of nothing else. I thought I might lose you in there. Or that you wouldn't be okay when you woke up.'

'It means a lot that you never left me all that time. I have been thinking about our discussion over Jen as well.'

Will's heart sank. He'd known this was coming at some point.

'I have chosen to believe you. I don't quite forgive you for covering things up, but let's hope that's a lesson for you. Never bullshit me over things like that again, and as Tom Petty says, "Time To Move On".'

Will breathed out. 'Thank you, Ruth. I am so glad we can put that behind us. I still feel terrible about it and it won't happen again. From now on: complete honesty and transparency.'

'Well, don't go that far, Will. If I ask you if I look nice when we are about to go out, I expect an affirmation. Otherwise we will never leave the house!'

'Ruth?'

'Yes?'

'You look lovely.' Will kissed her hand.

'Do you mean it?'

'Yes, of course,' he said with a mischievous grin.

***

Ruth was pottering about. An interesting concept that, roughly translated, meant keeping herself busy with various amounts of trivia and distractions. She felt tired after a couple of days with her parents, who were wonderfully enthusiastic but still had the tendency to treat her as if she were eleven years old. For example, her mum was obsessed with slippers. If Ruth appeared in bare feet, she would leap to accuse her of inviting cold germs to attack her. She would 'catch her death', apparently. Ruth was so bored by this that she did some research and could find no evidence that people had died from apparently not wearing slippers in the kitchen. It seems the human frame could indeed walk on B&Q linoleum without inviting significant health problems. There was acceptance that severe frostbite could become a major issue, but this required snow, ice and arctic conditions to take hold. And whilst her mum complained of the temperature regardless of the weather, there were few signs of frostbite taking hold in her kitchen.

At one point, Ruth pointed out that one foot was

mostly encased in bandages so only one would be in contact with a cold floor and therefore the likelihood of infection was reduced by 50 per cent. Her mum was not convinced.

Parents never lose something they learnt when their children were too small to talk. Ruth realised that when babies are unable to explain themselves, parents look for indications of wellbeing. Eating, sleeping soundly and colour in your cheeks become significant factors in determining the health of their offspring. Any deviation to the norm is met by Calpol in regular quantities. So, if Ruth announced she wasn't hungry this was met with sighs and concerns and a rummage through the medicine cupboard. It seems that parents never lose that caring instinct and are ready at any given moment to shovel in cough medicine and paracetamol.

Mum and Dad had also been popping out to do the shopping, which provided some interesting moments. They would come back with vast quantities of bread, potatoes and milk. Her mum also loved buying packets of cold meat. She would stock up on vast quantities of things like ham and chicken which had been 'formed' from ham and chicken. Ruth wondered what that actually meant. How do you take ham and form it into ham? She also bought corned beef, which prompted a discussion about what exactly is corned beef. And why is it sold in tins with a little key on the side? And why we don't have corned pork, chicken, turkey or ham? Ruth figured some things were best left as a mystery.

When her parents left, Ruth surveyed the fridge and the cupboards and decided that there was plenty of food and little she wanted to eat.

Ange arrived at lunchtime with flowers, some small, bite-size chocolates and body cream so that Ruth could feel pampered. Ruth was pleased to see her. Funny how it becomes easier to relax with some friends that it does with parents. Friends make a visit easy and Ange was a welcome sight on what had the potential to be an otherwise empty afternoon. Ange insisted on sorting tea and cleaning up the kitchen to make sure Ruth kept the weight off her feet. This was the first time they had seen each other since Ruth had come out of the hospital, so they had a lot to catch up on.

'So, how are you?' asked Ange when they finally settled.

'Yeah, good,' said Ruth. 'Ankle is a bloody pain to be honest, but it could have been worse, let's face it.'

'Too right it could but that doesn't make it okay, does it? Can I ask you something?'

'Sure.'

'Where does your head go after something like that? I can't imagine it.'

'Well, all over the place. Sometimes it all seems like a bad dream and can't possibly be real. Other times I get incredibly low thinking about it. I remember how furious my dad was when he had his car scratched by some random youth with a 50p piece and nothing better to do. This simple thing led him to a dark place where he was condemning the "youth of today". Imagine that but 100 times worse. You can sit in that chair and think the world is falling apart and there is evil on every corner. I also worry about ordinary people doing mundane things. Mum and Dad going to the shops, friends on the Tube. You realise there are horrible acts in the midst of routine. Christ, people should be able to walk to work without worrying about it. Sometimes I think I am better off just staying here and eating meat sandwiches provided by my mother. But then I snap out of it. The sun shines or a true friend calls and I realise I have a lot going for me. They have broken my ribs and ankle, punctured my lung, put me in a coma and left me with cuts and bruises, but I can get up and rise above it. Most of the time.'

'I can't imagine it, Ruth. I know I am still feeling vigilant as I go about my business. I don't know how long that will last. Are you talking to anyone about it?'

'Yes. I had a counsellor who came round and had a chat about it. It was nice to unload but I don't know if I need more sessions. I think getting on with life might be the best therapy.'

'And is Will looking after you?'

"Yeah, he has been brilliant. He took a lot of time off when I was in hospital so he is back at work now.'

'I saw quite a lot of him on the ward. He basically camped out there, you know. Have you sorted out your differences?'

'I think so. To be honest, I haven't forgotten all about it. I can't help wonder what he is doing for lunch today, for example. But I can't spend my whole life getting depressed about it. He has done enough to make me believe him. Plus, it has been a good test, hasn't it? Relationships are easy when things are new and going well. What happens when the shit hits the fan? Well, so far so good. I can't have been easy to cope with recently.'

'He never left you, Ruth. He couldn't bear the thought of you being alone in that place. I was there some of the time but mostly it was Will. He was rooted to the spot. I know he slept occasionally but mostly he was just sitting around, holding your hand, chatting away or fielding the visitors. I don't think my ex would have done that. I am pretty sure he would have popped in and then been pleased to put Sky Sports on the telly without interruptions. So … any plans?'

'When my foot has made a recovery, we might go away for a long weekend. Somewhere nice.'

'That sounds great. I am already jealous.'

'Hey Ange, Will told me how wonderful you were while I was on the ward. Thank you so much.'

'Don't be daft, anyone would have done the same thing.'

'Actually, I don't agree with that. I had all these cards and Facebook messages and text messages, and they all said basically the same thing.'

'Which was?'

'So sorry to hear about what happened. Hope you get better soon and let us know if there is anything you need.'

'That sounds okay,' said Ange.

'Yeah, it's great to know people are thinking of you, Ange, but what am I supposed to do? Ring up Debs from the office and say, "You know what, Debs, I could do with some shopping", or ring Uncle Aaron and say, 'Hi Uncle Aaron, I am a bit bored. Want to come over for a chat?" All I am saying is you get to know who your friends are. Acquaintances send kind words and it takes a few minutes. True friends think about the situation, they get their heads around where I am and then do helpful things. Like bringing the body cream just now, which was so thoughtful. Turning up with a smile and time for a chat. Making a cuppa.' She reached over and gave Ange a hug.

'I wish I could do more, Ruth.'

'You have been amazing.' The friends smiled at each other.

'By the sounds of it, Will has earned a few Brownie points, then.'

'Yes, I guess he has. We should give him a badge for hospital visitation excellence.' Ruth grinned.

'Or parental management,' Ange added. 'He sorted your folks out a lot as well, you know.'

'Yeah, maybe I should get him a badge. I think that would amuse him.'

'He's a good bloke, Ruth. Hold on to him.'

'I think I might.'

'Well if you change your mind, let me know. I might

join the queue.'

'Ange!'

'Just kidding.'

When Ange left, Ruth flicked through the cards lining her mantelpiece. It was lovely to feel needed. In the middle was one from Will. Inside was a handwritten message that Ruth kept returning to.

Dear Ruth,

I don't think I need to send you a card, seeing as I brought you home. But welcome home anyway. I looked at all the cards and flowers and had a moment when I realised I hadn't bought one myself. So please consider this the official 'Get Well Soon Card' from me. It has flowers on the front and the words 'Get Well Soon', so there is no mistaking it. I think the thing with cards is that what is written on them is one thing. But how you feel when you write them and send them also needs to be clear and apparent, so they have maximum impact. Trust me, I have spent many hours trying to think of the best things to say in cards in general. Anyway, I had a number of days to think about this one and have decided that the best sign off is:

Love and very best wishes,

Will xxxx

P.S. Now that doesn't sound very exiting but allow me to translate.

Love = I love you, Ruth

Very best wishes = I hope all your dreams come true and that I can be part of them

xxxx – Well, that's fairly obvious. I promise to wear slip-on shoes this time, though.

Ruth smiled to herself. He was quite a charmer with words, she felt.

Two months later

Will and Ruth decided to venture out for the first time in a long time. Convalescence had been hard, slow and painful. Her muscles had atrophied slightly during her coma and she remained weak for some time. She suffered persistent headaches, her ribs still hurt and the injury to her ankle was more complex and more difficult to heal than anticipated. If you say you have a broken leg, it sounds big, scary and complicated. If, on the other hand, you say you have broken an ankle, it sounds much smaller and more trivial. Unless, of course, it has happened to you and the reality of bone meeting bone and the weight distribution on that part of the body means plenty of pain and plenty of physio to treat a serious compound fracture.

In addition to the physical repairs, she had mental scars that emerged over time. It took a while to dawn on her that she nearly died that day. At first this gave a sense of euphoria and a joy for life that spurred her on. This was short-lived and was quickly replaced by deep melancholy and self-reflection. Will became a voice of reason and a confidant during tough discussions over the kitchen table.

With her leg well enough to make a journey, Will booked an Uber and decided to take Ruth out for dinner. Something special to welcome her back into the world. He wanted nice wine and great food. Flavours to savour. The cab took them along the Thames and along the South Bank. Will was well aware of where he was going. They stopped at the base of the OXO tower and Ruth hobbled towards the elevator. She knew the place, of course. 'I have had drinks up here but never eaten anything,' she said.

'I needed somewhere with a City view,' Will explained.

They left the elevator lobby and walked into the restaurant, where a well-groomed young man showed them to a prime window table overlooking the city. Right in the line of site was Waterloo Bridge.

Ruth gasped as it dawned on her what she was looking at. 'Why did you bring me here?'

'Can we get a bottle of Viognier and some sparkling water,' Will said to the waiter now hovering. 'We'll get a glass of wine and I will tell you. Have a look at the menu in the meantime. Be warned: this is a menu with intellectual food. No simple dishes here. Not for us a fish pie or conventional vegetables. This is the land of squid ink linguine, razor clam and champagne emulsion,' said Will, reading from the menu.

'What the fuck is champagne emulsion?' Ruth grinned.

'I have no idea, but we can order chips with it if you like.'

The waiter arrived and showed them the bottle. It did indeed look like wine and had the word Viognier written on it.

'Yes, that's the one' said Will, enjoying this rather bizarre ritual. 'No, I don't need to try it, I am sure it's fine. Thank you. Okay, and now a toast.' As the waiter departed, Will raised his glass. 'I need you to look down at that place and think about it for a moment. Down there was hell on earth. Some madman ruined the lives of many and nearly took you from me.'

'I don't need reminding,' Ruth interrupted.

'Give me a minute,' said Will, 'this is important. I came here to bring some perspective. Here we are, looking pretty good. We have colour in our cheeks. We have some very nice wine in our hands and we are about to dine on squid ink and champagne emulsion. And while we dine, we rise above the memory of that place. We drink to celebrate. We drink to remember and we savour every mouthful and every scent and every moment. Here's to you. I love you, Ruth.'

Their glasses kissed first and their lips quickly followed.

'Will, can I ask you a question?'

'Sure.'

'Will you marry me?' said Ruth. 'I mean, you don't have to say anything now but I am thinking it's a good idea and I have learnt that it's best not to wait too long for these things.'

'Ruth, I can't believe you've just done that. Will looked angry and called over the waiter. 'Jesus, this was so fucking perfect. How could you do that, dammit?'

Ruth's stomach dropped as the waiter made his way across the busy restaurant. What had she done?

'Can we have the cheeseboard now, please?'

'Now, sir?'

'Yes, now.'

'Will, what are you up to?'

The waiter arrived with a cheeseboard containing a selection of Neal's Yard British and Irish farmhouse cheeses, and a small box tied up with a bow.

'Open it,' said Will.

And Ruth already knew what was inside. She slipped the ring on her finger and the light from the diamond solitaire danced across her face. 'Oh Will, that is lovely.'

'Yes, but I had a big moment planned, Ruth. I had briefed these guys. They were all ready to help me with my beautifully planned romantic proposal. And you fucking beat me to it! I even asked them to play Van Morrison's 'Have I Told You Lately' when they brought this out.'

Now she came to think of it, the song was indeed playing in the background.

Ruth wiped a tear from her eye. She didn't know

whether to laugh or cry, but it seemed appropriate to do both. 'So is that a yes then?' she said, giggling.

'Yes, Ruth, of course I will marry you,' said Will, smiling through his own tears.

'Well, it's a yes from me,' said Ruth. 'We have too yeses.'

They reached across the table to ripples of applause from those near enough to see what was going on.

'This is great, we can start planning a wedding,' said Ruth.

'Let's not be so hasty,' said Will. 'No need to rush.'

'Actually there is,' said Ruth. 'Bloody white vans everywhere. Plus, you'd better marry me before someone else does. I quite like the idea of a barn or something rustic. I don't want some shoddy hotel with stuffy waiters and no seat coverings.'

'What, no seat coverings?' said Will. 'You can't possibly have a wedding without seat coverings.'

***

And so we move above Will and Ruth as they plan their next great adventure in the restaurant in the OXO tower. We rise above the skyline and look down to the traffic on Waterloo Bridge, which is flowing freely. Across the City people carry on with their busy lives, their work and their play. Meanwhile millions of digital messages land on the capital carrying news, trivia and proposals. Each one of them has the potential to change lives and the course of events. If we look closely, we can see one with Will's mobile phone number programmed into its core and heading his way. We can only wonder what it says and how he will react.

THE END (perhaps)

A Deconstruction of the Song 'Have I Told You Lately' by Van Morrison and its Relevance to the Essays In Love soundtrack

Published in Twelve Essays In Love by Andy Matheson

'Have I Told You Lately' is a romantic ballad written by Northern Irish singer-songwriter Van Morrison and recorded for his 1989 album, Avalon Sunset, and the song that Will chose for his proposal of marriage. It is easy to see why this is one of the most popular wedding dance requests of all time. Many people connect with the words and interpret this song as the ultimate in romantic ballads. It has been performed countless times and has been the first dance for thousands of happy couples.

There is, however, a different interpretation of Van's lyrics. The song is rich in religious references and words that would not be out of place in the book of common prayer. *'At the end of the day / We should give thanks and pray to the One' is a clear celebration of God. In addition, 'Fill my heart with gladness / Take away my sadness / Ease my troubles, that's what you do'* is not about a loved one but about the power of faith and how this can impact on self-worth and meaning. I am sure that most people who have chosen this song for a wedding are unaware of the religious connection that runs alongside the melody.

The final chapter, 'The Glory Of Love', and the song of the same name on the album both pick up on this dichotomy and we raise a question about whether it is modern medical care or love and faith that drives the final moments in this story.

Songs clearly mean different things to different people. Often the author's intentions are misunderstood or simply reinterpreted to suit the individual. A couple of quotes come to mind here. One is from Dave Grohl of Foo

Fighters who said, 'You can sing a song to 85,000 people and they'll sing it back for 85,000 different reasons.'

Then we have Paul McCartney being interviewed about his own songs. The interviewer mentions that people had been poring over his lyrics and extracting meaning that Paul might not recognise. Paul acknowledged this and said, 'Well I didn't think that when I wrote it. But maybe they're right,' in other words, acknowledging the interpretation of the song as a viable meaning.

I guess Dave Grohl is right and people will give the song their own meaning and interpretation. As we reach the last chapter and the closing words, we can leave you with some final questions for discussion:

• Are the chapters sequential or does the story stand up if you chop them up into a different order? Perhaps life is more like the chopped-up version?

• What saved Ruth in the end? Was it love, divine intervention or medicine?

• There is much we don't know about Will and his life. The only information we have about him is based on what he chooses to divulge. Do you believe in him as Ruth does?

• How much of Will and Ruth's emotional state is based on reality or perception?

• How has technology changed the nature of relationships and what was the role of technology in the story?

• Has God taken control of text messages and levels of power in phones as a means of controlling the population?

• Will Ruth and Will live happily ever after?

- How will Will respond to the text that has just buzzed in his pocket?

Actually, you don't know the answers. Perhaps no one does – not even me. But I give you, the reader, permission to decide for yourself. And then that decision becomes the truth.

The Essays In Love Album

This book started life in song. As a musician and songwriter, I took inspiration from Alain De Botton's book of the same name and began to construct songs that contained a classic love story. The more the songs took shape, the more the characters became real. It seemed inevitable that Will and Ruth should emerge from the chords, verses and choruses, and appear in print. In that way, this whole book had a clear structure before a word was written. Each chapter has a song on the album (apart from the last one, when Van Morrison needs to be added to the playlist). These songs help to set the tone for the narrative and perhaps vice versa.

In my head, you should read the chapter and then reflect on it while playing the song, as the two are intrinsically linked. Whether or not you do so is, of course, up to you. I have included the song lyrics here and perhaps their poetry will suffice.

Andy Matheson, April 2018

For more details on The Explorers, visit
www.the-explorers.co.uk
The album, *'Essays In Love'* can be purchased from iTunes and Amazon

'Essays in Love'

The lyrics

These Four Walls

These four walls are closing in
These four walls are paper thin
And these four walls have nothing much to say
These four walls and ceiling tiles
Have no reports or genuine smiles
These four walls will listen as you pray

But oh, oh, oh my heart is calling
Oh, oh, oh I heed the warning
But oh, oh, oh

These four walls would like to know
The outcome of the dreams you show
These four walls will listen from within

These four walls are covered with
Pictures of the days you've lived
Blu Tack dreams and memories wearing thin

But oh, oh, oh my heart is calling
Oh, oh, oh I heed the warning
But oh, oh, oh

The time is right to tear down the posters
Put on the light and banish the monsters
Open the window and welcome a beckoning day
To take a good look at the girl in the mirror
Stop wishing for beauty and ways to be thinner
Banish the magazines and throw all the papers away

But oh, oh, oh my heart is calling
Oh, oh, oh I heed the warning

Close Encounters

I was only dreaming I was half asleep
The world was right beside me now
I'm standing on the corner but my feet don't touch the
ground

How come you're smiling when the rain falls down
Who puts the light in your eyes
I know you're right behind me so I best go in disguise

The wind blows ... and you may forget my name (it's still
the same)
My heart knows – the feeling grows – I will never be the
same (it's such a shame)

Standing on the corner was a nice idea
No one here will see me now
But the signs on my features they give me away somehow

Who needs forgiveness when you fall in love
Who needs a minute more
Trying to recover when your feet don't touch the floor

The wind blows ... and the darkness knows my name
My heart knows – it comes and goes – I can never be the
same

Nobody will see me if I hide away
Nobody will see my tears
Realisation and the thoughts of a thousand years

I was only tempted now I'm hypnotised
I am in a vacant trance
Reputation crumbles and I'm ready to start the dance

This Is The Moment

This is the moment – a perfect moment in time
This is the moment I fell for you
This is the moment – a simple moment in time

This is the moment I fell for you
Do you feel it too? (Do you feel like I do?)

I wasn't made to be alone
Pick up your bag and grab the phone
Light the beacons on the hill
Just look at me and say you will

And don't you know the things I've said
Are hidden signs of etiquette
I don't believe a word I've said
I no longer feel alone

This is the moment – a perfect moment in time
This is the moment I fell for you
This is the moment – a simple moment in time

This is the moment I fell for you
Do you feel like I do?

You must be the alphabet
My A to B since we first met
You rearrange the words I've said
You are now my letterhead

And even when the day is done
You write my words and sing my song
And tell me I can do no wrong
And all my thoughts have been undone

This is the moment – a perfect moment in time
This is the moment I fell for you
This is the moment – a simple moment in time

This is the moment I fell for you
Do you feel it too? (Do you feel like I do?)

Feels So Good

It feels so good – don't worry about the way you look
It's so good – there is no peace of mind mid the dust and
the grime
It's so good – and I'm breathing in emotion and you know
you should
Don't you feel the whirlwind turn you round
Don't you feel like heaven's bearing down
And it feels so good
It feels so good – there is someone I'm
depending on
It's so good – And I'm standing at the
entrance and I must be strong
It's so good – And you give me inspiration
and it's understood

It feels so good – will not drive you crazy it will keep you
sane
It's so good – never press for answers ask you to explain
It's so good – Always right behind you as you said you
would

And the light will shine for all of those who wait
One-time captive opens up the gate
Hair shines brightly and reflects the sun
And you celebrate innocence a natural one
Take a long, long ride to the world outside
A shield of compassion firmly at your side
You have the strength to move a mountain at will
As you shake off repentance as a natural ill
Circle is broken and the stone is cast
Wiping dust from the window see the world at last
New day dawning and the dew will fall
Those once forgotten will now heed your call
Case is now over and the jury retired

Verdict is granted you have God on your side
You stand and reflect and you know that you should
It's been a long time and it
Feels so good

Mad About You

I didn't want to say goodbye, simply needed to catch your eye
A minute seems a thousand hours
As we walked our different ways my head was full – in a mixed-up haze
Not making sense but searching for a meaning

Light shines bright – but the night is calling
Flowers bloom – but is winter morning
Time goes by – but with seconds stalling

Crazy but it's true, I guess I'm mad about you
I feel in love it's true, and all I want is you

I stood and watched as you walked away, I thought I saw you glance my way
I wanted you to change mind and direction
I nearly followed you down the lane, across the road and then back again
A thousand thoughts but none of them have reason

I feel strong – but with weakness showing through
I can't speak – unless you can hear me too
I don't exist – unless you tell me true

Crazy but it's true, I guess I'm mad about you
I feel in love it's true, and all I want is you

Hold me close – but don't suffocate me
Feel my heart – but don't patronise me
Believe in me – but set my soul free

Crazy but it's true, I guess I'm mad about you
I feel in love it's true, and all I want is you

Jealousy

Jealousy you hide beneath my features
Jealousy you sit behind my eyes
Jealousy you offer up my weakness
Jealousy you've taken on my mind

Baby it's all right
I know it's all right
Baby it's all right to cry
Baby it's all right
I know it's all right
Baby it's all right to cry (to say goodbye)
My love I don't know why

Jealousy you wrap me round your finger
Jealousy you tie me up inside
Jealousy you hide away the meanings
Jealousy you take away my pride

See You Again

Mood has been broken my heart was on fire
Mind has gone crazy, paved with desire
Who tore the pages, cast out predictions
Away from a guaranteed history line

But I would forgive every word that you say
If you'd smile for a minute and stay
I would protect you and take you away
From the cold and the pressure, undying rain
And I hope I can see you again

A minute is passing, an hour has gone by
Listening to sound on the street and you're trying
To memorise features, bring forth a picture
Of what you are missing, while you are waiting

But I would forgive every word that you say
If you'd smile for a minute and stay
I would protect you and take you away
From the cold and the pressure, undying rain
And I hope I can see you again

It's way past eleven, my mind is still reeling
Writing the words that I've already written
This song is only expression of feeling
Wanted to tell you, I'm never leaving

The Last Goodnight

Hold me
Come on and hold on to me
Hold me close tonight
Need you near me
Come on and be here with me
Till the day turns to night

This is the last goodnight I'll send you
I ask myself how could it come to this
I close my eyes and think of you forever in my dreams
This last goodnight is sealed with a kiss

Take hold of me
Need you to be there for me
Unfold me tonight
See right through me
I need you to be here with me
Be true to me tonight

Release me
I don't need you to please me
Don't dream of me tonight
Time is leaving me
No need to be here with me
Don't talk to me again tonight

Four In The Morning

The moon's at my window
Wind howls at my door
And it's four in the morning and I can't sleep any more

My head feels so restless
I breathe out with a sigh
And the streetlight shines down with displeasure without asking why

There's a ghost on my pillow
Shadows of you on the wall
And a space in the mirror
And echoes of you when you call
I hear no voice at all

And I need an answer
But questions keep coming to mind
And all of my tears mingle with fears in the night

What if I'm lonely
What if no one is there
I am a hard one to love but ready to show that I care

But oh, oh, oh where did our love go wrong
But oh, oh, oh how can my heart be strong

There's a tear on my pillow
There's a sign on the wall
And a smear on the mirror
No one to hear when I fall
And echoes of you when you call

I don't know if I'm guilty
I can't face the look in your eyes

But I'm ready for something
But not really saying goodbye
In the morning I rise

Smile in My Eyes

You are the memory all summer long
You sit behind this disguise
You come to mind like the words of a song
You are the smile in my eyes
Gotta hold on to something
The wind whispers words in my ear
I can cry over nothing
And all of my dreams disappear
You are the memory that hangs in the air
You are the cloud in the skies
You come to mind like the words of a song
You are the smile in my eyes
And time waits for no one
And photos will curl and will fade
I can flick through the pages
Where emotions and moments are saved
You are the memory scent on my skin
You are the moon on the rise
You are the radio playing our song
You are the smile in my eyes
Some time on my own now
To turn off the lights and to hide
The roses have wilted
None of the love and affection has died
You are the memory eight summers long
You sit behind this disguise
You come to mind like the words of a song
You are the smile in my eyes
You are the memory that hangs in the air
You are the cloud in the skies
You come to mind like the words of a song
You are the smile in my eyes
You are the smile in my eyes
You are the smile in my eyes

The Glory Of Love

I want to shout about it
Scream about it
The glory of love

I can't live without it
Breathe without it
The glory of love

I need to be beside you
Live inside you
The glory of love

I wanna dream in colour
Live through another
The glory of love

Come on baby take my hand
I will never understand you
Disappear together we are meant to be right here, me and
you

You are the only
One I care for
The glory of love

You are the one
I save my breath for
The glory of love

You are the reason
You are believing
The glory of love

You are the season

Every beginning now
The glory of love

Come on baby take my hand
I will never understand you
Disappear together we are meant to be right here, me and
you

You are the light
At the end of the dark days
The glory of love

You are the answer
End of the old ways
The glory of love

Dedication and thanks

My Mum was a great reader of books and probably my biggest supporter and fan. I know she would be proud to see my name in print and so this book is dedicated to her memory.

The novel is set in central London and many of the locations, bars and restaurants are real. I recommend them all in what is probably the greatest city in the world.

Thanks to Bryony Sutherland for being a most amazing editor, to Caroline Goldsmith from Goldsmith Publishing for cover design and presentation and Justine Solomon from Byte The Book for the advice, networking and connections. Thanks to Barbara Walker for making sure my medical references are authentic. Finally thanks to all family, friends and colleagues who have helped shape these characters and their story.

About the author

Andy was born in London and now lives on the South Coast. He divides his time between writing and business consulting. He also plays in a band and has recorded two albums. 'Walking In Slow Motion' by Andy Matheson and 'Essays In Love' by The Explorers - both available on all platforms.